INTENSE
PLEASURE

By Lora Leigh and
published by Pan Books

INTENSE PLEASURE

Lora Leigh

PAN BOOKS

First published 2017 by St Martin's Press, New York

First published in the UK 2017 by Pan Books
an imprint of Pan Macmillan
20 New Wharf Road, London N1 9RR
Associated companies throughout the world
www.panmacmillan.com

ISBN 978-1-4472-5803-2

1 3 5 7 9 8 6 4 2

A CIP catalogue record for this book is available from the British Library.

Printed and bound by CPI Group (UK) Ltd, Croydon, CR0 4YY

Visit **www.panmacmillan.com** to read more about all our books
and to buy them. You will also find features, author interviews and
news of any author events, and you can sign up for e-newsletters
so that you're always first to hear about our new releases.

INTENSE
PLEASURE

PROLOGUE

She had to leave.

Summer Calhoun, the woman the world knew as Summer Bartlett, was smart enough to know that this phase of her life was over. And though she wasn't normally one to run, or to give up, even she couldn't ignore the fact that she simply couldn't do this anymore.

Teeth clenched, battling tears and anger, Summer threw an armload of dresses into one of the suitcases lying open on the bed. Jamming the material into the leather bag, uncaring of the wrinkles and years of careful packing habits, she added more, pushing the frothy, girly material from the sides of the bag and stuffing them in before zipping the back with short, jerky movements.

She promised herself she wasn't going to cry.

Tears didn't help. They had never helped in the past and they damned sure wouldn't help now.

Nothing would help but getting away and running from the pain. Like serrated blades, the memories of the past few days sliced into her, tore at her.

God, how naïve she had been.

Four years with the CIA, two with various other agencies, and two more risking her ass in the private sector should have killed any naiveté she might have possessed long ago. Hell, she was certain it had done just that.

And how very wrong she'd been. So wrong that for eight years she'd believed an enemy was a friend, and that insults were just a brasher attitude than those Summer was used to in the South.

And because she'd let herself be fooled, she'd just spent three of the most hellish days of her life, two of them attending the funeral and burial of the very woman whose deceit and black heart had nearly destroyed far too many people Summer loved.

Easing to the padded bench at the bottom of the bed and propping her face in her hands as she rested her elbows on her knees, she tried to tell herself it was the price of ignorance. Of not seeing the true nature of the woman she'd known most of her life.

The woman Summer had killed.

The funeral had been somber, saddening, and subtly beautiful. Cascades of flowers, over a hundred friends and family mourning. Tears and heartrending testimonials for a woman no one had known for a traitor and a murderer.

Summer had remained tearless through the viewings she'd been forced to attend. She'd watched, listened, and taken her turn at the gleaming cherrywood casket where she stared into the pretty, silent features of the woman she'd been forced to kill. A woman who had hated her, whose jealousy and greed had destroyed so many over the years.

Summer had remained just as silent during the burial, her head lowered, so much anger burning inside her that keeping it hidden was next to impossible. However, she had no other choice. Because she'd killed the woman they were laying to rest. Because it was her bullet, not an enemy's, that had slammed into Gia Barrett's black heart. And God forbid that the world should learn about the woman's crimes, crimes that would shame her way too influential family.

Questions would be asked if Summer and the man Gia had turned her weapon on hadn't been there for the partner the world believed was so kind and warm of spirit.

Money talked, and the Barrett family had plenty of it. Enough to ensure that the world would never know the true reason their daughter was dead.

She could have refused to be there, Summer knew. She could have found a quiet place to nurse the wounds gouged inside her heart if it weren't for the man Gia was trying to murder when she was killed, and the man he called his brother.

Esteban Falcone, known as "Falcon," was the wild, Spanish bad boy whose pale blue eyes could burn with laughter and fun or turn icy with danger or disapproval. The partner whom both Summer and Gia had fought alongside for two years. Playful, sometimes dramatic, always protective and loyal. So protective, he'd had Summer dragged from the chapel seconds before security arrived to find Gia's body sprawled on the floor and Falcon holding the weapon that had killed her.

His half brother, John Raeg, had arrived with security. The half brother was nothing like his sibling. Older by only a few weeks, harder, colder, he'd handled everything and ensured the truth was buried so deep it never saw the light of day.

The truth that for eight years Gia had betrayed all of them. Friends and family alike.

Even more, she'd betrayed the friend Summer had

sworn to protect years ago. A vow that had been broken when she'd failed to keep Gia and those she was helping from nearly destroying Alyssa's life.

Because Summer had missed the signs, Alyssa had lost the two men she loved so much, and the unborn child she'd loved more than life. Because Summer had blinked and had refused to see Gia for the monster she had become.

At the sound of a quiet knock on her door, Summer jumped to her feet and quickly wiped away the dampness on her lashes. She couldn't bear that anyone see the tears, or the hurt.

"Come on in, god-daddy," she called out, expecting Alyssa's father, Senator David Allen Hampstead.

It wasn't her godfather who opened the door and stepped into the room though.

John Raeg, Falcon's half brother, entered the room instead, his gaze going over her coolly. Cold and hard, those eagle eyes missed nothing. His golden brown gaze swept over the room, finally coming to rest on the open bags on her bed.

Closing the door behind him, he just stared at her for long moments, disapproval and censure filling his gaze as he slid his hands into the pockets of his dark slacks.

"Running away?" His deep voice was completely lacking in any mercy or compassion.

But then, when had he ever felt any mercy or compassion for her, no matter the situation?

"Seems like the thing to do." She shrugged, turned her back to him, and laid the stacks of clothes she'd prepared the night before neatly into another case. "Besides, it's time to go home. Daddy's threatening to send Caleb after me and that's just trouble waitin' to happen."

Her older brother would go ballistic if he learned what had happened here.

"Maybe you should try being honest with your family for a change. That usually seems to keep Caleb calm," he suggested with such arrogant superiority it made her want to kick him.

He didn't know her family, not really. Just because he'd met Caleb didn't mean he knew what would work with them, or how they felt about her. Just because he disliked her didn't mean everyone did. And her family worried about her. Keeping them in the dark about the true nature of her work was getting harder by the year. It was time to stop it. But she was going to do it her way.

"Now, why would I want to go getting all honest with him?" She snorted, pushing back the thick, wavy fall of hair that slid over her shoulder as she continued to pack. "Besides, it doesn't matter now. I'm done. You will be happy to know I'm headin' home for good."

It was time.

She'd known since that debacle in Russia the year before that her luck was running out. If she kept tempting fate as she had been, she was going to end up dead. And Falcon would probably get killed as well trying to pull her ass out of some fire.

"And the fact that Falcon nearly sacrificed himself for you when he tried to take the blame for killing Gia doesn't matter, does it?" The savage derision in his tone sliced another wound across her heart. "You're just going to go back home and pretend none of it happened."

What choice did she have?

"Looks that way." She packed more of her clothing, keeping her back to him.

She didn't dare let him see how vulnerable she was right

now. It was bad enough the many ways he could unknow-ingly hurt her. If he ever learned just how weak she was, then the deliberate jabs he could inflict would destroy her.

What the hell was wrong with her? She couldn't stop herself from wanting him and Falcon. Knowing they shared their women, even knowing how deeply Raeg dis-approved of her, still, she ached for the experience, for the feel of both of them touching her.

"Looks that way?" he growled behind him. "I should have expected this out of you. It's about the most selfish act you could pull right now."

Oh, he so did not want to go there with her right now.

Turning, she flashed him a deliberately wide-eyed look of surprise.

"Well now, Raeg, I'd just love to stick around and try to see all this from your point of view, sugar," she assured him with brittle amusement. "But I just can't seem to get my head that far up my ass. So, if that's all you wanted, I'll just concede this little battle and you can get the fuck out of my room and let me pack in peace."

She expected to hear the door slam behind him, maybe with a smart-ass curse first. What she didn't expect was to be abruptly swung around to face him.

There wasn't a chance to blink back her tears or to dry the single trail of dampness that fell from her lashes.

She wasn't prepared . . .

Tears.

There hadn't been a sign of them in her voice. Raeg hadn't expected tears, so the effect they had on him was even more surprising.

Something dark and unfamiliar unfurled inside his chest, tightening the muscles there with a subtle pressure he found distinctly uncomfortable. And as he stared down at her, the deep, wounded violet color of her eyes darkened and another tear slipped free.

Involuntarily.

He knew Summer's tricks.

He bet he'd seen every one she knew to pull, but Summer had never used tears to try to sway him. She knew better.

"Let me go." She jerked her head to the side, blinking quickly as she tried to swallow back whatever emotion gave birth to her tears. "Please."

He gripped her chin with the fingers of one hand and forced her gaze back to him, ignoring her struggles to pull away.

"Stay still," he ordered her, his tone more clipped, angrier than he'd meant it to be.

"Don't do this to me," she whispered. The fine tremor that went through her was almost imperceptive. "Just let me go."

Another tear slipped free despite her efforts to hold it back.

She could use tears on his brother quite effectively, but Raeg had always seen through each attempt if he caught her working Falcon with a sheen of dampness gleaming in those unusually violet eyes. These tears weren't fake. Summer was hurting. And that pain actually had his chest aching as he wiped away the tear rolling down her cheek with his thumb.

"I need . . ." Her breathing hitched as she tried to avoid his gaze. "I need to go, Raeg."

"You cared about her, didn't you?" he asked her softly. "More than you're letting anyone know."

Summer had been like a robot during the viewing and funeral service. Cold and hard, refusing to speak or socialize as all the other mourners were. Not that he could blame her. The fact that she had been forced to be there was an insult to her that had caused him to cringe. He'd hated giving her the ultimatum from Gia's family, but he'd agreed it was the only way to keep any gossip or suspicion from arising.

"Why are you doing this?" Her whispered plea tore at his conscience. "Why do you want to hurt me?"

He covered those trembling lips with his, uncertain why he followed the impulse. For years he'd wondered how her pretty, pouty lips would taste, how they'd feel beneath his. He'd fantasized about them, hungered for them.

And she was leaving . . .

Slanting his lips over hers, he pushed his tongue past them as she froze beneath his kiss, for just a second. Just long enough for him to pull her closer, to taste the sweetness, the feminine surprise that had her lips parting for him. A second later a whimper left her lips and the heat of her response filled his senses.

Slender, silken arms went around his neck. Her fingers speared into his hair, nails pricking at his scalp, sending a rush of pleasure burning through his senses.

Every shred of common sense was yelling at him, warning him back. The mistake he knew he was making was tantamount. The biggest mistake he could possibly make with the one woman he should never make it with.

But damn, she tasted good, felt good. Sweet heat and shuddering response. She was burning like a flame in his arms and he wanted nothing more than to stoke that blaze higher. To have the freedom to touch her, excite her, as his brother restrained her . . .

Falcon stepped into the bedroom, his lips parting to call out Summer's name a second before the sight of her in his brother's arms stilled the sound. He closed the door,

taking in the scene before him as every drop of blood in
his body surged south. He was instantly painfully erect,
throttling the groan rising in his throat.

This was his most erotic fantasy come to life . . . or
part of it. The sight of Summer held firmly against his
brother, helpless within the pleasure she was receiving.
All that long black hair flowed down her back like a living cape, her slender body arched against Raeg, her arms
curled around his neck, fingers buried in his hair.

She looked so damned feminine, so delicate and sensual that the need burning inside him threatened to become an inferno.

Stepping behind her, Falcon lowered his head, his lips
just above her ear.

"Might I join you, Belle?" he asked gently. "Or is this
pleasure for you and Raeg alone?"

He couldn't imagine not being part of the very thing
he'd conspired to begin for years, the very pleasure that
he knew he hadn't craved alone. Raeg had battled the
need for her, battled his own emotions and hungers with
a strength Falcon couldn't have found in himself in the
same circumstances.

Summer froze, the erotic whimper rising in her throat
barely silenced, weakness flooding her, carnal sensuality rushing through her system.

She could barely breathe. She'd fantasized for far too
long, masturbated to the wicked thoughts of these two
men. There had been too many sleepless nights, too many
times she had tossed and turned, tormented by the unknown, but the need to touch, to taste the power and pas-
sion she'd imagined they could unleash on her senses.

Forcing her eyes open she was caught by the gold and
brown raptor's eyes watching her so closely.

"Oh, she wants," Raeg stated softly. "Those pretty eyes are full of how much she wants."

What was she doing?

Her hands fell from Raeg's hair to his shoulders, her fingers clenching in the material of his shirt as Falcon's broad hands rested on her hips. The heat of them sank through the thin material of the black sheath she still wore, sensation building in her skin beneath it.

Still caught by Raeg's eyes, she forced herself to breathe, not to whimper, as Falcon's hands slid slowly up her sides, curving beneath her arms, then drawing them up until he was placing her hands against the sides of his neck where he held them firmly.

As Falcon held her to him, keeping her arms raised, her body opened and vulnerable, Summer lost control of the moan trapped in her throat. Raeg's hands smoothed up her sides, his head bending as his hands framed the sides of her breasts, lifting them to further reveal the upper curves of her sensitive flesh.

The rasp of his lips over them, the stroke of his tongue, and the eroticism of the act drugged her senses. Helpless against the sensations surging through her, her eyes drifted closed and she had no choice but to let Falcon support her weight. Because it felt so good, because pleasure was racing through her with such a high, she was helpless against it.

"Summer, did you still want . . ."

Her eyes jerked open, and Raeg sprang back from her so fast that if she'd been depending on him for balance, she would have ended up on the floor. Thankfully, Falcon didn't seem nearly so ashamed to be caught by the senator.

"Oh well . . ." Davis Allen cleared his throat, his gray eyes filled with shock as they went from Summer to Raeg to Falcon and back to Summer. "Whenever you're ready dear . . ." Summer lowered her arms, the feel of Falcon's hands now at her hips kept her balanced as she found her feet once again, his hold possessively warm.

Backing out of the room, a flush suffusing his dark features, the senator quickly closed the door, leaving a heavy, suddenly uncomfortable silence behind.

Summer stared at Raeg's back where he stood across the room now, close to the door, rubbing at the back of his neck.

"Deal with this," Raeg told his brother, the brusque, cool tone of his voice tinged with regret. "I have to go."

And just that fast, he was gone.

Shame washed through her.

Whatever he'd meant to do, he definitely hadn't wanted anyone to know about it.

"God forbid anyone should believe he stooped so low as to actually touch the little Georgia hick," she whispered. "How embarrassing."

"Summer, that wasn't . . ."

"Just stop, Falcon." She turned to him, inhaling deeply at the tenderness in his expression. "I know you're going to defend him, and it's not needed."

She stared up at him, the cool, pale blue eyes that belied all the emotions she knew this brother hid inside. His Spanish nature rarely showed in his expression or his gaze, but they'd worked together long enough that she could often tell what he was feeling when no one else could.

"I need to go," she whispered, hearing the shakiness in her voice, feeling that trapped, smothering sensation that sometimes surrounded her. "Please. I just need some time . . ."

He laid two fingers against her lips. "I came to your room to wish you farewell, sweetheart, not to argue with you or attempt to change your mind," he told her softly. "But running isn't going to help. I know you, and we both know that's what you're doing."

"I need to rest." She was so tired. Summer could feel the weariness building inside her. She'd never imagined the past was as broken as it had been, and that those she'd been so loyal to could have betrayed her and those she cared about so easily.

She'd always known the world wasn't what others perceived it to be, but to learn it was even worse than that had shaken her to her core.

"Rest then." His hand cupped her cheek, his lips whispering across hers. "I'll wait for you. For a while. But don't forget to return Summer, or I'll come looking for you." His expression hardened then. "And you don't want me to come looking for you."

She had a feeling that it wouldn't matter.

As he left the room she stared at the clothes laid out, those waiting, and she just didn't have the energy or the patience to deal with packing. Her car had arrived earlier, and was waiting out front. All she really needed was her go bag and the small suitcase she always kept packed for emergencies.

Grabbing both, she then picked up her purse and left the bedroom without a backward glance before slipping from the house. She didn't tell Davis Allen good-bye, and she'd already talked to Alyssa that morning. There was nothing left to do but . . .

Run.

Raeg watched the little black cherry Ferrari leave the estate from where he stood at the window of the senator's office and tried to tell himself it was for the best. Just as he tried to tell himself she'd be back. He knew he was lying to himself on both fronts.

The feeling that Summer was finished with her life in DC left a heaviness in his chest he couldn't ignore, and hunger eating at his gut.

He could still taste her against his lips and he still ached for more of her. Ached in ways no other woman had ever made him ache. And that made her dangerous. It ensured that above all other women, this one was denied him. He couldn't allow himself to care, to allow his guard to slip, especially with a woman who had once been part of the CIA. An agent. A woman who would be perceived as the enemy. He didn't dare endanger his own soul in such a way again. He couldn't allow Falcon to do so, if there was a way to stop it.

Letting her go wasn't easy though.

The scent of her still lingered in his senses, the warmth of her body was a ghostly weight teasing against his chest, teasing his memory, testing his resolve. He had a feeling that forgetting those stolen moments in her suite would be impossible and he wasn't even certain if he wanted to forget.

He'd had a taste of the forbidden though, and now, he couldn't help but ache for more.

Chapter
ONE

FIVE MONTHS LATER

Well now, it would appear he owed his brother a sizeable payout on the bet they had, Falcon thought in disgust.

How the hell had she managed to fool him so easily?

The last time he'd seen Summer Bartlett, aka Summer Calhoun, she'd been lying sobbing in a bed in her brother's home in DC, long black strands of hair lying around her, her hair a neat little cap of jagged cuts no more than two or three inches long. All those long soft curls had been gone and he'd felt like a part of his heart had been cut from his chest.

He'd stomped out of the bedroom after warning her to get ready for an upcoming mission, so pissed that she'd cut her hair that he could barely stand to breathe, and it had been a damned ruse, nothing more. A trick. A carefully staged gimmick guaranteed to make him mad enough to stay away from her, for a while at least, when she slipped away again.

A month later there she stood on the balcony of a beach house she'd been staying in, nearly waist-length waves of raven black hair blowing in the ocean breeze, her slender, petite body clad only in a short nightie, allowing that breeze to caress tanned flesh as she tipped her head back in sensual enjoyment.

And she had him so damned hard it was all he could do to breathe.

"I warned you," his brother, Raeg snorted behind him. "Summer wouldn't cut her hair. She gets off far too easily on having you brush and braid it for her."

He slid a look to his brother, his jaw tightening at the scathing tone of voice. There were moments he wondered what had made him believe Raeg would be the best partner for this job. Perhaps he'd made a mistake in giving his brother first choice in accompanying him to inform Summer of the coming danger and protecting her from it. There had been other options. Options that would not have been so critical of the agent Summer had been, or the woman she was.

Was he wrong, he wondered, to believe Raeg's manner toward her held more than it appeared to on the surface? That the sensual enjoyment it seemed Raeg had found in Summer in DC was only in his own imagination?

Hell if he knew anymore.

"I didn't ask your opinion on her reasons why, they are obvious," he assured his half brother. "Searching for a woman with short black hair, made finding her more problematic if I continued searching for her. She would have known this."

"The point is, she ran, Falcon," Raeg pointed out, quite confident he knew Summer well enough to understand motivations that Falcon doubted even Summer understood. "If she gave a damn either way about how her abrupt absence affected you or anyone else, then she would have stuck around long enough to explain it."

Yes, she had run. Just as he had known at the time that she would do.

Evidently, Summer was serious about getting out of the covert and security work she'd been a part of for so long. Just as she was serious about refusing to return to the political social center that was DC.

But Raeg was wrong, she had attempted several times to tell him she wanted out, and Falcon had been so loath to lose her that he'd talked her into staying instead. That was a mistake he should have never allowed himself to make. A mistake he would not make again.

I'm so tired, Falcon, the note she had left at the house in DC stated. Tired of being shot at, tired of shooting at others, and tired of learning that friends were enemies and tried and true enemies could be friends.

Belle was being retired forever.

And could he truly blame her? In the space of only a few years, she had lost so much. The woman who had helped shape her as an agent and as a person had died unexpectedly, and she'd been forced to kill someone she had believed was a friend for most of her life.

To save him.

She had taken that life to save him, because he hadn't believed the woman would actually attempt to pull the trigger.

"I would be dead were it not for her," he reminded his brother softly. "She pulled the trigger when I could not, Raeg."

He'd kept his weapon holstered rather than pulling it and being prepared for what may happen.

Raeg said nothing. Instead, he lifted the water bottle to his lips and sipped as they stared at the vision still standing on the balcony, the sun's rays caressing her from head to toe, loving the breeze even as it loved her.

"I didn't say she didn't have her good points," Raeg finally stated with no small amount of ire. "I said she fooled you. You let her fool you."

Falcon pushed his fingers through his hair wearily, glancing at his brother and wondering if he could ever convince him that the reasons he fought so hard to find fault with Summer wasn't because she had the faults he wanted to see. Summer made Raeg see what he refused to acknowledge in himself. A man who hungered for a woman so much that he could not refuse who he was, what he was, if he was to have her. A man who knew that, even though he would have to walk away from her in the end, having her would be worth the agony of releasing her later.

If they could release her, Falcon thought, something he rarely allowed himself to consider because he knew too they'd have no choice but to let her go far too soon.

When Summer finally turned and reentered the house, Falcon hid his disappointment and continued to watch the area. Tonight, they'd sneak into the house and he'd have to tell her why he had chased her so relentlessly over the past month. She was running out of time and had no idea of the danger building with each day that she stayed out of sight. If he didn't tell her quickly, the consequences could prove disastrous.

"We will go in tonight," he told Raeg, hating the fact that what he would tell her would shatter any security she may have found in the past six months since leaving DC.

She was serious about getting out, he could see that now. He even accepted it, and after the past month of considering all the reasons why she would want out, he couldn't blame her.

She was a hell of an agent, but she was also a woman, and women did not see the world in the same terms, with the same logical choices that men saw it in. For a woman, friendships meant far more than they meant for a man in some ways. The rules were different in their hearts and taking the life of one she considered a friend would have altered everything she felt about the life she was living.

"You're not being logical about her, Falcon," Raeg advised. But Falcon heard the regret his brother tried to hide in his voice. "You know what you're risking. What both of us are risking."

The bleak lessons of the past couldn't be forgotten.

"Should I just allow Dragovich to kill her then?" Falcon turned to his brother, watching him curiously. "He nearly did in Russia. That was my fault because I all but begged her to take the job. Because of that, she was betrayed by Gia, her identity sold to the bastard and now he intends to finish the job." He couldn't even consider not protecting her, watching over her, after the many times she'd saved his life. But he understood Raeg's concern as well. "Why do you not go back to DC? I'll inform her of the problem and call Lucien Connor to come out and help me with this. She knows him, she works well with him."

Oh, he just bet she did, Raeg thought furiously, forcing back his anger at his brother's offer. She might get along fine with Lucien Conner, and that was all well and good, except for the fact that Lucien wanted nothing more than to get Summer into his bed.

"Why don't you just stop with the demands that I return to DC," Raeg snorted, "and stop making excuses for her."

"When you stop making excuses for yourself," Falcon stated with such disgust that Raeg could feel his frustration level rising. "For pity's sake, Raeg, protecting her from this will not endanger her from our enemy. Keeping her, loving her would. This will not."

Raeg couldn't convince himself of that, no matter how often he tried. He knew far better than Falcon the cost of forgetting the legacy that haunted them. He'd known a taste of that hell once already. He didn't want to revisit it. Especially not for a woman who affected him more than any other woman ever had.

And maybe that was part of it. She made him ache like nothing or no one ever had. She tugged at a part of him he hadn't known existed and made him admit to things he had never known he wanted, and all the while she'd bat those perfect, heavy black lashes of hers, smile with such feminine charm as those oddly colored violet eyes gleamed with seductive promise, right before informing him of what a prick she considered him. She could tear a strip off his hide in a voice so perfectly beautiful it made his dick harder than hell despite the insults she'd heap on him.

The fact that she was usually right, didn't count as far as he was concerned. He'd say he was a prick because she couldn't decide if she was a black-hearted agent or a sweet Cinderella wannabe, and he couldn't decide if he should make up her mind for her. The truth was, being a prick was the only way to keep her at arm's length.

"You still refuse to even discuss this," Falcon accused him, his voice low, his gaze still on the beach house. "Do you believe you'll be able to live in the same house with her and not eventually give into your needs? To what we both need? That, or you will make her hate you?"

Raeg didn't even deign to answer that question. He wouldn't touch it until he simply had no other choice and he damned sure wasn't going to listen to his brother lecture him on it.

"I think we should go in now." Placing his empty water bottle on the console of the vehicle they were sitting in, he narrowed his eyes on the house again. "She'll run again before nightfall."

"And you know this how?" Falcon bit out, frustration edging at his voice.

"She was on the balcony, full view for all the world, playing the lazy socialite," he pointed out. "We've been watching this damned place for two days, and you couldn't even tell anyone was there. It was a distraction. Any reasonable attempt to get to her would come after dark and she knows it. She intends to be long gone before that could happen, laughing her ass off because she fooled us again."

He knew her better than Falcon gave him credit.

His brother was silent, thoughtful. The explanation had at least gotten his brother off his back though, Raeg thought in relief. He didn't want to think about what he was going to do once they told her what was coming, who was coming. And he didn't want to consider the consequences of the only plan they'd been able to come up with to ensure she didn't end up dead.

Summer was a hell of an agent and he fully admitted that, but she wasn't Wonder Woman and she wasn't bullet resistant. And the enemy wanted to make a point, hence the reason a sniper hadn't been dispatched to just pick her off.

"We should go in now then," Falcon said softly, anticipation rumbling just below the soft tone of his voice as he started the Suburban and put it in gear. "She runs again, and we may not find her until she is but a corpse. If then."

That was a probability, Raeg thought, pushing back the arousal and the anticipation he couldn't help but feel.

It had been five months since he'd seen her. In the past eight years, five months had never passed that he hadn't seen her, argued with her, touched her, even if it was in the most impersonal way. She always seemed to bring the sunshine with her, he thought wearily. What was it Falcon called her sometimes? Summer-shine. That was what it was like, feeling the warmth of that season when she was around, whether she was charming them to distraction or driving Raeg insane with the sugary little jabs.

And Summer was like a drug. Didn't matter if it was the argument or merely seeing her now, her physical presence lit up a room with her smile and her bright violet eyes. It was still a fix, and he hadn't had his in far too long.

"Fuck this up, Raeg, and you and I will have words." Falcon surprised him, not just with the warning, but also with the fact that he was dead serious. "Do not antagonize her to the point that she refuses to allow us to watch her back."

Raeg stared at his brother thoughtfully. In all the years they'd argued over Summer, Falcon had never given him an ultimatum before.

"We're always having words where Summer's concerned," he finally pointed out, knowing even as he said it, it was a mistake. "What would make this time any different?"

"This time, I doubt I would forgive you. Especially if she's hurt because of it." Falcon flicked him a determined look as they turned into the drive leading to the beach house. "And I will definitely not forgive you should anything happen to her because of your animosity toward her."

And that, Raeg knew, Falcon wouldn't threaten lightly. The fact that Raeg was going to eventually lose the woman was a definite, but he never considered losing his brother as well.

Dammit.

Now things were just going to get complicated.

"And if something happens to her because we *are* trying to protect her?" he asked his brother. "What will we do then?"

Falcon shook his head. "As far as we know, the past is dead."

"The past never really dies, Falcon," he sighed heavily. "Only its victims. Let's try to keep that in mind until we at least have Dragovich taken care of."

Then, maybe, he could ensure Falcon at least stayed with her, if that was what he decided to do. Raeg couldn't discount the possibility. If he simply played the third, hid his own ever deepening hunger, his own need for more, maybe, he could protect his brother and the woman both of them ached so desperately for.

Dammit.

Now how had Falcon managed to find her?

Summer stepped into the private beach house before throwing a glare back at the white curtains billowing in the breeze and blowing through the open French doors.

He should have never found her so quickly. Hell, he shouldn't have even been looking for her after the last run-in she'd had with him.

Evidently Esteban de la Cortez Falcone, or "Falcon" as most who knew him, called him, was far more stubborn than she'd believed him to be.

But five months?

Really?

After four months he should have given up. Especially after believing she'd committed the unpardonable sin of chopping off all her hair to only a few inches in length. He'd always sworn he'd never forgive her for that.

Not that she would ever dare cut more than just the ends of her hair. Her family would just disown her, she was sure, if she did such a thing. Besides, she loved her hair. There wasn't a chance she'd willingly mutilate it in such a way.

Making Falcon believe she had, then running, would be enough to convince him to just go home and give up. She was certain of it.

She'd obviously forgotten how stubborn he could be. That was her bad. Now, she'd simply have to deal with it. And if she knew Falcon, she *might* just have enough time to get dressed.

Maybe.

She'd make certain to throw his little system into overdrive and just wear the nightie if she hadn't glimpsed someone in the vehicle with him. God only knew who he was working with now, and flashing an unknown male wasn't her favored sport.

At least, not this week.

Thankfully she knew how to be quick as well.

The short, casual white chiffon skirt and matching white cami tank were already laid out, along with strappy, flat thong sandals. She'd intended to pack and leave after she'd had her coffee and a piece of the crumb cake she'd made the night before for the drive home. It was a good thing she'd made a full pan rather than just a few muffin-sized ones.

Brushing her hair, she pulled it over her shoulder and quickly braided it. Maybe while he was arguing with her, Falcon would braid it for her. Her hair hadn't been properly braided since she left Arlington, come to think of it. She hadn't had a chance to get to her favorite hair-

dresser either. But Falcon had always found such pleasure in playing with her hair that she actually found it
quite relaxing.

Damn, this was messing with her intended schedule.
Her family was expecting her home soon. She was supposed to leave in a matter of hours if she wanted to get
there tonight in time to get some sleep before Sunday
breakfast.

She'd promised her sister Aunjenue she'd been there
tonight as well. Evidently Auna was having problems
with some guy and wanted to talk to Summer about it.
Auna, love her heart, had far too many admirers.

Finishing the braid and tying it off, Summer checked
the mirror quickly. No makeup was required, she didn't
believe. She was going for casual yet relaxed. She looked
fine.

Good enough for a former partner and his current
partner at least.

The thought of that current partner had her inhaling
without regret, but still, a bit of bitter sweetness. She
and Falcon had worked very well together. The few times
he'd convinced his brother Raeg to join them, Raeg had
actually put aside his animosity for her, and they'd func-
tioned so well that when he'd left, she'd found herself
missing him.

When Raeg wasn't being a prick, when he wasn't trying to make her feel like she wasn't only helpless, but just
shy of an actual IQ quotient, then she'd been fascinated
by him. He was quick, as intelligent as Falcon and just
as instinctive on a mission. He could look at the opera-
tional plan, pick its flaws apart, and by time he and Falcon finished yelling out the strengths and weaknesses of
each move, it was flawless.

Senator's chief of staff indeed. She suspected he did

far more for Davis Allen than any chief of staff had ever been wrangled into. She remembered her godfather nearly having a melt-down when Raeg had mentioned resigning the year before and perhaps doing something else. He hadn't just gotten a handsome pay raise as incentive to stay, but several exceptional perks as well.

And when he and his half brother, Falcon, were together, it was like finally getting a glimpse of the heart and soul of both men. Apart, they simply lacked something that came together whenever they worked side by side.

They were an interesting combination. Unfortunately, she'd only had a chance to work with them together a few times. Once Raeg returned to his duties with the senator, the prick came back in full strength and it was like trying to get along with a rabid wolf.

A roughly handsome, sexy-as-hell, but still entirely rabid wolf.

Smiling at the analogy she left the bedroom and swept through the beach house. The wide hallway, open living room, dining and kitchen areas had seaside views, full-length windows, and a multitude of French doors left open, long white sheers fluttering in the sweet breeze drifting through the house.

She could have actually stayed a few more days before heading to her hometown, just to be certain she wasn't being followed. There was an odd certainty she might be, but once she'd glimpsed the Suburban Falcon used for long-distance trips, she had a pretty good idea who was shadowing her.

He just wasn't giving up . . .

Sweet Jesus.

And here she thought she was one of his favorite little Southern girls.

If that were the case, Falcon wouldn't be standing in the kitchen as she stepped from the bedroom with the one partner guaranteed to give her a headache. Because if she wasn't on the mission with them, then she was still public enemy number one.

This wasn't a mission, which meant Raeg was going to make her completely insane. And no doubt, the second his lips opened . . .

"And here Falcon blubbered into his beer for hours over the mutilated hair," Raeg snorted, leaning lazily against the white wood and marble counter, a smirk tilting his lips as his gaze went over her. "I even felt sorry for him."

From the corner of her eye she watched Falcon shoot his brother a hard glare. A warning. Which wasn't exactly unheard of between the two of them.

"I see he survived it." She lifted a brow as she shot Falcon a grin. "None the worse for wear, right?"

Falcon merely snorted. She'd one-upped him, he wouldn't be angry over it, but she'd never get away with it again.

Damn, there were days she was certain she just might love Falcon far more than she suspected. He hid his powerful, stubborn will with an easy charm that even managed to keep her at ease, and had a habit of charming her out of any anger she might feel far too quickly. Wicked and sensual and filled with teasing warmth, she'd missed him more than she wanted to admit.

But then, she'd missed his exasperating, infuriating brother just the same.

"He was fine after I convinced him there wasn't a chance in hell you'd cut your crowning glory." Raeg slid his brother a mocking look. "I'm disappointed he didn't know better at the time though."

Mr. Know-It-All, she thought. No wonder Falcon was glaring at him.

"I'm just curious how *you* knew I wouldn't cut it," she muttered, moving for the coffeemaker on the kitchen island. "You must have taken your smart pill that morning."

Wasn't she the lucky one that he didn't take one every morning?

Raeg merely grinned rather than rising to the bait.

What the hell was up with him?

"You disappoint me, Summer," Falcon told her, shaking his head as he shot her a teasing frown. "Trying to trick me rather than talking to me was not nice."

She glanced toward the Heavens. God love his heart, talking to him had never gotten her anywhere before. He'd just end up sweet-talking her into wherever he needed her to go at any given time.

"Since when did talking to you work when you didn't want to hear what I had to say?" she asked him, dumping some coffee beans into the grinder. "I was tired of talking, Falcon."

She flipped the grinder on.

No one spoke as the scent of freshly ground coffee filled the air. Once it finished, she leveled the finely ground beans into the coffeemaker's metal basket and turned the machine on.

"You didn't have to make me think you had cut all your beautiful hair," Falcon informed her, moving to the cabinets to collect their cups. "I was grieving, Summer. I believe I may have wanted to cry."

She believed he was full of it.

"He was pathetic," Raeg agreed in disgust. "Cursing and whining. Then he was waxing poetic. In Spanish even."

In Spanish?

She slid Falcon an amused look. He rarely used his native language, but when he did, it was worth listening to. Though waxing poetic wasn't normally his style when he erupted into a full-scale Spanish temper tantrum as she'd seen him do. It was usually some of the most inventive curses she believed she'd probably heard in her life.

Then there were the times he'd use all five languages he knew in one eruption of enraged sentences. She admitted those displays were completely mesmerizing. An education even when he really got into it.

"I'm sending him back to Arlington." Falcon nodded toward his brother. "In a body bag. Next time I bring him out to play it will be in a muzzle."

She almost laughed. Yeah, she could really see that one happening. There were many, many times she wished she could put a muzzle on Raeg herself. Sometimes, he actually deserved to be in one.

"I didn't ask to be included this time," Raeg seemed to remind him, his expression darkening.

"And I didn't invite you," Falcon retorted without any true anger. Yet. "But now that you are here, stop being an asshole and figure out where she'd be hiding that cake. I can smell it."

She shot him an infuriated look. She simply couldn't believe him.

Damn him. She had really hoped to get by without him detecting that cake.

"Oh for pity's sake," Summer muttered, pulling open the oven door to reveal the aluminum tin filled with the cinnamony fresh crumb cake. "You're like an old hound dog sniffing out bones."

Raeg chuckled, though Falcon dived for the pan.

"One day, I will kiss your momma's cheek," Falcon

promised as he pulled the sweet treat from the oven as though it were gold.

He was just too easy to please sometimes.

"Too bad Summer can't bake," Raeg pointed out mockingly. "Or cook. I thought all good Southern mothers taught their daughters to cook before they were ten?"

Summer merely shrugged. Let him say what he wanted, she and her momma knew the truth, and that was all that mattered.

"If she baked this delight, we would marry her," Falcon swore with almost gleeful pleasure. "Perhaps I can convince her momma to marry us. I think I could do so if I thought she'd bake for us often."

Summer just dropped her head and stared at the floor, shaking her head. Just when she had managed to convince herself to forget the fact that it was one for all and all for one with those two, one of them just had to remind her.

At the sound of the coffeemaker completing its cycle she poured the coffee into the cups Falcon had placed next to her, aware of Raeg searching the cupboards until he found dessert plates and forks.

Carrying the three cups to the table, she placed one in front of Falcon as he guarded the cake pan—no doubt terrorists worldwide were after her cake—while Raeg set a plate and fork by each cup.

"You think he's going to share that cake?" Raeg asked as they took their chairs and stared at Falcon expectantly.

Falcon cut the cake though, placed generous portions on each plate, then immediately dug into his with the most sensual sound of pleasure. That little hum of love went straight between her thighs and sent a pulse of aching need through her entire system.

Damn him. Far too charming by far.

"We're going to have to make this a quick visit," she told them. Evidently they had no intentions of telling her why they were there.

"And this would be why?" Falcon spared her no more than a quick glance as he forked another bite of cake into his mouth, obviously in no hurry to finish the sweet.

"Because I have to leave. I'd already be packing if I hadn't spotted the Suburban parked in the carpool area where you thought you were hiding." She gave them both a chiding look. "Really? Did you think I wouldn't see you there?"

Evidently, that was exactly what they thought.

"How did you know who it was?" Raeg leaned back in his chair regarding her curiously rather than hatefully as he normally did.

Maybe he was ill this week.

Or maybe he was working an operation with Falcon, which meant her former partner had no intention whatsoever of paying attention when she said she was finished. Not that working with both Raeg and Falcon couldn't be fun, because it could be.

She simply knew it was time for her to get out. To continue heading out knowing that would be the same as signing her own death warrant.

"Falcon keeps forgetting to have the Suburban painted, and the scuffs on the front are very distinctive. And they show up real good in sunlight," she answered Raeg.

Falcon was too busy stuffing his face to do more than roll his eyes at the reminder. But since his hair had drifted over his brow, falling to partially obscure one eye, and he looked too damned sexy for words, she wouldn't hold it against him.

"This cake . . ." Falcon sighed, tipping his fork toward

the few bites left. "I am in love with your momma, Summer. She has stolen my heart. I'm telling you, Raeg and I will marry her. I'm certain we could slip her right past your father and steal her completely away."

Once again, Raeg simply slid his brother a doubtful look.

Sipping her coffee to hide her smile, she ignored the look Raeg turned on her then. God only knew what he was thinking. It was equal parts suspicion and chiding amusement, and not a look she'd ever received from him. As though he knew far more than she wanted him to know, and had every intention of using it to his advantage. The look actually excited her more than it should have and left her just a tad breathless.

Remaining silent while they finished their cake, Summer sipped her coffee, merely picking at her own portion. She knew Falcon and Raeg had something on their minds, and she was terribly afraid that saying no to both of them would be impossible.

A hunter always knew when it was time to find their hole and learn how to hide, Summer thought painfully. They realized when they couldn't handle the blood and the death, the lies and the danger any longer. She'd reached that point before the Russian operation, but she'd kept going because she hated walking away from Falcon and Raeg forever. And it would be forever, she'd known. Whatever haunted the two men, she'd never learned, just as she had no idea how to get past it.

"Falcon, you seem to be ignoring the fact that I told you I have to leave," she finally told him gently when he'd nearly finished his cake.

She didn't want to argue with him. In the time she'd worked with him, she'd glimpsed a gentleness, a warmth in him that both intrigued her and endeared him to her.

"Summer . . ." he began.

"Falcon." She leaned forward, staring back at him imploringly. "I don't want to have to run from you again, but I just can't do it anymore. You didn't want to listen before. You keep hunting me down, and all I want is to find some peace. If I go out again, feeling this way, I'll die, and we both know it."

She had to make him understand before he began making his play for her to join them in whatever job they had taken.

"I realized that when I saw the lengths you would go to in escaping me." Pushing his fingers through his hair, he sat back and regarded her silently for a moment. "I wish I could continue to leave you to find your peace, sweetheart. Raeg and I both do. But that isn't possible now."

"You don't want me going out on a job with you ever again," she advised him painfully. "Don't try to convince me otherwise. I'll end up getting both of us killed."

"I know this, Summer."

"They why are you here? With him?" She gestured angrily to Raeg as he sat silently, simply watching her, his eagle-like gaze far too intent. "For God's sake, Falcon—"

Raeg smacked a picture down on the table.

Staring down at it, Summer felt everything inside her freeze in shock as she recognized the girl.

And she knew. In that moment, Summer knew peace was once again elusive, and hell was waiting instead.

Chapter
TWO

The picture was of a younger version of herself. Barely eighteen, her eyes more blue than violet, her smile more open, filled with warmth and joy. The young woman stood in front of a Main Street clothing store with several other girls, their expressions animated as they stared at the long, formal dress in the window.

"Aunjenue." She whispered her sister's name.

It wasn't the only picture.

The four-by-six photos Raeg tossed onto the table in front of her featured her family, from at different times. Her brothers—though the picture of her eldest brother Caleb wasn't there—Momma and Daddy, cousins, several aunts. And two of her mother shopping with Aunjenue.

They were surveillance photos.

"The envelope these came in was addressed to me," Raeg told her quietly. "Inside was this note."

He placed it carefully on top of the photos.

Summer Calhoun, Cliffton, Georgia

Not Summer Bartlett. Summer Calhoun.

"Who? How?" She shook her head.

She had been careful. Very careful. Even the name Summer Bartlett wasn't ever used on an operation. Her codename Belle was the only one she'd ever used.

She was caught by Raeg's gaze, the piercing golden brown predatory color was cool, watchful, waiting. Waiting to see if it was her fault? To point out how she'd messed up? She hadn't messed up. She was too careful for that.

"Who did this?" she whispered, lips numb, fighting to process how this could have happened. "How did they do this?"

The implacable expression on Raeg's face never changed as he answered her. "Dragovich."

The word struck at her with a force that caused her to flinch.

The Russian crime lord had come in on her as she was retrieving a flash drive from his laptop at his office in Moscow that contained sensitive military information. Information he'd paid a premium for.

He'd shot her in her shoulder from the back as she jumped through a second-story window to the balcony. Falcon had been waiting in the SUV just below the edge of the balcony, and when she managed to drop to it and into the open sun roof, he'd sped away, ensuring no one identified her. When they'd finally managed to get out of Russia, they'd left enough suspicion that she'd died that she was certain he wasn't even looking for her.

"How?" Linking her fingers together at her lap, she clenched tight, pulling back the shock, the fear to find that center where the cool agent rather than the woman torn with panic existed. "How did he learn my identity? Find my family? No one knew I was there but . . ."

That was all it took—the knowledge of who had known her identity and the fact that Dragovich would pay just about any price to acquire it.

"Just the team," Falcon confirmed. "You, me, Gia."

Gia. The friend Summer had been forced to kill to save Falcon.

"She sold Dragovich the information just after your arrival at that last job the three of you took to protect Alyssa Hampstead," Raeg confirmed. "Payment was made and the file sent electronically just days before . . ."

Raeg paused then, his lips tightening at the memory. He'd been enraged when he learned Gia had nearly killed his brother.

"Before I killed her." Summer tonelessly finished the sentence, staring at her uneaten portion of cake on the table in front of her.

Of all her enemies, Dragovich was the most brutal, the most arrogant. He would never stop coming after her. And if he couldn't get to her, he would eventually go after her family, starting with Aunjenue and her parents.

God, her brother was going to kill her.

"We have to call Caleb."

"How do you think we found you?" Raeg stated coolly. "We've already been to the farm looking for you, Summer. Caleb's aware of the problem."

Yeah, her brother was going to kill her. No wonder Aunjenue kept texting to make certain she'd be home.

She ran her hands over her face. How was she going to protect them? Cliffton, Georgia, was home. Damned near everyone who lived there was related to her in one way or another. Aunts, uncles, cousins, her friends . . . her life.

It was all there in Cliffton.

She roughly pushed back from the table, nearly upending the chair she was sitting in before Raeg caught it. Wrapping her arms around herself, she turned her back on them and fought to control the fear, the overwhelming guilt surging through her.

Damn Dragovich. This was the reason Falcon had so carefully plotted the appearance that Summer had died in Moscow—they knew he'd never stop looking for her.

When he was pissed off, he was like a damned dog searching for a particular bone. And he had enough money to get whatever he wanted. Evidently her former teammate had enough hatred to sell information to him too.

"When he couldn't find you, he sent two men to Cliffton," Raeg informed her. "They're watching the family and watching for you. You did the psychological profile on him. You know him better than anyone, Summer. What will he do?"

He would begin killing her family off one by one until she showed up. Once she did, he'd want to play with her. Dragovich was a demented son of a bitch. The evil he possessed was so black and ice cold, there was no mercy at all within him. But he also considered himself smarter, stronger than his opponents. Because of that, he made a game out of everything.

"He'll play with me," she told him, keeping her back to him. "No matter where I go, no matter how I try to draw him away from the family, that's where he'll stay, just to torment me. He'll want me there, want me fighting to figure out who he'll go after first and how to stop him."

She'd spent months on the profile she'd built on him. Even her mother, a former CIA analyst herself, had helped her pull together the information she'd needed on the Russian warlord. Not that her mother had known Summer was going after him. Her family still seemed to believe that she worked as an analyst and profiler only.

They had no idea she was in the thick of danger whenever possible in the past years. When she'd left the CIA
she had never actually informed them that she was doing
fieldwork. She'd just stated that she was doing more or
less as she had with the Agency.

"Who will he go after first?"

Who would he go after first?

"If I go home, he'll focus on me. He'll want me to
worry, to suffer, then he'll send his men in to take me and
a family member, though more than likely he'll take more
than one. Once he has me in custody, he'll make me
watch while he kills a few of them before he lets me die."

He'd start with Aunjenue.

"I have to go back home." She sighed. "I was going
back anyway, but . . ."

She'd have to face Caleb, convince him to make certain protection concentrated on the family and allow her
to face Dragovich, though she really didn't see that happening. That wouldn't happen.

What have I done to my family?

"I was getting out," she whispered. "I knew it was
time. I thought I was going in time . . ."

In time to save herself, in time to find some peace.
She shook her head at the thought. She should have
known better. After learning how destructive, how completely corrupt Gia actually was, she should have known
that the other woman had done something like this. She
should have been prepared, should have kept it from
happening.

She knew how people worked, knew how people like
Dragovich and traitors like Gia connived and manipu-
lated information and the people around them. She should
have never been caught unaware by this, or allowed her
family to be in this kind of danger.

She should have been prepared . . .

"Thank you for letting me know." She turned back to them, the ice that filled her freezing her clear to her soul. "You should return to Arlington."

Falcon and Raeg remained at the table. Falcon glanced at his brother with a sort of mild assurance, as though they had already expected her response, while his brother's expression went from implacable to prick in about two heartbeats.

"Do you think you can do this alone, Summer?" Raeg snorted, mockery filling his voice. "Or that Caleb can protect you against Dragovich?"

She knew he would try. Caleb, her brothers Bowe and Brody, her father and her mother and even Aunjenue, they would try to protect her. Unfortunately, they would be Dragovich's targets as well if he couldn't get to her. Aunjenue would be the most vulnerable. Her father was a former Delta Force soldier, Caleb was former Special Forces, but Bowe and Brody's training, though less conventional, was just as extensive. Even her mother was former CIA, and one of the best shooters Summer had ever witnessed.

She actually suspected her mother, like herself, had been far more than an analyst while employed by the CIA.

"Caleb can protect the house." She toyed absently with the braid that fell over her shoulder. "Momma and Daddy, Aunjenue, our brothers." She nodded at the thought. "I'll protect myself. I have my own place but . . ."

"I told you she was fucking crazy." Raeg turned to his brother, glaring at him before Summer could finish. "Didn't I tell you she'd come up with just this? She's a suicide wish disguised as a sex kitten. I warned you."

A sex kitten?

Summer turned to him in surprise, her eyes widening. Where the hell had he come up with sex kitten?

"Raeg . . ." Falcon's voice was its own warning.

"Don't you 'Raeg' me." His brother pushed from the chair, turning a brooding look of simmering anger on her. "You're right. The best place to face Dragovich is right there where he's focused. You leave, he'll focus on your family anyway. Go back, let him see you there. Face the first attack, then he'll come after you himself. He won't be able to help it."

"That's exactly what I said." Her hands went to her hips as she frowned back at him. "And how is that a suicide wish?"

He had never made any sense to her. Ever. He was a walking, talking puzzle she couldn't figure out no matter how hard she tried.

"Because you think you can do it alone?" His craggy features were filled with anger now. "Because you keep thinking you're Wonder Woman and Supergirl all rolled into one?"

Fury snapped inside her. He was staring at her again as though she was too stupid to live, as though he had all the answers and he knew her all the way to her soul and found her completely lacking.

This was why the two of them could not get along. He was a prick on a good day and a complete asshole at any other time.

And he didn't know a damned thing.

"If we're talkin' superheroes, sugar, I always preferred the Black Widow myself. She was just so much more interestin'," she informed him with an exaggerated drawl. "And if I needed your opinion I would have asked for it, now wouldn't I? Now go home and let me fix my own mess if you don't mind."

Let her fix her own mess?

Raeg could feel his head getting ready to explode.

Be nice to her, Falcon had demanded.

Be understanding, his brother had told him a dozen times if he'd told him one.

Well "nice" and "understanding" just didn't get it with this woman. She was like a damned tornado if she wasn't reined in, and Falcon simply refused to see it. Hell, his brother was so blinded by emotion and lust he couldn't see it if it knocked him on his ass.

"You say that as though you actually have a hope in hell of facing that bastard and surviving." He couldn't help that his voice was rising, or that incredulity was filling it. "What you'll do is end up straining Caleb's resources, and all of you will end up dead."

Her eyes widened instantly, outrage filling them.

"Shame on you." The violet hue of her eyes snapped in fury as her nose lifted with insulting disgust. "You think I've learned nothing in the years I've been covert? Trust me, Raeg. I do know how to handle acquiring my own security and I'm really not too damned proud to do so."

She knew how to do what? Hire some fifty-cent fucking personal protection agents who'd never gone against the likes of Dragovich? Who had no idea what they were facing? Good God, she'd lost her mind. She was a crazy woman and his brother simply refused to see it. Hell, even he hadn't realized the lengths she'd go to in her insanity, now had he?

He turned on his brother, glaring at him expectantly and seeing only Falcon's cool, observational look in return. Why the hell was he so calm now? Where were the Spanish curses? The little temper tantrum guaranteed to ensure Summer at least paid attention to the fact that she was completely fucking up?

"Why the hell are we even here then?" he demanded, disbelief adding volume to his voice. "You should have sent her a fucking text and been done with it."

"My thoughts exactly!" Summer yelled from behind him. "Especially considering how much we both know you alone hate me. I'm surprised you're not gloating your ass off. Poor Falcon, you just set him thinkin' you came to help him. You probably just came to get your rocks off at the sight of me tremblin' in fear. Well, I don't tremble, do I, hot shot?"

He jerked around to her.

She had not just said something so ridiculous, had she? She couldn't believe he hated her, could she? That he'd ever, in a million years, allow anyone to physically harm her, that he could even bear the thought of it? And were those tears sparkling in her eyes? She made his dick so hard it was like iron, shredded his temper, and she thought he hated her? Thought he'd get off at the thought of her hurt, or worse, dead?

Disbelief warred with self-disgust as he stared at her, realizing she believed just that. That over the years the anger and sharp comments hadn't been because he was dying to touch her and couldn't, but because he hated her. And nothing could be further from the truth.

"Just go, Raeg," she demanded, her voice lowering, thickening, before she swung around to stare out at the ocean once again. "I'll figure it out."

And Falcon wasn't saying a word. He was watching both of them instead, his pale blue eyes icy, all emotion or thoughts hidden as he sat, his forearms resting on the table, simply watching silently.

Raeg knew that look, knew his brother wouldn't intercede unless forced to. Instead, he was dissecting them, and Raeg hated it when Falcon tried to dissect him.

Damn him.

"Do something," he ordered his brother. "You're the only one who can handle her."

Falcon's brows only lifted curiously.

" 'Handle' me?" Summer swung back around then, anger filling her expression, her eyes. "No one 'handles' me, John Raeg, especially not Falcon. And damned sure not you."

"I believe it," Raeg snarled when his brother did no more than shrug when he glared at him. "I think it's the other way around. You make damned sure you control him instead." He flicked Falcon a disgusted glance. "She leads you around by your dick, and makes you love every second of it."

Falcon's lips only quirked to match the gleam of amusement that suddenly appeared in his eyes.

"Jealous, asshole?" she snapped behind him. "Maybe if you learned how to control that ugly attitude of yours, you'd be so lucky. Maybe then you wouldn't have the disposition of a wounded gator."

He turned to her, seeing the confrontational stance. One hand on a cocked hip, her nose lifted disdainfully, her expression so damned superior even though those tears glittered in her eyes, refusing to fall. And he wanted nothing more than to jerk her to him, lift her to the counter behind her, and fuck her until the only thing she could do was whisper his name in exhaustion.

"You are completely unreasonable," he ground out, feeling the pressure on his molars as his teeth clenched.

She made him crazy. She refused to listen to reason, refused to listen to him.

Damn her.

He should head right back to Arlington as she demanded, but he knew that wasn't really an option. He couldn't let it become an option. He'd be leaving his brother and Summer to face a Russian warlord alone, uncertain of the backup they may or may not have.

They worked well together, but he remembered what happened the last time they'd gone against Dragovich without adequate backup. Their former teammate couldn't be considered "backup," let alone "adequate."

Son of a bitch.

He couldn't do this, yet he had no other choice.

Summer was chaos and she made him insane.

She was everything he and Falcon had ever wanted in a woman and everything they couldn't have, couldn't afford to lose. And she thought they were just going to walk away and leave her to face this alone? Leave her to trust some damned stranger to cover her back, someone Raeg had no idea if they could be trusted or not?

It simply was not going to happen.

"I need to pack." Tension filled her voice, but at least she was no longer on the verge of crying. "The two of you need to go home. Thank you for letting me know what's going on, but I can handle this from here."

She could handle it from here, could she?

And Falcon simply snagged Summer's dessert plate, and began silently eating her cake as though his brother and his former partner weren't about to strangle each other.

As though whatever Summer decided was law.

Before he realized what he was doing, before Summer could evade him, he was in her face, nose to nose, ignoring her surprise.

"Go ahead and fucking pack," he snarled. "We head out in an hour for Cliffton. And by God, I don't take orders from a spoil-assed little Southern socialite I can't seem to keep my damned brother away from. I guess you're fucking stuck with me."

Her eyes narrowed. "You are handling that F-word far too often." She sniffed disdainfully. "And I don't have to worry about you staying long. You won't make it five minutes around my family, and you'll be stealing all Dragovich's fun when you kill them yourself. Or they kill you."

With that, she swept from the kitchen in a cloud of subtle spicy scent and affronted feminine anger.

And Raeg had a feeling he just placed the first nail in his own coffin.

"She bakes those goddamned cakes herself, you moron," he snapped at his brother when there was no one else to yell at. "When are you going figure that out?"

Falcon scooped up the last bite with relish before lifting his brow with a knowing smile. "Since the first one I ate? Try learning how to deal with her, Raeg, maybe then she'd cook for us. I hear she's quite good at it. I'll be waiting in the car. Make sure she doesn't run."

"Me?" he growled. "Why me?"

Falcon shrugged, moving for the door. "Because. You're the one who pissed her off."

Chapter
THREE

Her brother Caleb was waiting for them when they stepped into the kitchen from the attached garage of her house. The low light from the counter illuminated the large, country-style room with its wide work island, breakfast nook, and multitude of cabinets and windows.

She'd had the house completely remodeled after she'd bought it from her brother. She was an agent, with all the paranoid tendencies that went with it. Exterior walls were lead-lined, windows were bullet resistant, shades made to screw with infra-red and heat-detecting technology. The inside window shutters were merely added security.

The security system wasn't just installed by her brother, it was created by him as well, right down to the footfall detector on the walk leading to the porch and on the porch itself.

"So far, there's no sign of a sniper," Caleb informed them as he carried a pot of coffee to the table as Whitt, one of his former Special Forces team members, collected cups. "Watchers are having problems watching the houses," he grinned. "They don't care much for the alligators that creep around the grounds at night."

"Who needs security guards?" Summer murmured.

Caleb chuckled at the comment. Even in the low light, his eyes—nearly the same color as hers—gleamed in the near darkness. Short black hair, beard, and mustache. He looked like a pirate. He had been known to act like one on occasion too.

"We'll go over everything I've pulled in since Falcon and Raeg showed up in the morning," he promised. "Daddy's expecting all three of you at the house before breakfast. He likes to chat on the front porch over coffee, and Momma likes Summer's help in the kitchen." He gave them all a warning look. "That's you and Falcon as well, Raeg. You don't want the major to come looking for you."

Oh God.

That was going to be a disaster.

Her daddy would take one look at Falcon and Raeg, then give her one of those disappointed looks she hated so badly. And that was just the beginning.

Her daddy knew her, could read her like a book. That meant she was *really* in trouble.

"Daddy's askin' questions, Summer," he warned her next. "Especially about the work you've been doing with Falcon and Raeg that had Dragovich coming after you. He was on the phone with Davis Allen when I left the house earlier."

That was not a good thing. It was bad. It was so very bad, and she was just in so much trouble.

"Daddy will take a switch to me," she groaned. "I am such dead meat, Caleb."

She was aware of Raeg frowning at her and Falcon's curiosity as they listened to the exchange.

"Eh, not this week," her brother promised, highly amused. "His knees are acting up. Just run. Hell, you could outrun him in those four-inch heels you wear if you wanted to."

Her momma would do it then.

"Breakfast, boys." Caleb lifted his hand and headed for the garage door. "I'd get there early, Summer. Help Momma with breakfast. You know how she likes that. Then she might not chase you down for Daddy when he mentions that switch."

He just wasn't going to be nice to her tonight, was he?

"You're bein' ugly to me, Caleb," she sighed, pretty much resigned. "And that is so not fair."

Without answering the accusation, he shot her an amused grin before he disappeared into the garage. Seconds later a muted beep to her cellphone had a map flashing on screen of the yard, showing his and Whitt's progress.

At least the security system worked.

Rising from her chair she stared at the cups still on the table and the coffee pot Caleb hadn't returned to the maker, and held back a sigh. Collecting them, she quickly washed them in the sink, aware of both Raeg and Falcon as they moved through the house. They checked the security system as well as the footfall alarms on the wraparound porch and cement walk.

By the time they finished, she was getting her luggage, wondering why the hell Caleb always managed to forget his manners with her. He should have carried them right to her room himself. She was going to tell their momma on him first thing. Maybe she could be distracted from being put out with Summer by getting put out with her son instead?

Doubtful. But she could hope.

"Here." Falcon grabbed the two suitcases she was struggling to haul from the Suburban. "We loaded them, dammit, did you think we wouldn't unload them?"

The tone was completely irate and Falcon was hardly ever irate with her.

"Now *you're* gettin' ugly with me?" she asked as she grabbed her makeup bag and headed into the house. "Just what I need, you in a bad mood too."

It always took a while to settle in when she arrived home, Summer remembered as she led the way to her upstairs suite. The transition was always a pain in the ass.

"Summer, do you always have to travel with half a dozen bags?" he asked, more amused than irritated as her brothers or even Raeg could get. But his expression was still a little tense.

"I try to travel light." She shrugged, wandering to the balcony doors and unlocking them before stepping outside.

And there it was.

The fog was rolling in from the swamp, steamy and thick, coming in as floating tendrils, fingers of humid moisture reaching out and creeping across the backyard.

She could hear the gators, bellowing out an eerie sound into the night. In the distance, a big cat called out—panthers or even cougars were known to wander the Okefenokee.

When she was younger, her daddy had tracked a cougar that had killed one of his calves. He'd never caught it, but he'd come back with tales of monster alligators, panthers stalking him from the tops of the trees, and a fog so thick and heavy he swore it moved him through the swamps as if it had a will of its own, for miles at a time.

Watching it now, the thick threads reaching closer

to the house, she could well imagine such a thing happening.

"Now that is eerie as hell," Falcon whispered as his arms slid around her, pulling her closer to his obviously aroused body.

Summer let her head settle against the chest behind her, her hands resting against his linked ones where they came together low on her stomach.

It took everything she had to control her breathing, to fight back the heat that rose inside her whenever he touched her like this, whenever he let her feel how much he wanted her. But it also calmed her whenever he held her. No matter how upset she was or how worried, when he pulled her against him, Summer could almost feel herself drawing on his strength and his power. Sometimes, those qualities seemed inexhaustible in Falcon.

"It's beautiful," she whispered. "Soon, it will surround the house like a blanket, ghostly white, that little bit of moon giving it a glow that sends chills up the spine if you're not used to it. And those fingers of fog will seem to be probing at the seams of the door, the windows, as though hungry to reach the inside and consume it as well."

She was used to it, and still, she'd been known to give a little shiver.

Aunjenue would actually sit out on her balcony sometimes when it came through as though soaking up the moisture, enjoying the tendrils that wrapped around her. Summer avoided them. Not that she was scared of them, or spooked by them, but the curious-like threads of moisture always seemed far too sentient to her for comfort.

"You've missed being home," he murmured. "I was seeing it in you before we took that job with Davis Allen."

She had missed home. Learning her dearest friend in the world was in danger had been far more important though. Home was always waiting, but Alyssa might not be if she didn't get there in time.

She'd gotten there in time, but that job had gone to hell so fast she still had trouble acclimating herself to the consequences.

"I always miss home," she revealed, something no one but Alyssa had known before now. "When I'm away for too long, I begin to feel off balance. The person you've always known isn't who I am, Falcon," she revealed sadly. "This is where I'm me. This is where all my hopes and dreams began and where I hope to live to an old old age. This is where I took my first breath and it's where I want to draw my last breath."

"Think I don't know that the woman that flits and flirts around DC isn't really you?" he questioned her softly. "Do you think I don't know the sweetness that exists beneath the woman you show the world?"

Perhaps he did. Falcon always saw deeper, probed at the layers of a person until he could reach the inner parts. Not because he was nosy or because he felt they were being secretive as Raeg did. He did it because he genuinely cared about people. He wanted to know who they were and what they were.

"Maybe you do," she sighed, watching the fog come closer. "I hated leaving you though. As bad as I wanted to be home, I want you to know that. I hated walking away from you."

And Raeg. Though she left that unsaid. Falcon would know, just as he'd known she wasn't the person she showed the world.

"You didn't come straight home." He rested his chin against the top of her head, meeting her gaze in the reflection of the glass door. "Why not?"

Why hadn't she?

It had been six months, and there had been times she'd ached to find her own bed, to hear her momma's laughter, her daddy's booming voice, in person rather than on the phone.

She'd needed to heal first though, she'd thought. She hadn't been able to shed the person she was in DC as easily as she had in the past, because the wounds that had been left in her soul had seemed to fuse that part of her to the woman she was inside. She couldn't face her family like that. She wasn't herself. Just as she never showed the inner woman to the world, she never allowed the agent she was while in the world to return home with her, where her dreams and laughter awaited her.

"I was too ragged," she finally answered honestly. "If I had come home then, Momma and Daddy would have worried and Caleb would have headed straight to Arlington to demand even more answers from you. I couldn't be me, yet. And I didn't want them to see or to know who I was away from them." Her eyes closed as his head bent further, his lips brushing over her bare shoulder.

"I would have avoided him just as I always do," he promised her, the light Spanish accent he still carried washing over her senses. "I would have protected your secrets if I could have, Summer. Caleb knew them though. When we arrived here to warn him of Dragovich and see if he knew where you were hiding, he already had all the answers. I warned you long ago he no doubt knew exactly what you were doing."

Yeah, that sounded like Caleb. He'd ask questions even when he knew the answers. That was just his way. And she should have known he was aware of what she was doing. He was too nosy. There had just been no indication of it, so she'd hoped he'd accepted her explanations.

Her eyes closed as Falcon's lips moved closer to the sensitive column of her neck. In the next heartbeat she forced herself to step away from him and turn back to the bedroom, only to come to a stop.

Raeg stood leaning against the wall, just on the other side of the bed, his expression shadowed but not enough to hide the lust she could see in his face.

For once, there was no sense of anger or judgment coming from him. As though he were simply enjoying the sight of her and Falcon, of hearing them talk, their voices low. Could he find pleasure in that? Was that part of what caused these two men to share something so intimate as the women they both desired?

"Falcon knows where the guest rooms are," she told him, uncertain now what to say, or what to do. "There's one on each side of this suite, and they're comfortable."

"From the looks of things, Falcon doesn't need a guest room," he pointed out, though without a sense of jealousy or even his normal insulting, snide attitude.

"Falcon is not nearly that lucky," his brother grunted, pausing to kiss the top of her head before walking across the room. "Just sometimes, when I'm a very good boy, she allows me to pet her a little." He shot her a teasing smile over his shoulder before turning back to his brother.

Raeg still held her gaze, his dark eyes probing, intense. If he said something nasty to her, she simply didn't know if she could handle it.

His gaze moved over her, and Summer felt her breasts swell further, her nipples aching, her sex melting. And how futile was the arousal rushing through her, flooding her body and her senses? Falcon would never take her without Raeg, and Raeg despised her. Oh, he became aroused by her occasionally, but actually touching her was something he wanted nothing to do with. He'd made that plain over the years.

"Good night, Summer," he told her softly, nodding his head before straightening and leaving the room ahead of Falcon.

"He hates me," she whispered as Falcon paused, then turned back to her. "Why?"

His expression softened, his pale blue eyes, normally cool even when he wasn't, darkened with those shadows she'd always glimpsed in both him as well as his brother.

"He doesn't hate you." There was a heaviness to his voice that left her confused, aching to know the origin of his pain so she could soothe it.

"I think he does." She used to hope he didn't, had tried to tell herself he didn't. But now? Now, she just didn't know.

Falcon shook his head. "And I know he does not. What he does feel though, we may all have to work through eventually." His gaze touched hers. "And that may be far more dangerous to us than we ever imagined Dragovich being."

With that, he left her bedroom, leaving her to stand in the darkness alone as the fog reached her balcony doors, spreading over them, easing against each crack and crevice, searching for an entrance that didn't exist.

That was how she felt sometimes, as though searching for an entrance into the hearts of two men who wanted her, but were determined to keep her from being a presence in their lives.

What had Raeg once told her? He'd join her and Falcon, if she wanted to give into his brother's seduction, for a night or two. But she wasn't the type of woman he'd ever give his heart to.

And how that had hurt.

It still hurt. She was certain she'd spent a week crying into her pillow whenever she was supposed to be sleeping. He'd stripped her bare with those words. And even though it had been years since he'd given her the warning, she'd never forgotten it. Just as she'd never forgotten Falcon's warning that he and Raeg did share their lovers, and that should one of them ever marry, then she could count on the fact that it would be both of them the wife would be sharing her bed with.

And she wasn't in the running for a wife. Raeg had made that one clear right from the get-go.

So what the hell was her problem?

She'd known him since she was sixteen, two years before he ever went to work for the senator, and they'd been fighting for just as long. He'd snipe at her and just get as mean as a feral cat. She'd scratch back, then they'd stay at each other's throats whenever possible.

Putting away the last of her clothes, she snagged a nightie and matching robe before heading to the shower. By the time she crawled into bed, she gave a weary sigh at the knowledge that life was about to get crazy again.

Tomorrow was just going to be hell, and there was no help for it. This was what she got for waiting a year to come home, and when she did return, bringing Falcon and Raeg with her. Hell, this was what she got for giving a damn if Falcon and Raeg were with her. If they meant nothing to her, then her daddy would just give them a few warnings about playing with his little girl's heart and leave it at that.

But her daddy knew her, just as her momma did, and they knew what Raeg or Falcon would never guess. They meant far more to her than just friends. Far more than she should have allowed them to mean to her. And if she wasn't very, very careful, she'd end up loving them.

She almost thought another bullet in her shoulder would be preferable. She was damned sure it wouldn't hurt near as long.

And it would destroy all her plans too.

She was tired of aching for two men she couldn't have, and she was tired to being so alone, of ignoring the dreams that had slowly grown inside her during the long nights she'd spent with no one to lie beside her.

The dream of returning to Georgia, of having a family of her own, babies of her own. If she was ever going to let go of the fantasy she knew she couldn't have, then she was going to have to start looking at what she could have. She could have a husband and babies. One husband would be far less complicated than two men sharing that role, now wouldn't they? And she could live with caring for a man instead of giving him all of her. She could make do with that, because she knew she couldn't have the two men she longed for. It wasn't settling for second best when there was absolutely no chance at first choice. Right?

Lifting the remote next to the bed, Summer turned on the television and sat crossed-legged on the bed with her brush. As the late-night world-events anchor discussed yet another DC scandal, she pulled her hair over her shoulder and began brushing the heavy mass.

If she tried to sleep without braiding her hair, she'd probably be strangled in her sleep.

Just as she began brushing, she was surprised by a low knock on the door a second before it swung slowly open.

Falcon had showered as well. His hair was still damp, the elastic band of the loose, gray pants he wore rested low on his hips, and he wasn't wearing a shirt.

But he was carrying a brush identical to the one in her hand.

Without speaking, he strode to the side of the bed as Summer scooted to the middle of the mattress and sat cross-legged while he settled in behind her. A heartbeat later, pleasure began singing through her body. The stroke of the brush through her hair, the caressing tug against her scalp, and the rhythmic, steady movements erased every tension, fear, and wariness.

She'd always found this incredibly sensual. Falcon brushed her hair with an enjoyment that always surprised her, but never failed to please her.

He was one of the reasons she refused to cut her hair, not some vain pleasure she found in it. Falcon seemed to love it. The very mention of cutting her hair was enough to have panic gleaming in his pale blue eyes.

"Had you actually cut this beautiful hair, I believe I might have spanked you with your own brush," he sighed, causing a smile to tug at her lips.

She actually believed him too.

"You should have known better," she murmured as he laid the brush aside and began to slowly pull her long strands into an intricate braid that he left loose enough that it wouldn't leave her head aching from the pressure, but would keep the long strands from tangling or from strangling her.

"You owe me for making me believe you had done something so cruel to me as to cut this beautiful hair." The humor in his voice was always contagious.

And maybe he was right. She had known that if he had actually believed she had cut her hair, he would be furious. Maybe even hurt.

"Okay, I owe you," she agreed, the feel of his fingers working her hair, pulling her into a drowsy, sensual haze.

As good as he was making her feel by just braiding her hair, she thought how good it would feel to be touched by him, to have his fingers stroking over her body, touching her. To be allowed to touch him.

"Hmm, what should I demand as payment?" he asked, his voice just a little rough, the dark sound a pleasure on its own.

"Whatever you want," she murmured, her senses drugged with the sensations.

She could feel him binding the end of the braid with the elastic band, and wanted to moan in regret. She wasn't ready for it to end. Not yet.

"I've missed this." His hands caressed her bare shoulders, the slightly calloused warmth of his palms sensitizing the nerve endings beneath her flesh. "Sitting with you, braiding your hair, feeling you against me."

He never stopped at just braiding her hair. Maybe that was why she had missed it herself. Falcon liked touching her, and she so loved the feel of his hands on her, stroking and caressing her.

· "Raeg says you're addicted," she said, reminding him of the accusation Raeg had made the previous year.

"Such jealousy he harbors," he chuckled, the sound of it gentle, filled with the affection she knew he felt for her. "We feel sorry for him, don't we?"

"He would probably disagree with you." Her head lowered as his fingers began rubbing against the top of her spine, sending waves of exquisite pleasure rolling through her.

Oh yes, she had missed this. The calloused pads of his thumbs working the muscles beneath, firmly massaging her neck, draining the tension right out of her. It sent another type of tension invading her, but even that she looked forward to. Those sensations intensified the pleasure of his touch, heated her, and reaffirmed the fact that she was indeed a woman. A woman who ached for a touch denied her far too often.

"I bet he wouldn't," he whispered, his warm breath caressing her ear. "Raeg may fool you with his attitude, but he doesn't fool me, sweetheart. If he could be right here, right now, touching you like this, feeling you soft and sweet, he would be as addicted as I."

Her breath caught as his lips brushed against the shell of her ear, pulling her deeper into the sensuality building inside her senses.

She was just weak enough, she thought hazily, just needy enough actually, to sit there like a crazy woman and let her body burn for him. She could feel her breasts swelling, her nipples becoming so sensitive, so needy for his touch as her sex melted and wept for touch as well, that there was no hiding her need for him.

"How is he fooling me then?" She bent her head to the side in an invitation for him to continue those little brushes of his lips a little lower.

"How does he keep you at arm's length?" It was the edge of his teeth that rasped against the sensitive skin of her neck rather than his lips, and the sensation had her fighting to hold back a moan.

"What are you up to, Falcon?" she sighed, aware of the slow, steady seduction of her senses and that he was touching her far differently than he normally did, allowing himself to go much further in his caresses.

"Besides seducing you?" The edge of amusement in his tone should have pissed her off; instead, she felt herself softening further against him.

It wasn't a good idea and she knew it. Both of them were approaching that point of no return, and she couldn't seem to make herself care.

"Get on with it then," she demanded on a sigh, knowing she had slipped far too deeply into the spell he was weaving around her senses.

A dark chuckle met the demand, and rather than doing as she suggested, he slid from the bed and stared down at her, his gaze filled with a carnal hunger that had her heart racing.

Yes, she was in too deep, but she suddenly wondered exactly how deep she was allowing herself to be drawn into this sensual web she could feel restraining her, holding back common sense or any desire to consider what she was about to do. And she was going to do it. She couldn't even consider denying the pleasure she could sense he'd give her.

Dark lashes lowered over pale blue eyes, the intense sexuality and dominance in his expression stole her breath for a moment. Normally veiled, the dominant, strong-willed man he usually kept hidden wasn't hiding anymore. He was right there, and the sight of it sent a wave of weakness rushing through her.

She'd been so long without a lover that she could barely remember what it felt like to be taken, to have her flesh penetrated and stretched with sensual pleasure. The dominance and lust in his expression assured her that once he took her though, she'd never forget what it felt like.

If Falcon took her, he'd do far more than simply part her responsive inner flesh. He'd make her burn, take her to a place no other lover ever had, and she knew it.

The muscles of her vagina clenched, rippling in a silent demand for the erotic pain she knew his possession would give her. It was something she'd never considered before, something she'd never ached for before. But the proof of his erection tenting those pants assured her that that was exactly what he was going to give her. He'd do far more than fill her, he'd give her an edge of pleasure she'd only suspected existed.

"Why tonight?" she asked, her fingers clenching in the blankets beneath her as his gaze went over her. "Why wait 'til now, Falcon?"

Why ambush her without warning? Why wait until they were in her home, in her bed, in a place where he'd haunt her for the rest of her life?

His gaze moved to her breasts, her heavier breathing rough, lifting her breasts against her gown and rasping her tender nipples against it. The quick, hard breaths had his expression turning positively carnal.

"I actually thought I'd just braid your hair," he replied, his voice deeper. "That I'd be satisfied with just touching you for a moment, then I could return to my own bed once again, just as I always have before."

She couldn't breathe. She had no idea how to handle Falcon like this. She'd never seen him like this. He wasn't teasing and subtly asking permission. He was confident, powerful and aroused, and he wasn't asking anymore.

"Why?" She could barely push the word past her lips.

He didn't even bother to try to hide the tenting of his pants as his cock pointed toward her, long and thick, holding her attention despite that inner voice screaming at her to run.

Oh yes, he was going to give her more than she'd ever had before and she wasn't certain how she'd survive once it was over, once he and Raeg left her life forever.

He was suddenly far more than she was certain she could handle, and not just physically.

"I dream of all that long, pretty hair," he told her. "Of holding it back and watching those pretty, pouty lips parting for my cock. That's why I braid it so loosely. That way, I'll be able to thread my fingers in it and show you how the slightest, firm little tugs against it could increase your pleasure if I ever managed to convince you to let me fuck those pretty lips."

Lust slammed into her senses, not simply arousal. Pure. White hot. It struck her womb with a force that stole her breath.

"I love brushing your hair because the feel of it is a memory I can pull up as I jack off thinking about it." His voice was hoarse now, guttural. The sound combined with the explicit words drugged her senses so fast, so deep, she was dazed. "Imagining the feel of your lips, your hot little mouth wrapped around the head of my cock, moaning and sucking me, your face dazed with the hunger to taste me."

Her breathing was harsh now, labored, as she slid to the edge of the bed and reached out, pulling at the elastic band of his pants and easing them over the hard shaft before Falcon discarded them completely. After stepping from the pants he wrapped the fingers of one hand around the base of the broad shaft, tightening on it as a drop of creamy moisture eased past the tiny slit on top the crest.

The dark, flared head pulsed. Thick, ropey veins throbbed along the shaft, and Summer knew the fight was over. She'd lost the battle to keep her heart from being shattered, if they survived Dragovich.

"Take the gown off," he demanded.

It wasn't a request, and acknowledging that had her reacting instinctively. Lifting herself enough to pull the material over her hips, she gripped the hem and pulled it over her head before dropping it to the floor next to the bed.

His gaze dropped to her breasts, lashes shielding his eyes though his breathing was deeper now, heavier.

"Lie back across the bed, Belle." The demand was softly voiced.

Demand, or request? She couldn't differentiate, but the sound of it had her fighting back a whimper, fighting just to breathe as she moved to the center and stretched across it, pulling the braid out of the way instinctively.

"No fight?" he asked, his knee pressing into the bed as he lifted himself to her, coming down beside her.

"Do you want me to fight?" She watched warily as he gripped her wrists and pulled them over her head, staring down at her breasts as he did so.

"I want you to let me give you exactly what I know you need." His head lowered, his lips brushing over hers, their gazes locking.

His hand tightened at her hip, the other slid into loosely weaved strands of hair, gripping them with erotic pressure. The wicked tug and subtle restraint had her stilling, shock surging through her as some inner core of feminine submission sent a wave of pure bliss shuddering through her senses.

The contradictory, completely unfamiliar sensations left her reeling, uncertain whether to orgasm or panic, and as she stared back at Falcon, she knew, *knew,* somehow, that she'd given him exactly what he'd wanted, but hadn't been certain he'd find.

She wasn't entirely certain that was a good thing.

There it was.

The steel core of sexual dominance Falcon had always hid from her rushed forward when she stilled beneath him and those violet eyes darkened, flaring with the unconscious sexual submission that only a strong, otherwise dominant woman could possess when beneath a lover she sensed could harness and control all that wild hunger inside her.

"Maybe this isn't a good idea." Panic, it was there in her eyes, in her voice.

"Should we continue to play games instead?" he asked, tugging at her hair once again. "Go back to pretending we are not dying for exactly what burns between us at this moment?"

Sweet Summer.

Confusion filled her pretty eyes. She did not even know what she wanted so desperately, why no other man had ever given her what she'd known he and Raeg could give her. And it was exactly what he needed himself to sate the greedy lust that always rose whenever he was around her.

If he gave her time to think about this first, then her fears would pull her back. And that he simply could not allow.

Before she could make another protest, his lips covered hers. Slanting over the soft curves, Falcon took the taste of her with greedy hunger as her arms wrapped around his neck, her body arching to him.

Catching her wrists, he drew them over her head, holding them with one hand and cursing his brother's stubbornness. Had Raeg been there he would have restrained her, held her arms above her head and helped Falcon to give her a pleasure she could only know with both of them. A pleasure he couldn't give her alone.

It would take both of them to fully sate this woman's hungers. He had always known this.

She arched against him, moaning into his kiss, her tongue dueling against his, challenging for control. Taking her alone would be more pleasure than he'd known in his life. But how much better could it be?

Pulling back, he stared down at her, taking in her flushed features, her passion-drugged gaze, the arch of her swollen, flushed breasts and cherry red nipples.

"Do you wish he was here as well?" he asked, grimacing in hunger at the thought as he cupped the silken weight of her breast. "That both of us touched you?"

For a moment something so hungry and tormented flashed in her gaze before it was gone.

"Does it matter?" she whispered, her voice filled with need. "He's not here."

Her nipples darkened, became harder at the thought of it though.

"If he was," he told her, "we would hold you between us and both sweet nipples would know the hunger we have for them."

His head lowered, his lips covering one hard peak, teeth raking it, then his lips closing on it as he sucked the tempting morsel into his mouth.

The low strangled cry was not quite enough to draw Raeg's attention. But it would be, Falcon swore. Very soon, it would be.

Keeping her arms stretched above her, he sucked, nibbled, teased her nipples. Suckling kisses were given to the tight little buds, each caress drawing her deeper into the hunger building between them, loosening her restraint and her fears of being overheard.

Control was always the issue for Falcon when taking a woman alone, especially one he knew would begin instinctively fighting the need for pleasures she had never imagined hungering for. Restraining her kept her focused on her own pleasure rather than pleasuring him. She had no choice but to let her senses fill with each sensation.

Gripping the tender nipple between his teeth and exerting just enough pressure to create that pleasure-pain that shocked the senses, he licked over it, adding to the sensations before he released it and sucked it firmly. The taste of her skin, the hardness of the little bud against his tongue, the throb of reaction a little pulse in the tip, making him hungrier for her.

He'd known she'd respond to that edge of sensation between pleasure and pain. That place where a woman's sensuality became far too curious and her inhibitions surged free.

Summer's moans went from strangled to unrestrained. Her head tossed against the bed, her body shuddered, perspiration slickening her flesh as he alternated his caresses, soothing, fierce, sucking hard and tight against the sensitive flesh, then licking it, easing it before making it burn again. From one nipple to the other, he tormented each in turn, wondering how much more she would have loved it had Raeg been there to concentrate on one breast as he had the other.

Soon, her cries echoed around him, and still Raeg was not there.

Regret and disbelief that his brother could be so stubborn filled him. Summer wasn't the only one who would fight what she knew would complete her. Even Raeg, it seemed, was determined to wage that battle.

It was her cries.

Stepping from the bathroom into his bedroom, a towel around his hips, Raeg felt his dick go rock-hard instantly at the sound of them.

Iron. Spike. Hard.

Hungry, desperate cries. The faintest sound of them,

hoarse and resonating with such pleasure it couldn't be contained, hit his senses like a sledgehammer. It was a sound he thought he'd never hear, from a woman he'd tried to convince himself he couldn't have.

He knew that sound, knew the edge of confusion, of dazed uncertainty that filled each cry. He knew, and he was helpless against it. It was a sound that had filled his fantasies, his darkest dreams, and filled every hungry desire he had for Summer.

Leaving the bedroom, Raeg walked to Summer's room, the open door an invitation he couldn't resist. Didn't resist. He then stepped into his greatest fantasy.

Summer, spread on the bed, her wrists captured in one of Falcon's hands, the hard tip of a breast being sucked firmly as Falcon drew her slowly into a pleasure she couldn't know was coming.

"Now," she demanded, breathless, that edge of desperation in her tone an assurance that the need Falcon had struck a match to, she was going to instinctively fight it. Raeg could hear it in her cries, her plea that his brother take her now. She would fight each level of pleasure she would be drawn into, and that struggle would only intensify his and Falcon's pleasure in taking her.

And he knew Falcon. His brother would struggle against the demands, but his hunger and hers would make it difficult to pull her into that dark edge where she'd begin craving sensations one lover alone would find difficult to harness.

As he watched, Falcon's free hand moved slowly over her thigh, the silken, slick bare flesh between her thighs drawing his touch. He couldn't resist it, not alone, not without a reminder that it wasn't quite the time for a deeper, more intimate touch yet.

"Falcon." Raeg spoke firmly just before his brother found the sweet, heavy juices spilling from her. "It's too soon."

Summer shuddered. Raeg saw the hard, rippling response to the carnality and nearing orgasm that nearly exploded inside her at the sound of his reminder.

His brother released the hard, reddened nipple, his blue eyes several shades darker with the needs he was fighting.

"Do you require a third?" Raeg asked, desperate to touch Summer, aching for it. Every muscle in his body was strung tight, tension radiating through him as his hunger burned hotter than he could ever remember feeling it burn.

"A third?" Falcon snapped, his voice darker, deeper with the struggle to hold back his lusts. "I don't need a damned third, I need an equal."

A commitment to Summer, to her pleasure, to the woman and the needs waiting for them to unlock inside her. An integral part of the relationship, free to take her with or without his brother. She would be as much his as she was Falcon's. And the thought of that was like a heady drug rushing through his senses.

"Very well," he agreed, barely hesitating. "An equal."

The second he acknowledged it he felt a shift inside him, a knowledge he simply couldn't face at that moment. Later, he decided. He'd consider it later, when his mind wasn't clouded with his needs as well as Summer's.

Moving around the bed as Falcon shifted position and moved behind her head, Raeg met her violet gaze with a slow smile.

"Is she going to fight it?" he asked his brother as he dropped the towel from his hips and watched the haze of sensuality intensify in her expression.

"Every step of the way," Falcon assured him, the obvious satisfaction in the knowledge echoing in his voice.

Still holding Summer's gaze, he let his hand slide up the inside of her thigh. Reaching the saturated flesh between her thighs, he let a single finger slide through the heavy juices. Finding her clit, Raeg exerted just the slightest pressure, nearly pushing her into release, and held it there.

He had every iota of her attention now.

"One word will stop this," he told her. "One word only. When you say it, we'll both walk away. Understand?"

Defiance flashed in her eyes.

Glancing up at Falcon, he watched as his brother's lips quirked. He had caught the look as well.

"All you must say is no, love," Falcon assured her. "If you are frightened, if anything causes you pain, then you tell us. But when you say no, this ends. It will mean you do not desire what we hunger for. What we know you hunger for. That your fears are greater than your need."

Just "no."

They wouldn't hurt her. She knew they would never hurt her. Not physically. There were worse ways they could hurt her though.

"I believe she understands," Raeg stated softly, lifting his finger from her clit and causing sensation to streak through the tender knot of nerves.

Her hips lifted with an involuntary cry, a tremor racing through her as she fought to find the wave and let it carry her into release.

"She's far too close," Falcon's voice was strained, as strained as she knew her own would be if she attempted to speak.

"No, she's fine," Raeg assured him, kneeling between

her thighs and watching her closely, the heavy length of his cock throbbing imperatively. "Aren't you, sweetheart?"

There was a challenge in his gaze, a dare that said she couldn't possible take whatever they decided to dish out. And why the hell she was going to let them dish it out, she wasn't certain.

"You're a tease," she accused him.

"Think that's all?" he asked her, a dark, heavy eroticism filling his expression. "Shall we see?"

That was all he could do, she told herself. Tease her. The tugging of her hair was good, that bit of heat mixing with the pleasure had been shocking for a second, but it was gone now.

His gaze moved across her slowly, leisurely.

"What's your greatest fantasy?" he asked then, pushing her legs further apart. "When it's dark and you're alone with only your fingers for pleasure, what do you fantasize about?"

What did she fantasize about?

"Both of you," she whispered. She didn't have to lie about that—they already knew she wanted them.

"Separately? Together?"

What did he want?

"Together." She frowned up at him, breath catching as Falcon bent to her, his tongue licking over her nipple as he knelt next to her.

Her gaze moved to his cock as he laid on his side, stretching to his lower stomach, so hard, throbbing.

"Together," she repeated, fighting to breathe.

She'd touch him, but he still held her wrists, restraining her, keeping her from reaching out to him.

She jerked in reaction as Raeg's teeth scraped over her thigh, far too close to the sensitive, needy flesh of her sex.

"Together how?" His voice was lower now, a gentle

croon, nothing threatening, nothing to distract from the desire to taste the hard length of cock just beyond her reach.

"However you want me," she moaned, licking her lips. "Every way."

"Falcon." Raeg's tone firmed. "Put her on her knees." On her knees?

A second later she was being rolled to her stomach, Raeg's hands gripping her hips, pulling her to her knees as Falcon released her wrists to allow her to hold her position.

"Give her what she's so hungry for," Raeg told his brother then. "Fuck her mouth. I'll see how much of a tease she can take on that pretty pussy."

Falcon's fingers gripped her hair, surprising her, holding her in place as the head of his cock pressed to her lips, pushed past them, and filled her mouth with the taste of iron-hard male heat.

At the same time, Raeg's head pushed between her thighs, his body stretched out beneath her, both hands reaching up to cup her rear and draw her hips to him.

Raeg's tongue licked through the sensitive wet folds of her pussy at the same time his hand landed on the curve of her rear in a heated caress.

Heated. Fiery heat snapped through her senses as his tongue circled her clit.

She tried to jerk back from Falcon, tried to make sense of what she'd just felt whipping through her senses. But before she could process that need, Falcon's hands clenched in her hair, the head of his cock filling her mouth again.

The moan that slipped past her throat was part cry, part whimper.

In the next breath, it was a strangled scream.

Raeg's tongue pushed inside her, thrusting hard past the clenched entrance to her pussy as his hand landed on the curve of her ass again, that blooming heat attacking her senses, mixing with the pleasure and sending shudders tearing through her.

And it didn't stop. Each lick, each thrust of his tongue was another heavy caress to her rear. Always in a different place. Some landing heavier than others, all of them tearing past a reserve she hadn't known she possessed and opening a hunger inside her she couldn't have imagined.

Slowly, too slowly, the heated pleasure intensified, the burn building to a pleasure-pain she hadn't imagined existed. Her hips writhed, pushed to his too playful tongue, only to still as the caress landed harder, chastising her for trying to take her pleasure before he was willing to give it to her.

All the while Falcon's fingers tightened and released her hair close to the scalp, his cock shuttling between her lips, working past them in slow, measured thrusts that gave her just enough time to believe she'd soon taste his release only to take it from her once again.

Already dazed, desperate for them, Summer felt the need for that mix of pleasure and pain begin rising. It built in a part of her sexuality that she'd never imagined existed until now, then spread through her senses like a tidal wave.

Each surge of pleasure from his tongue, his sucking lips, was followed by his heated caresses. Caresses that soon weren't enough, the heat dimming, the needs for more only growing.

And she needed that harder caress.

Damn him, why wouldn't he just go ahead and spank

her? Just give it to her? If the heavy caresses were this good, what would a spanking actually do for her?

His hand landed harder then and dazed satisfaction began over-taking her. Between each burning caress his fingers would stroke and caress the curves of her ass, part them, and send flares of sensation streaking through her anal opening.

As the pleasure-pain began to burn, to build, she sucked Falcon's cock, working her mouth over the engorged head, sucking and tonguing it, desperate for the taste of his release.

She had never had a man spill between her lips.

The slow measured thrusts between her lips moved deeper, pulling a strangled cry from her as the engorged crest flexed and throbbed against her tongue.

"Raeg, I can't last much longer,' Falcon groaned. "Her mouth is so sweet. So sweet and hot."

Raeg's tongue speared inside her, retreated, circled her clit again. The heated, heavy caresses to her rear came closer together, and each time his hand landed, the pleasure-pain of it filled her senses, drugging them further, pushing her closer to her own release.

"Your ass blushes so pretty," Falcon groaned. "Dark pink, clenching with each little slap . . ."

She cried out around his cock, needing, aching . . .

"I want to fuck your mouth just like this, Summer. Fuck it slow and easy while you scream around it, and I will watch him work his cock up that sweet, tight ass . . ."

Raeg's lips surrounded her clit, his tongue swiped over it. His hand landed with such erotic, wicked heat . . .

Ecstasy exploded through her.

Her mouth tightened on Falcon's cock, her tongue undulating just beneath the head. Orgasmic explosions ripped through her senses, jerked through her body, and sent her hurtling into chaos.

No more than a heartbeat later, Falcon's hands tightened further in her hair, amplifying the pleasure before she felt the first, rapid pulse of semen fill her mouth, shocking her senses.

That first taste, and she wanted more. Each rapid taste of male heat, slightly salty, reminiscent of a Georgia thunderstorm. It filled her taste buds and added to the explosions tearing through her.

And with each, hard detonation of pleasure rocking, Raeg's lips and tongue were there to catch, to taste, the release of her juices spilling from her.

It was never-ending, only to end far too soon.

Falcon's still-erect cock pulled from her lips, his voice soothing, deep, as Raeg eased from between her thighs. His lips and tongue were no longer tormenting her, driving her deeper into that climactic storm.

Collapsing to the bed, the sweetest lassitude swept through Summer. Stealing over her, dragging her into a quiet, dark place where nothing existed but the warm peace she'd been craving.

Finally . . .

Chapter
FOUR

Summer's eyes opened as Raeg turned her onto her back. He watched her breath catch, need still simmering in her dark violet eyes as he pushed her legs apart. He lifted her knees, placing them over his spread thighs as he knelt between them. Sliding his hands to her hips, and rather than coming over her, he dragged her body forward, her hips tilting until the wide, flared crest of his erection kissed the naked folds of her saturated pussy. Pleasure shot up his spine and drew a ragged groan from his chest.

"How fucking pretty," Falcon's voice sounded like a growl as Raeg watched his brother lie beside her, his hand smoothing over her stomach, his broad palm stroking against her abdomen. "I want to see this, baby. To hear your pleasure. This is what we dream of, Summer, seeing all the hunger and need inside you, and stoking it as hot, as wild as it can go."

She was pretty. So damned pretty it was all Raeg could do to breathe when he saw her sometimes. And now— his gaze lowered between her thighs, watched as the glistening folds of her pussy parted, embracing the broad crest of his cock.

He had to clench his jaw to hold back. His teeth locked together so tight they ached. The slick, juice-laden flesh cupped the end of his cock, the narrow entrance flexing, heat easing from the inner channel as he began pressing forward. His hands clenched on her thighs as he watched, felt the brutal pleasure beginning from the head of his dick to his balls as they drew tight at the base of the shaft.

"Oh God . . ." She tried to tighten her thighs as her pussy flexed, caressing each inch of his flesh as he worked it inside the snug channel.

"Hell, she's so fucking tight," he groaned, pushing in deeper, easing back, then forcing inside her by slow degrees once again. Each inner contraction around the sensitive crest was destructive.

So hot, so damned good . . .

Her fingers fisted in the blankets beneath her, hips arching as strangled cries left her lips.

Flushed features were dazed with her pleasure, those pretty violet eyes so dark, so wild with her climb to release that they were nearly black. Dazed, her face suffused with the intensity of sensation. And he was mesmerized by that look, torn between watching as he pushed inside her and watching her face as each inch stretched her inner flesh.

He'd told himself he could keep this from happening, could maintain the distance, could keep her so angry that she wouldn't let him touch her. But he'd known, he thought fatalistically as a groan tore from his chest, that he was lying to himself. Lying to himself and endangering her in ways he'd never wanted to. Just as he was endangering his own soul.

Because Summer wasn't the only one mesmerized by the pleasure. *He* was dying from it. With each shallow thrust, each clench of her snug pussy around the head of his cock, his sensations became sharper, his pleasure deeper.

"That's it, baby," he whispered as her hips jerked in his grip, trying to push him deeper as her cries of pleasure filled his senses. "You're so sweet and tight. You like that little burn, don't you? That little bit of pain mixed with the pleasure."

His gaze slid to Falcon, watching as his brother kissed his way down Summer's perspiration-dewed neck to the tight, hard points of her nipples. The flushed, pebbled tips were cherry red, flushed and swollen and drawing Falcon's attention as Summer arched against the tight, controlled thrusts of Raeg's erection inside her.

"Please." Her voice was low, her body straining as he worked his cock deeper inside her in slow, controlled thrusts, easing inside her, torturing himself with the pleasure, with the heat searing his flesh and tightening around his erection.

He wanted to enjoy this. Every sensation, every cry from her pouty, reddened lips, the sight of her struggling to accept a pleasure so extreme it was tearing through her senses.

As Falcon's lips neared the swollen point of a nipple, Raeg eased back, pausing, his cock resting just inside the entrance of the snuggest grip he'd ever known in his life.

The second his brother's lips covered the sensitive tip, Raeg pushed inside her in a long, hard stroke. The pleasure suddenly gripping the sensitive length of his cock was violent.

Each time Falcon's cheeks drew in, creating a firm

suction on her sensitive nipple, her pussy flexed and rippled around Raeg's erect flesh, the action sending warning strikes of raw pleasure racing straight to his balls.

"Oh God, Raeg . . . please . . ." Her hips jerked against his grip, each thrust a little stroke against his cock that resulted in devastating pleasure.

Tilting his head back on his shoulders, he fought for control, fought to remain still, to just experience the feel of her pussy sucking him from base to crest, clenching, flexing, tightening around his erection, stealing his control. He'd never known pleasure this sharp. In all his sexual life, he'd never known these blistering, overwhelming sensations.

"Move . . ." she cried out, thighs tightening again, fighting his hold on her hips as Falcon's lips lifted from her nipple only to lick the tip before gripping it between his teeth and tugging it gently.

A strangled scream of pleasure tore from Summer's throat, her expression drugged, dazed with the pleasure she couldn't fight, couldn't hold back from. A pleasure she was transferring to him through the heated grip of her pussy.

Moving was becoming imperative though. As much as Raeg wanted to linger, wanted to just feel her, just experience the feel of her pussy gripping him, sucking at his erection, hunger was overcoming the need to just relish the pleasure.

He glimpsed Falcon's lips covering her nipple once again, sucking at it with the deep, hungry pulls of his lips. Summer jerked against him, that slick, hot grip of her pussy tightening further.

Raeg lost the ability to simply experience the feel of her. His hips jerked back, then slammed forward, the friction of hot, slick flesh tightening around him drawing a groan from his chest and fraying what was left of his control.

Before he could stop himself, before he could regain enough control to take her slow and easy, to experience the feel of her, the pleasure he knew only she could give, he was pumping inside her hard and deep. Quick, heavy strokes that built the burning pleasure, the furious, brilliant pinpoints of sensation racing from his shaft to his taut balls, and clenching the muscles of his abdomen.

Her cries of pleasure, of need, filled his head and sliced through any defenses he might have maintained. Nothing mattered but Summer, her pleasure, her need, touching her, stroking her, protecting her from everything but himself.

Everything but his hunger.

At that moment, she stiffened beneath him, a smothered wail of ecstasy escaping her lips as she began coming around him, her pussy like a vise, milking the last fragile remnants of restraints from his grip.

Slamming inside her, Raeg froze, his release exploding from him, shooting from his cock, his semen jetting inside her in furious pulses of blinding rapture.

Teeth clenched, his muscles bunched and tight against the power of each ejaculation, a groan escaping his lips, he gave himself to it. Let himself feel, just feel for the space of time it took for the rippling flesh surrounding his cock to suck the last pulse of release from his balls.

Distantly, he heard Falcon's groans, knew he'd found his own release, and he knew both of them were doomed. No other woman had ever affected them like this. No other woman had ever caused so many contradictory emotions to rise inside him.

She was his weakness.

She was Falcon's weakness.

And he may well have doomed both of them because of the very lack of control that had him collapsing over Summer now, holding her, covering her until he could catch his breath, until he could find his strength once again.

Maybe, in the search for his strength, he'd be able to recover his heart as well. He had a feeling though that he'd lost both to the far too delicate, far too stubborn woman he feared would be the death of not just him, but his brother as well.

Their weakness.

Sometimes, Falcon thought as he felt his brother silently leave Summer's bed nearly an hour later, the complications of life could strip a man so painfully bare, the truth of his soul could only be faced in the midnight hours.

Staring up at the ceiling bleakly he wished he could allow Raeg the time he needed to come to grips with whatever had caused him to lose control and give into his hunger. Unfortunately, he didn't consider that an option at the moment.

He hadn't wanted to leave the bed yet either. Summer was a warm weight against his side, her soft breathing calming. He'd been pretty damned close to sleep when Raeg decided to leave the bed.

Restraining a sigh, he eased from Summer, then rolled from the bed. Locating the cotton pants he'd worn after his shower, he pulled them on and left the room. He knew where he'd find his brother. The same place he always found him when the past haunted him. Where Raeg also found him when the past come calling as well.

Making his way downstairs, he found Raeg standing next to the glass doors leading to the back porch, a drink in hand as he watched fog swirling on invisible currents of air.

Raeg was fighting to contain himself again, Falcon knew. All that cool, careful calm his brother showed the world came with a price and a battle to maintain it. The same fiery Spanish blood Falcon possessed ran through his brother's veins as well. Raeg had learned to harness it for the most part though. At least, until it came to Summer.

"She still asleep?" Raeg asked, not turning from whatever he was watching within the night.

"She is," he said softly, leaning against the wall on the opposite side of the doors and crossing his arms over his chest as he watched his brother. "We should be as well."

Raeg lifted his glass and took a healthy swallow.

It wasn't really often that Raeg drank, though, when he did, Falcon knew it was because whatever was bothering him wasn't something he'd come to peace with easily.

"Why the hell does she keep coming back here?" Raeg growled, staring into the glass for a moment before once again turning his gaze to the night. "Her father let some bastard nearly rape her, beat her, and still, she's run home every chance she's had."

The bitterness in his voice came from more than just the memory of Summer that long-ago night when Margot and Davis Allen had flown to Georgia to take her from her parents' home and bring her to DC for the summer.

"I told you that was not as it was told," Falcon reminded him. "Whatever happened that night, there was far more to it than her father allowing anything to happen. And this isn't about Summer's father. It's about—"

"Don't say it," Raeg growled, his voice low. "Don't give him that title or I won't be able to control myself."

Their father.

No, Roberto Falcone hadn't been much of a father. A monster. A murdering bastard, but not much of a father.

"It's been a lot of years, Raeg," Falcon reminded him, just as he often reminded himself. "And the circumstances are far different. Summer is not an agent assigned to gain information from the young man she'd coerced into falling in love with her. She's no danger or threat to us personally. You keep forgetting that."

"And if he decides to see it different?" his brother asked. "Could you live with Summer's death on your conscience, Falcon?"

No, he couldn't. Not like that. Never like that.

"Let us deal with one problem at a time," Falcon suggested. "We take care of Dragovich, then we'll tackle the other. For now though, she's in no danger from our past as long as Dragovich stalks her."

Silence settled around them then. Falcon was beginning to believe his brother had nothing more to say when he watched Raeg slowly shake his head wearily.

"And when this is over?" Raeg asked. "When it's time for us to walk away from her, will you be able to do that?"

It would kill him. It would rip his soul from his body and leave a ragged, gaping wound in its place.

"If that's what I have to do," Falcon assured him. "If it comes to that choice, Raeg, I'll make it. I won't do it unless we're certain though. And I don't think you can either."

He'd walk away from her before he'd see her harmed by the man who had sired them. That didn't mean he'd survive it. He'd let her go five months before, believing she'd be back, that she'd return to their lives as she'd always had before. When she hadn't, he'd known they were losing her. He was losing her.

Finishing his drink, Raeg continued to stare into the night, his expression brooding. Falcon knew that the conflicts still raged inside, tormenting him. Both of them possessed that broodiness, a quiet, dark intensity that gripped them whenever they were forced to deal with emotions they couldn't or wouldn't accept.

Summer had always brought the broodiness out in them, Falcon had always thought with a grain of amusement. The woman was like a whirlwind of emotion, and she never failed to affect them with it.

"Eight years is a long time to ache for a woman," Falcon told him softly. "I'm tired of longing for her, of trying to imagine she's the woman we're taking whenever we take a lover. I'm tired of wondering, of being tormented by the unknown where she's concerned. And I'm tired of living in the past. Once this is over, I'll go hunting him in earnest, Raeg. If I find him, he dies."

The flash of regret Raeg couldn't quite control flickered over his expression before it was pulled back. Falcon had always known that dealing with this issue had the potential to destroy both of them. Because of that, he'd let the situation go. Even after he'd acknowledged what Summer meant to him, still, he'd held back. Raeg hadn't been ready to accept the fact that Summer belonged to them, that this woman that made him crazy belonged to them.

His brother knew it now though.

"He wouldn't kill one of us," Raeg sighed heavily. "But we'll never get close enough to kill him either. Summer's our weakness, Falcon, and he'll know that." There was no way they could hide it, and no way to stay with her. "He won't allow that weakness to exist if we fuck up and reveal it to him. You know that as well as I do. Once Dragovich is taken care of here, I won't risk her that way. I'll leave."

"And I'll find him," Falcon assured him, knowing he would have no other choice. "I won't live my life beneath that threat any longer. It will be my life or his. And I will have nothing left to lose once I lose her. Neither of us will."

Turning, Falcon made his way through the dimly lit house and back up the stairs to the warm bed and the even warmer woman awaiting him.

He'd waited too long for her. He knew that once this was over he would never be able to stay away from her again. That left only one other option. He'd have to find Roberto, and once he did, one of them would die, because there would be no peace, and no assurance of Summer's safety otherwise. And that he simply could not tolerate.

Raeg remained silent as Falcon left the room, that parting shot echoing in the silence around him.

I knew this was coming.

He'd known for years that once he and Falcon had a taste of the woman who haunted them, there'd be no turning back. It would change them.

The fact that he was right didn't comfort him in the least. The suspicion that the man who sired them was far closer than they believed couldn't be shaken away either.

It was a feeling, a gut reaction that he knew better than to ignore.

Roberto Falcone was a ghost, a highly elite, specialized soldier trained by the CIA, then turned loose on a world that couldn't have suspected the killer that would move among them. Certainly his and Falcon's mothers hadn't known when they became involved with him, then conceived his two sons. Yet they'd stayed. Even after their sons had refused to have any contact with them because of Roberto and their continued connection to him, they'd stayed. Falcon's mother had even had another child. A daughter.

Their mothers hadn't given up though. Letters, emails, messages to phone numbers they should never be able to access, even attempts to meet with them when they knew they'd be at a certain party or event. And Raeg and Falcon didn't dare allow that connection once again. Roberto shouldn't have been threatened enough by the agent Raeg was sleeping with all those years ago to kill her. But he had. They wouldn't risk their mothers as well, and they couldn't risk Summer once Dragovich was taken care of either.

Raeg couldn't allow it.

The past.

He shook his head wearily, wishing he could understand it, that he could make sense of it. He'd learned years ago that there was no doing either. And now, all that mattered was protecting Summer from it.

Because if there was one thing Roberto hated more than he hated the CIA, it was CIA agents. Especially female agents he believed were a risk to his sons. And Raeg knew well how Roberto dealt with those female agents.

That knowledge lived in his nightmares, and he didn't think he could survive if Summer became a casualty to it.

Actually, he *knew* he wouldn't survive it.

Chapter
FIVE

What had make her think that anything would change with Raeg? Summer wondered the next morning after she woke to both him and Falcon already up, showered, and dressed.

Falcon had been watchful, but as charming as ever. Raeg was in a mood though. A very odd mood. One that left her feeling uncertain and off-balance. So much so that she insisted on leaving for her parents' the moment she joined them downstairs.

Not that either of them argued with her.

If they wanted to pretend that last night hadn't happened, then she'd just help them right along with that, she decided after leaving her house and walking the distance to her parents'. She'd gotten real good at ignoring Raeg, anyway. She'd perfected the art over the years. At least, that was what she told herself as she stepped onto the back porch where her father was sitting comfortably in his rocking chair. "There's my baby girl." Daddy, or Caleb "Cal" Calhoun Sr., opened his arms for a hug that enfolded Summer in a secure and loving gentleness she'd felt only with her parents.

Raeg and Falcon stepped onto the porch behind her, waiting patiently as father and daughter hugged.

"And there's those friends of yours. Caleb was certain they wouldn't make it this morning." There was a watchful tension in her father's gaze that almost caused her to cringe with worry.

Daddy could be a problem when he got that look. It meant he was curious, and his curiosity could become a problem if her momma didn't keep it reined in.

At sixty, Cal was still a force to be reckoned with despite his claim of bum knees and a busted shoulder and she knew it. And it worried her.

His face was lined from his years in the military, but his dark blue eyes still held a twinkle of amusement and, sometimes, downright fun that never failed to draw others in.

His black hair was heavily layered with silver, his brows were still a raven's black, his farmer's tan giving his face a dark, leathery look of a lifetime spent in the weather. He was still fit though, shoulders broad, his frame perhaps not as muscular as in his youth, but her momma seemed right proud of how well built he appeared.

Her daddy had always been strong in her eyes though, even at a time when he seemed lost within himself. He was still the man who had taught her how to protect herself from the time she could walk until the time came that training would require harder lessons than he was comfortable teaching her. Because of him, she'd saved herself more than once instead of needing someone else to save her.

He and his "bride," as he still called her momma, were still crazy in love and had managed to raise three boys and two girls that were, as he put it, "wild as the wind but damned good kids."

"Good morning, sir." Falcon shook hands with her father first. "It's nice to see you again."

"Mr. Calhoun." Raeg nodded, shaking Cal's hand as well, though the fact that he was remaining as aloof and distant as possible was easy to see.

She hoped Raeg knew how to mind his manners with her daddy, otherwise, she might have to find the black iron skillet in the kitchen and teach him better.

"Raeg." Her daddy nodded. "Davis Allen speaks highly of both ya'll, but he seems especially fond of you."

"Thank you, sir." Raeg nodded back. "I've gotten kind of used to him as well."

Now, didn't he just sound about as enthusiastic as a hound over a rock bone? Damn him. He was scooting close to being offensive to her daddy.

"Why, Davis Allen just loves Raeg," Summer stated with wide-eyed sweetness as she shot him a warning look. "He's saying all the time how his chief of staff is just a political natural."

And it wasn't a compliment. Though only Raeg and Falcon likely knew it. Because didn't her god-daddy just think a political natural was an asshole to the core and too damned hateful to even discuss the weather with?

She smiled at Raeg, an innocent smile as she clasped her hands behind her back and tilted her head to bat her lashes at him ingenuously.

He didn't appear overly impressed with her though, now did he?

"If she comes up missing, it's because I've fed her to

the alligators," Raeg grunted, though his expression was anything but teasing.

"Her brothers threaten that daily." Her daddy chuckled before turning back to her and centering his attention on her.

Uh oh, there was that look in his eyes again. That was definitely her cue.

"I'll just go help Momma . . ." she said, trying to escape.

"You just wait a minute." Cal caught her shoulder gently as she was about to pass him, leveling a firm look down at her. "You have something to show me, little girl?" her daddy asked her then, frowning down at her from his six-foot height, his expression stern.

"Something to show you?" She shook her head, confused. "I don't think so."

And she wasn't a forgetful sort of person either.

His dark blue eyes narrowed on her. "Turn around, little girl. Your brother told me about that bullet you took in the shoulder. I wondered why you stopped wearing those dresses with those tiny straps last year."

He pushed her around, gently but firmly, as she restrained a groan of defeat.

She was killing Caleb, she decided.

Killing him. Her momma was going to lose a son right fast.

It was with gentle fingers that her daddy lowered the wide strap of her dress just enough to find the scar that marred her shoulder, his calloused thumb brushing over it.

"I have an appointment in a few months with a plastic surgeon," she mumbled. "He'll just make it all go away, Daddy. I promise. We won't even know it was there."

He wasn't happy. She could feel it.

"Only animals shoot little girls in the back." He pushed the strap back in place. "Get in the house, girl. Your momma's waitin' for you."

She went. Too quickly. She knew that tone of voice, and it was not one she ever argued with.

The minute she saw Caleb, she was going to kick him. A killing was just too good for him. He damned certain wouldn't suffer enough.

Raeg watched her go, a little bemused by the fact that she did everything but ask her father how high when he told her to jump. She didn't even obey Davis Allen like that, and from what he'd seen, the senator was like a close and favored uncle to her.

She called him "god-daddy." And though she respected him, she damned sure didn't obey him.

"Surprises you, does it?" Cal asked him gruffly, lowering himself into the rocking chair on the back porch Summer had led them around to from the front of the house.

"Excuse me?" Raeg turned to the other man, watching from the corner of his eye as Falcon took a seat on the thickly padded porch swing, eyeing it like a damned kid who'd never seen one before as Summer's father returned to his rocker.

"That she gets, when I tell her to get." The older man frowned up at him. "And sit down, dammit, don't make me squint up at ya."

Looking around and ignoring Falcon's amusement, he chose a chair across from Cal, so he wouldn't have to squint or turn his head.

God forbid he put the old man out. "I stopped questioning Summer's actions a long time ago," he answered as he sat down, ignoring Falcon's frown. "It's nice to see

she listens to someone though." And that was a damned
lie. It actually irked the hell out of him that she obeyed
anyone without question as she'd just obeyed her father.

He hated it that she would bow and scrape to a man
who had allowed himself to slip so deep into a drunken
stupor that his child had been beaten so severely she'd
thought she was going to die, and he wouldn't wake
up. Beaten because she'd fought back when a nameless,
faceless monster had tried to rape her.

And Raeg had caught the warning in her gaze. Dis-
respecting him would come with a price he might not want
to pay. But it would hurt her. Pissing her off was okay, it
always had been, but hurting her was another story.

Cal rocked silently for a moment as Falcon put a little
swing in the seat he was sitting in. What the hell was up
with that? The two of them were just rocking and enjoying the motion like there was nothing better in the world.
He glanced at his brother, seeing the warning in his eyes
and the disapproval on his expression.

What had he done to upset his far-too-playful brother
this time?

"She'd listen to ya more if ya actually put some sweet
in your voice," the father grunted, surprising Raeg at the
advice. "Though to be honest"—the other man glanced
between him and Falcon—"maybe it's a good thing ya
don't."

Summer's was no man's fool, Raeg thought with sudden insight. The fact that her father was seeing something
none of them wanted him to see wasn't lost on Raeg.

"I'm actually very sweet to Summer, sir," Falcon
assured Summer's father, his expression holding its typi-
cal grin as he obviously tried to distract Cal. "You may
ask her. I worship at her very tiny feet every chance she
gives me."

Raeg closed his eyes and shook his head slowly. His brother . . . One of these days that penchant for drama would get both of them in trouble.

"I can tell you let her think you're wrapped right around her delicate little pinky," Summer's father grunted, giving Falcon a doubtful look. "Boy, I have a feeling you're a menace."

Raeg actually had to hold back an amused snort. No truer words had ever been spoken.

Falcon looked up at the chains that attached his seat to the ceiling. "This is secure, is it not?" he asked, obviously determined to ignore the observation.

Cal narrowed his eyes on Falcon, rubbed the side of his nose with his thumb, and shook his head, almost hiding the tug of a grin at his lips. He continued to watch Falcon until pale blue eyes met darker blue a bit warily.

"You're the one, the reason that girl was in Moscow, I understand?" Cal stated. The expression on his face was anything but approving. "Tell me what happened, boy. Caleb swears he doesn't know, but that boy lies for his sisters every chance he gets. Let's see if *you* can be honest with me."

Raeg almost laughed at the thought. "He lies for her as well, Mr. Calhoun," he informed Summer's father. "Probably more often than Caleb does."

Falcon lied to his brother all the time where Summer was concerned, Raeg mused. They fought over that often.

"I do not lie for her," Falcon assured both of them, enjoying that swing a little too much as far as Raeg was concerned. "I simply refuse to tell you what is none of your business." He turned to Summer's father. "But you are her father, sir, and so I am at your disposal. Ask what you will."

"What the hell happened would be a good place to

start," the older man demanded. "How the hell did my little girl end up with a bullet in her shoulder and some damned Russian psychopath hunting her?"

Amazingly enough, Falcon answered him. Thankfully, he did so briefly without his usual flare for the dramatic when it came to a story. Dragovich had bought stolen American secrets and he and his team, Gia and Summer, had been hired to recover them. As Summer was slipping from the office, Dragovich burst in, obviously warned at the last minute of the recovery. He shot, Summer jumped into the SUV, and Falcon raced to a safe house outside of town where the bullet had been removed by a surgeon Raeg and Davis Allen knew in the area.

The bullet hadn't gone straight through.

Yes, there was quite a bit of bleeding.

And yes, she had developed an infection but at no time had Falcon thought she would die—a bald-faced lie, Raeg knew.

Raeg and Davis Allen had been leaving the airport to fly to Russia and get them back to the States before Summer's fever killed her. It had broken and begun lowering just as they'd been packing the vehicle with needed weapons and supplies for the ride to a nearby military base.

The pain and anger that flashed in her father's face surprised Raeg, as did the other man's desperately clenched fists resting beside his body, pressed into the cushion beneath him.

"As she said, she meets with the plastic surgeon soon and he is certain there will be no sign of the scar once he is finished," Falcon reiterated. "My agency is covering the cost of the procedure as it occurred while she was on a job."

Summer's father was quiet for long, tense moments.

Finally, Raeg saw his fists unclench as the other man took a slow, deep breath.

"Feel guilty as hell over it though, don't ya, boy?" he asked, clearing his throat.

"I still have nightmares," Falcon stated simply.

Cal nodded slowly before a brooding look filled his gaze and he looked between them, obviously not in the least worried about upsetting his daughter with his questions. Raeg wondered why he was still worried about the answers he might give . . .

"Think I haven't checked the two of you out since you came here looking for Summer?" he grunted. "I know quite a bit about your wild ways in DC. Once I knew what to ask, Davis Allen wasn't about to lie to me. Why am I sensing both of you think you can play those games and claim my baby girl while you're protecting her? You think that's going to work here?"

Falcon stopped the swing, his blue eyes icy, his expression not nearly so open and friendly now. "You may ask me anything about Summer but that, sir. Let's not hurt her with questions that will cause the three of us to become out of sorts."

Summer's father turned to him then, and Raeg wondered why he hadn't just obeyed his first impulse and stayed at the house. "You got an answer there, young man?"

"He's a young man and I'm a boy?" Falcon protested then, obviously desperate now to change the subject.

Raeg and Cal both ignored him.

He wouldn't lie, but he didn't have to tell the other man the truth either. He was the senator's chief of staff for a reason. And he was damned good at his job.

"I have no claim on Summer," Raeg answered carefully, his voice low. "And to my knowledge, neither does Falcon."

Summer's father was quiet for long tense moments.

"Summer?" he said quietly then.

"Yes, Daddy?" Her quiet response wasn't hiding the hurt he thought he could hear in it.

Damn her father. The son of a bitch.

Raeg's gaze jerked to the screen door. She stood there, simply staring at him, her eyes like wounded violets. He'd hurt her, just as he hadn't wanted to do. Just as her father had fucking led him into doing.

"Could we get some coffee, since you're prone to eavesdroppin' this mornin'?" her father ordered more than asked.

"Yes, Daddy. But I wasn't eavesdroppin'. Breakfast is going on the table. Momma just put your coffee there," she said, her voice low, the hurt in her eyes causing his chest to tighten at the sight of it.

Her father smiled then, his gaze meeting Raeg's.

The bastard had known Summer was standing there when he'd asked if they thought they could claim her, had known she'd hear Raeg's answer and it would hurt her.

He needed alcohol, not coffee, Raeg decided, though he was sure they'd consider it too early here for whisky.

Surely it was five o'clock somewhere?

"Come on, boys." Cal lifted himself from the rocker, his voice far more jovial than the look he gave her. "My Leasa is a hell of a cook. You don't want to be late to the table, those boys of hers are like human vacuums when it comes to food. They consume it afore you even know it's there."

Following the older man into the house, Raeg caught

Summer before she reached the table, his fingers curling around her upper arm.

"Summer . . . ?" he began.

She shook her head and pulled her arm out of his grip. "Not now. Please don't embarrass me, Raeg."

She moved away from him, taking her seat as Raeg turned and caught her father watching them broodingly.

The son of a bitch. Damn him.

Breakfast was as crazy and loud as any elementary school lunchroom, Summer thought as she sat between Raeg and Falcon. The fact that she'd ended up there hadn't been lost on Momma and Daddy, or on brother Caleb.

Her other brothers Bowe and Brody were there alone, a rare enough occurrence, just as Aunjenue had evidently dissuaded any friends from showing up that morning. Besides Falcon and Raeg, only Clay, her brother's farm foreman, wasn't family—but he'd been there long enough that her momma and daddy considered him family.

The fact that Falcon and Raeg were simply not used to a family-style breakfast, with steaming bowls of food displayed in the center of the table, then passed around, was evident. Falcon caught on quickly. Raeg, despite his cool, confident appearance, wasn't nearly so certain about jumping right in. The paltry amount of eggs and the few pieces of bacon he put on his plate were going to hurt her momma's feelings.

When he went to pass the bowl of silky sausage gravy to her brother without taking any himself, she quickly pinched his thigh.

His gaze jerked to her.

"My momma worked all mornin'," she muttered, her voice low. "Don't you dare hurt her feelings by not eatin'."

He glanced at her plate, lips thinning, then spooned a small amount on the half pieces of his biscuit.

From then on, he was at least considerate enough to try the foods she placed on her own plate.

Thankfully, breakfast went by without too many problems. Falcon flirted with Momma and Aunjenue equally, keeping both women laughing while Daddy and the boys discussed the farm. Raeg ate silently, as did Summer. His declaration that neither he nor Falcon claimed her shadowed her mind no matter how many times she reminded herself that this was something she was already well aware of.

She'd already made her plans anyway. She didn't need them sticking around too long and messing up not just her head but her heart as well.

It proved the suspicion that her daddy truly did read minds though, she thought heavily. No one could have known the sexual tension that fired between her, Raeg, and Falcon when others were not around.

Yet, her daddy knew.

Thankfully, breakfast ended. As everyone rose from the table, Summer joined Aunjenue and their momma in gathering the dishes and moving them to the sink.

"Falcon, Raeg, put those dishes right straight down." Her momma's firm voice had Summer turning, watching, as they slowly lowered their plates and cups to the table, their gazes moving to Summer questioningly. "Aunjenue, fix these two young men another cup of coffee. They can wait for Summer on the front porch."

The subtle order wasn't lost on Falcon or Raeg.

Both men glared at Summer.

"What should we do on the porch?" Falcon finally asked her mother charmingly. "It would be quite boring out there."

Raeg slid him a hooded glance; whether he agreed or disagreed, Summer wasn't certain.

"Summer's gentlemen callers take coffee on the porch with her daddy after breakfast." Her momma was firm despite the pretty smile she flashed. "Aunjenue, get that coffee. Summer, come help me with the table."

That first mention of Summer's gentlemen callers had Falcon and Raeg both pinning her with their gaze.

Restraining her smile, she merely lifted her brow and reached for the nearest plates and cups.

"Daddy's waitin' for ya'll," she told them softly. "Mind your manners though," she suggested, meeting both their gazes warningly. "And don't forget, I know many ways to kill you and dispose of your lifeless carcasses if you get me in trouble. Hear me?"

She didn't wait for an answer. Dishes in hand she turned toward the sink, the sound of the screen door smacking smartly closed a second later. She shot Aunjenue a little wink as her sister stared back at her in awe.

Not that she wasn't well aware that Raeg and Falcon both would make her pay for the fact that they had to endure a much longer interrogation by her daddy now that breakfast was over.

That was just her daddy though. She contented herself with the fact that it shouldn't get worse than what she'd heard earlier. Not being claimed by the men who spent the night wearing her into exhaustion with the pleasure they gave her was about as hurtful as it could get after all.

"You are in so much trouble," Aunjenue snickered as she eased over to the sink where Summer was placing dishes in the hot sudsy water her momma had run to wash them in. "They don't even know about the parties yet, do they? Let alone why—"

"Shh," Summer hissed, glancing quickly behind her.

Falcon and Raeg both were far too sneaky for her peace of mind. "I'll figure it out."

"Yeah, I can't wait to see how you do that one," Aunjenue snorted, on the verge of laughter. "Can I sell tickets?"

She was in so much trouble.

Thankfully, no one mentioned the upcoming parties, or "socials," as her momma was calling them. And when she stepped out onto the porch, her daddy wasn't frowning and her brothers weren't gloating, so she decided Raeg and Falcon might get to live another day.

"I'm going home, Daddy." Stepping next to him, she leaned down and kissed his cheek as he patted her shoulder fondly.

"See you later, baby girl." He nodded, his gaze somber and filled with worry. "Caleb and Bowe can walk over with ya'll, make sure the house is still secure."

Her brothers were rising the second those words came from their daddy's lips, as did Raeg and Falcon.

"Tell them to be nice to me or I'm sending them back in body bags," she informed him, knowing her brothers for the troublemakers they were.

"Be nice to her boys," he ordered them firmly. "Let her get used to bein' home before the three of you start drivin' her crazy."

That was the best she was going to get, and she knew it.

Glancing over at them, she caught their promised looks of retaliation and reverted back to the childish habit of sticking the tip of her tongue out at them before giving them a smug smile.

"Love you, Daddy."

Raeg remained quiet after Summer stepped onto the porch. Even when she stuck the tip of her tongue out at her brothers with childish glee, he managed to keep his shock hidden.

Never, in all the years he'd known her, had he seen this side of the woman he'd been so combative with. She'd infuriated him, drove him insane with the need to fuck her, made him crazy with her mysterious smiles and the knowledge that she was hiding something important, something no one ever saw, away from the world.

This woman resembled the Summer he knew in looks only.

The loving daughter—even though that father of hers likely deserved very little of her devotion—and the playful sister. There was a vulnerability he was seeing now that he'd never seen before.

Returning to the house with her, her brothers trailing behind them, Raeg left her in Falcon's care as he and her brothers checked the house carefully. Despite the closeness of the two houses, the tree line separating them made it impossible to watch Summer's house from her parents'. That made it harder to be certain no one had managed to slip past the security Caleb had installed.

They were playing a waiting game, and Raeg knew the odds were not in their favor. They had no idea when Dragovich would strike, where he would strike from, and how much help he'd have, if any. They were currently vetting all the employees who worked on the farm, but several of them were actually part of Caleb's Special Forces team, and Summer's brother had already vetted the others extensively before he hired them.

Which meant absolutely zero. Just because a man hadn't been offered a bribe to betray a friend didn't mean he wouldn't take it once offered. That was a lesson Raeg had learned the hard way.

Once the house was checked thoroughly, and after a

few teasing insults thrown out to their sister, the brothers
left as Falcon disappeared upstairs for a video confer-
ence.

At least, that was his excuse.

Surprisingly enough, Summer kicked off her sandals
and padded barefoot into the kitchen where she pulled a
covered baking dish from refrigerator, pushed it into the
oven, and set the temperature.

Raeg watched her silently, uncomfortable returning to
his room and leaving her downstairs alone. God only
knew the trouble she'd get into if he left her completely
to her own devices.

"Momma put us a chicken casserole together this
morning and had Caleb bring it over." She grinned, turning to him. "At least we won't starve this evening."

At least they wouldn't have to make the trek back to
the other house to eat, he thought with some relief.

"You really don't know what to think about my family
do you?" Leaning on the center island, she stared at him
in amusement. "All those balls and dinners you go to in
DC, and my family just about makes you shake in your
boots."

Her humor at his expense really wasn't appreciated.

"Your family is different—" He had to stop there.
Hell, what did he know about families, his wasn't exactly
conventional, now was it?

His lips quirked rueful as her smiled widened, her
violet eyes shining with mirth.

"They're not what I expected," he amended, hating the
thought of taking that bright, fun-filled laughter from her
eyes. "You're different here. It was unexpected."

She wasn't hurt as she had been earlier, that shadow
of betrayal wasn't filling her eyes and he didn't want to
see it again.

"I'm at home here." She looked around the kitchen with a fondness that maybe he *should* have expected. "I bought the house from my brother and then had it completely remodeled." Her gaze met his once again and the shadows he'd always glimpsed in her eyes in DC weren't there now. "It's my home."

And it felt like a home. Despite the fact that the atmosphere of the house had seemed lonely the night before, today it seemed anything but. There was a sense of peace here now, a settled feeling that was hard for him to put his finger on.

His mother always said a house reflected the owners, a home reflected those who shared it. Summer loved her home, and she loved being there, he realized.

"Even the kitchen?" he arched his brow, hiding the grin that wanted to tug at his lips. "You know Falcon's on to you, right? He knows who makes those damned crumb cakes."

Summer straightened at the information, her eyes narrowing on him in promised retaliation. "Who told? You? I bet god-daddy told you, didn't he? And I bet you told Falcon. You're a snitch, Raeg. You know that, right?" She was only barely holding back her laughter.

"Never try to con a con, Summer," he snorted, crossing his arms over his chest as he shook his head at her. "Falcon's been on to you since long before you went to work for him. He just lets you think you're getting away with your shenanigans."

Her eyes were sparkling with laughter now, her face filled with happiness. He'd never seen her like this. Never seen so much warmth and joy filling her face and her eyes, warming him from the inside out.

A little pout formed at her lips though teasing humor

filled her eyes. "You're lyin' to me, surely. He would have said something."

She and Falcon shared that warmth of spirit, he realized. The teasing charm and sense of drama, yet, he realized, he didn't feel left out of it, and he didn't feel that his brother possessed a part of her he didn't. It felt right somehow. The two of them needed someone to keep them out of trouble when they were together. He would have been good at that, he thought somberly. He would have enjoyed it. If he could have had the chance to do it.

"He likes playing with you," he answered rather than allowing her to sense the darkness of his thoughts.

Acknowledging how much Falcon enjoyed playing with Summer over the years had been hard for him though. It had taken a while for him to realize how much he enjoyed watching her and his brother playing, teasing each other.

Her lips twitched. "I like playin' with him too."

There was a softness, a sudden hint of vulnerability in her expression.

"You like fooling us," he said, hating the ache in his chest. "Playing games."

She straightened at the accusation, and he told himself that wasn't a shadow of pain he'd caused that flashed through her eyes.

"Games? You think that's all I am?" she asked, anger flashing in her dark eyes. "You think I play with Falcon because I like games?"

He wasn't going to answer that question. He couldn't. Damn her though, if it wasn't games, then what was it? And why the hell did he have to say anything about it, take that laughter from her eyes when he'd been determined not to.

"Your whole family seems to excel in them, Summer," he pointed out, remaining calm, that feeling of being off-balance, of not understanding something and wanting to himself, bugging the hell out of him. "You play the happy, loving family, but that's not the truth either, is it?"

Her nostrils flared, the pout on her lips tightening to a thin line.

"Why don't you just tell me what the truth is, then, Raeg?" she suggested with silky heat. "What do you think you know about me and my family?"

They were facing off again, and despite his regret, despite the fact that he didn't want to hurt her—he never had—by God, he wanted the truth for a change.

"You've run back here every chance you've had for as long as I've known you." He flattened his hands on the counter and leaned toward her. "But I was there that night Davis Allen and Margot brought you back to DC, beaten half to death because your father was passed out drunk when you were attacked. And you act like he never betrayed you. That he didn't leave you defenseless. You fucking idolize him and I want to know why."

Her chin jerked up, her eyes darkening until they looked like bruised violets. Her delicate nostrils flared, and the pain he saw in her eyes was because of him, not because of her family.

"He didn't leave me defenseless, Raeg." There wasn't so much as a hint of that accent in her voice now. "Whoever attacked me got a knife buried in his balls because Daddy taught me how to protect myself." Her face flushed, anger burning hot and bright inside her along with a glimmer of pain that had him wanting to kick himself. "You don't know me and you don't know my family." She pointed her finger to him furiously, the slender digit shaking with whatever she was feeling. "And as far as

I'm concerned, you don't even deserve the chance to know any of us. Why don't you just go back where you belong and leave me and my family alone!"

Before he could stop her, she turned, stalking through the doorway on the other side of the kitchen, through the dining room, then up the stairs.

"Fuck!" The curse slipped past his lips as he shoved his fingers through his hair and pivoted on his heel, intent on returning to the living room.

As he turned, he glimpsed the figure standing on the porch, the tall, broad form of Summer's father as he stared silently through the open kitchen window.

Raeg hadn't known he was there. Had no idea the older man had managed to slip up onto the porch.

Dark blue eyes stared at him emotionlessly from an expression carved in granite.

Cal didn't say a word, just turned and, with military precision, moved across the porch and down the steps to the walkway leading back to his own house.

Wonderful.

This was just fucking wonderful.

Chapter
SIX

The bastard.

Deceitful. Conniving.

He'd just been waiting to slice her open with that one. To rip into the happiness she was feeling and make certain he destroyed it.

She slammed the bedroom door behind her, so furious she was shaking.

He had no idea what had happened all those years ago, or how hard it was for her to come home, to understand what had happened that night and to accept it. Still Raeg hadn't cared a damned bit to cut her open and watch her bleed with it though, had he? He hadn't even asked for an explanation, just made all his accusations like they were the only truth that could possibly exist.

He had to leave.

That was all there was to it.

She was going to have make Falcon understand that.

Swinging around, she was heading back to the door to go inform him of just that when it opened and Raeg stalked into her room, his expression dark and filled with his own anger.

"We were not finished," he informed her, his tone as hard and savage as she'd ever heard it.

"Oh, weren't we?" Her hands went to her hips as she faced him, fingers clenching as she fought to keep from throwing something at him. "Why Raeg, we were finished months ago," she informed him, the brutal anger slamming through her in waves of hot emotion. "Or did you somehow miss the fact that I left? Didn't write. Didn't call." She gave a sharp little wave of her hand before clenching it on her hip once again. "That should have been your first clue that I was completely finished with your superior ass and snide-assed mouth."

"You have got to be the most stubborn, infuriating woman I have ever met in my life," he snapped, stalking to her until she was forced to tip her head back to glare up at him. "I'd rather face Congress than deal with you in a temper."

"Me?" She jerked her thumb back toward herself in incredulity. "In a temper? What the hell do you expect when you go spoutin' off your bullshit and don't even know what you're talkin' about?" she demanded. "You have no more right to judge my family than you have to judge me."

The muscle at his jaw was throbbing, the dark gold lights in his eyes piercing. Damn him, he should not ever be sexy when she was this damned mad at him.

"I wasn't judging you—"

"The hell you weren't. If you're judging my daddy, then you're judging me. That's my family, Raeg. Mine." She lifted herself on her tiptoes, still far too short to go nose to nose with him. "And you will keep your ugly-ass attitude contained. No, forget that. You will leave." Slapping her hands against his chest she shoved against it, hard.

And he didn't even budge.

"Just get the hell out of my house now!" She couldn't ever remember being so mad in her life.

"Will you settle down and talk to me?" He gripped her upper arms when she pushed at him again, holding her in place as she imagined all the different ways she was going to skin him out.

"Talk? About what? Your nastiness with me and my family?" she exclaimed, pushing against him and coming into full contact against his body.

His very aroused body.

A hard, mocking smile pulled at her lips, suspicion clouding her mind like a heavy, smothering fog.

"Summer . . ."

"I know what your problem is. I've always known." She sneered up at him, hating him, hating herself and all the impossible things he made her feel. "You hate yourself because I make you hard. Poor Raeg. He just can't stand it because he wants to fuck the little Georgia hick who just isn't good enough for him and all his fine aristocratic blood." She laughed mockingly. "You think you're too damned good to fuck the likes of me. But that dick of yours has other thoughts, doesn't it, stud?"

She'd tried—Good Lord above she'd tried for as long as she'd known him to be nice to him. To be sweet—even when she was insulting him. Her momma had taught her early how to be a nice little Southern girl, and her godmother, Margot Hampstead, had taught her the fine of art of slicing through the bullshit with a smile. None of those lessons were helping her deal with Raeg though so she resorted to pure Calhoun temper.

Raeg's eyes narrowed on her, sexual tension fairly singing through his body.

"Stud?" he questioned her softly.

"Stud," she enunciated clearly. "I don't remember stuttering. From what I understand, that hard cock of yours is in high demand. I guess I'm the only one who has to deal with your prick-ass attitude to get a taste of it. Aren't I so lucky?"

It was gossiped about by every woman she knew that had ever shared a bed with him and his brother. She hated every floozy that had ever described just how good he and Falcon were as they giggled with the remembrance of satisfied pleasure.

"Summer, now would be a real good time to just shut the fuck up," he warned her, his low, carefully modulated tone just pissing her off more.

"What? That hit too damned close to the truth?" she charged, the rush of blood, anger, and the hated need she felt for him clashing inside her senses. "I knew I liked Falcon better for a reason. His standards must not be nearly as high as yours, I guess, because I actually think he enjoyed being in my bed last night. I guess he can stomach fucking me a little better than you can. Right?"

God help him. If she didn't stop saying "fuck me," he was going to come in his jeans. Every time the words slipped from her lips his cock seemed to harden further, his balls tightening with the need to take her again.

She did this to him.

Every damned time a confrontation rose between them, every damned time they began striking sparks off each other, his cock hardened like iron and his senses became consumed with the need to touch her, to taste her.

They were combustible, he'd always known that. Last night had only proven it.

"I believe I did far more than just stomach it," Falcon spoke from behind Raeg, a curious, waiting sound in his voice, almost a question. "I was only awaiting an invitation for more." He sighed heavily. "Instead, I see you've managed to anger Summer yet again. How did you manage it this time?

Raeg wasn't certain what had flashed in her eyes—a vulnerability? A flash of pain? Secrets, to be sure.

Her secrets made him crazy. There were always hints of them, shadows of them, but learning them was next to impossible.

"An invitation?" she directed the furious question to Falcon. "You wanted an invitation? People in hell want ice water. Your chances are about as good as theirs." Her gaze shot back to Raeg, filled with anger and disdain. And that damned shadow of pain.

She was hurt far worse than he'd suspected, and God knew he hadn't meant for that to happen.

"I'm not stupid enough to wait for a fucking invitation," Raeg growled, sliding one arm around her waist and jerking her against him.

He didn't give her a chance to curse him, to think, or to consider a damned thing. Swiftly lowering his head, his lips covered hers, parted them and tasted the fiery sweetness of a kiss he couldn't seem to get enough of.

Like setting a match to gasoline.

She should be kicking his ass out of her house, off her property, out of Georgia.

Summer whimpered. Her inability to resist Raeg's touch, Raeg's kiss, and the dark dominance that filled him, shocked her. It shouldn't be like this. She had never had a problem resisting any man when she wanted to. There hadn't been a kiss or a touch she couldn't deny no matter the circumstances, until Raeg and Falcon.

Now, she ached, she burned for them, even when she wanted to hit Raeg over the head with a frying pan.

Her fingers clenched in the material of his shirt as she felt her knees weakening, her senses clouding with need as her body sensitized, preparing for the overwhelming pleasure she'd experienced the night before.

Another whimper left her lips as he cradled the side of her face with one hand, holding her in place while his kiss ravaged her senses. One arm moved around her hips, pulling her against him, the hard length of his erection pressing against her lower stomach.

She tightened her hold on his shoulders as his kiss tormented her. His tongue forged past her lips, licked, stroked, feeding from her need as she felt his hunger burning out of control. Releasing the material of the shirt that covered his arms, she moved her hands to his chest, tearing at the buttons, desperate to touch him. She needed to touch him, feel the warmth and heat of his body.

Fabric tore, the sound barely penetrating the dazed lust that had her shuddering with hunger as his groan urged her on.

Pushing the material apart, she let her hands stroke down his chest, feeling the rasp of his chest hair against her palms, the heavy beat of his heart, the heat of his flesh. Stroking lower, she encountered the band of his jeans and the wide leather belt cinching his hips.

She wanted more of him, wanted to stake her own claim on his senses just as he'd staked his on hers.

Struggling to release his belt, she tore at the leather, then the metal buttons until the denim parted and she could free the hard length of his cock.

"Damn, Summer." His head jerked back from his possession of her lips, dragging in a hard breath as the groan escaped his throat. Thick and hot, heavy veins pulsed beneath silky flesh. Iron hard and powerful, the memory of the pleasure he could give her had her stomach clenching, her womb flexing, as silky heat spilled to the sensitive folds between her thighs.

Staring up at him in dazed hunger, Summer licked her lips slowly and, as he watched, his gold and brown gaze gleaming with lust, went slowly to her knees.

Raeg gripped the base of his cock in one hand, his expression turning fierce as he slid the fingers of the other into the hair at the top of her head. Raeg didn't intend to wait for her to take possession of him either. The second she was on her knees, she found her mouth filled with his wide, flared crest as it pushed past her lips.

"Ah fuck!" he cursed, his thighs tightening beneath her palms as she braced herself against him, his gaze darkening, flaring with savage lust now. "How fucking pretty. I've dreamed of fucking your mouth."

The earthy male taste of his cock infused with a hint of a storm, intoxicated her senses.

She could feel Falcon watching them, hear the subtle sounds of him undressing, and it only pushed her arousal higher, the feeling of drugged lust deepening.

Raeg's fingers tightened in her hair, the little sting of sensation against her scalp as he thrust between her lips, dragging a muffled cry from her throat. And she only wanted more.

His cock stretched her lips, each shallow thrust only amping her need higher as the wide head throbbed imperatively against her tongue.

"Your mouth is so damned good, baby," he groaned, his gaze completely carnal now. "So tight and hot."

Her tongue flicked over, beneath the broad head as it shuttled between her lips, the pure eroticism of the act sending pulses of sensation to attack the swollen bud of her clit.

Suckling him deeper, she was rewarded with the salt and male taste of pre-cum spilling onto her tongue as the feeling of dazed lust and hunger increased.

Her breasts were swollen, nipples so sensitive that each rasp of her bra against them was incredibly erotic. Between her thighs her juices spilled, hot and slick, coating her throbbing clit, preparing her for him.

"You're killing my control," he groaned, staring down at her as she forced her eyes open. "I'll come between those pretty lips, Summer."

She would taste his release against her tongue, feel each fierce ejaculation.

That worked for her.

"You little hellion," he groaned as her hold on him tightened. "Come here, let me show you how much better it can get."

Pulling back, Raeg forced her to release the broad crest as Falcon gripped her shoulders, pulling her to her feet before drawing her back against his naked chest as he captured her wrists, holding them in one hand behind her back, her head rested against his chest.

"Let's get you out of these clothes, Belle," Falcon whispered as Raeg began doing just that.

Confident, sure fingers released the tiny buttons that ran down the front of her dress. Pushing the edges apart, he then flicked open the front clasp of her bra. As he pushed the dress and straps of her bra over her shoulders, the material slid down her arms, then to the floor when Falcon released her only long enough to remove the clothing.

Falcon turned her to him then, his lips lowering to hers, taking them possessively. Summer arched into his hold, the feel of his cock throbbing against her lower stomach intensifying the arousal burning through her. A moan broke from her throat as his lips slid from hers and moved down her neck. Then, arching her to him, his head lowered further to a tight, swollen tip of a breast. His teeth rasped over the sensitive point, causing her to jerk in reaction, pleasure searing her a second before it exploded through her senses. His mouth covered the hard point, drawing on it with hard, hungry pulls of his mouth and quick flicks of his tongue.

"Falcon. Oh God, what are you doing to me?" she cried out, a wild, uncontrollable rush of adrenaline rushing through her.

She was going to explode. She could feel it. She was going to orgasm from the feel of his lips on her nipple alone. Her pussy clenched, the involuntary rush of sensation spearing through the aching depths almost violent in its response.

It was better than the night before, more wicked, more carnal. Hotter, more extreme, releasing that wild, wicked part of her that she'd always kept contained.

When his lips lifted from her nipple, Summer was shaking, weak with the languorous sensuality burning through her senses.

As she stared up at Falcon, a cry was torn from her, the feel of Raeg's fingers tugging the last barrier of her panties from her hips so damned sexy that it just didn't make sense.

His teeth raked over the curve of her buttock as his hands guided her to step from the lacy material. Then he was stroking up her legs, one hand sliding between her thighs, his fingers glancing over the sensitive folds between them.

"Wet, baby?" Falcon whispered as another shudder tore through her and Raeg's touch eased back.

Lifting her in his arms, Falcon carried her to the bed, placed her in the center of it, and eased her back to the mattress. He laid her out before them, their gazes going over her with savage, relentless lust.

Falcon stretched out beside her, his lips lowering to hers once again, his kiss drugging her senses further as she felt Raeg pushing between her thighs.

Falcon caressed her breasts with one hand, his fingers tugged at her nipples, exerted and exciting pressure on them even as Raeg destroyed her senses.

His tongue stroked through the swollen, saturated folds between her thighs, lapping at the heavy excess of moisture, stroking around the painfully sensitive bud of her clit. His hungry lips and tongue burned her senses, broad fingers thrust past the snug entrance of her pussy, filling her, destroying her.

Falcon broke the kiss depriving both them of oxygen, only to steal it again as he covered her nipple with his lips.

Raeg's tongue lashed at her clit, the enflamed, swollen bud throbbing madly with the need for release.

"Oh God, Falcon . . ." Her head tossed against the mattress, her wrists still held in his grip, keeping her from touching him, from holding onto him to center herself amid a storm she hadn't expected.

The heavy thrusts of Raeg's fingers inside the clenching depths of her vagina were destructive. His lips on her clit, his tongue rubbing around it . . .

"Please . . . please . . . Oh God, it's so good." And she

needed to come now. She was dying to find that pinnacle of sensation that would consume her senses with ecstasy.

"She'd come so easy," Raeg groaned, lifting his lips though his fingers still filled her, working inside her, pushing her higher. "Her pussy's so tight around my fingers and creaming so sweet and hot."

She was dying. Panting, moaning with the need for more, on the verge of begging.

"I'm going to come on the damned sheets like this," Raeg snarled.

He moved back from her so quickly she couldn't process the desertion before she was being lifted, eased over Falcon, as he stretched out on the bed.

She couldn't wait. She was no virgin in need of guidance. Gripping the thick shaft as she came over Falcon's body, she impaled herself on the iron-hard stalk of flesh, crying out at the lash of pleasure-pain, the burning stretch and feeling of invasion as the broad head pierced the inner flesh.

That was it. That burn. That lash of pain mixing with the pleasure was what she was so desperate for. The wild, carnal mix of agony and ecstasy defied description.

She didn't stop with that first strike of fiery sensation though. Rocking her hips, bearing down as his hips thrust between her thighs, a shattered wail of blazing pleasure escaped her when his full length lodged inside her, buried to the hilt, thick and throbbing in the tender channel.

Desperate lust consumed her as her body slowly adjusted to the penetration, her muscles flexing and rippling around his cock.

Hard hands clamped on her hips when she tried to

move on him though, holding her still, keeping her in place.

"Just a minute, baby," Falcon groaned.

A minute? She needed . . .

She froze.

Raeg moved in behind her, one hand parting her cheeks, his heavily lubricated fingers finding her rear entrance.

Waiting, breathless, uncertain what to expect, she wasn't prepared for what came. The slow, measured invasion of his fingers inside the nerve-laden channel seared her senses, burned through them like wildfire.

Each additional finger, each stretching stroke sent shuddered tearing through her as she jerked in Falcon's hold, crying out their names, lost in the extremity of each sensation erupting through her mind.

"Fuck, Belle, you're going to destroy our minds," Falcon groaned as Raeg moved behind her again, his fingers easing from the grip of her body. "Sweet baby . . ."

His arms wrapped around her, pinning her to him, holding her in place as she felt the head of Raeg's cock press against the tight entrance he'd prepared so carefully.

Her nails bit into Falcon's shoulders as she fought to breathe. The steady, firm push past resistant tissue sent waves of ecstatic pain ripping through her senses, dragging her to that edge of carnal intensity she hadn't known she needed, hungered for. The determined penetration of her rear, the slow filling of the heated depths, tightened the muscles further around Falcon's cock by steady degrees. When the broad length pierced that heavy, ultra-tight ring of muscles and buried in her rear to the hilt, Summer screamed with the hot mix of sensation exploding through her body.

She could feel every inch of their iron-hard erections filling her, throbbing inside her. She was stretched around them so tight, the erotic grip she had on their cocks, the milking ripples of each channel stroking along the heavily veined shafts and destroying any illusion she'd had of surviving it when they left. It was wicked, forbidden. It was everything she'd ever hungered for.

Then they began moving. Practiced years of sharing their women, perfecting their ability to work the female body and give the maximum amount of sensation was apparent. It was destructive. Each coordinated thrust, each retreat and return stroked inside her with heated friction and violent pleasure mixed with the sharp, electrifying jolts of erotic pain.

Her nails dug into Falcon's shoulders as she fought to find something to hold onto. Harsh male groans, muttered exclamations of their pleasure, blended in with her own ragged cries, her own pleas for mercy, her own pleas for more.

The heavy thrusts inside her were tearing her senses apart, invading her mind deeper than they were invading her body, and she had no idea if she could survive it. The sensations were almost terrifying, the spiraling waves of ecstasy and agony tore her from any preconceived idea of what being taken by them would be.

Each impalement, gaining in speed, in friction, caused her muscles to tighten, the spiraling storm growing inside her, whipping through her, over her, tearing past any hope of control . . .

The shattering, violent explosions of ecstasy sent her hurtling into orgasm. They ripped through her body, causing her to jerk in their embrace, to cry out in desperation and a sense of foreboding certainty.

Each hard punch of sensation burrowed past any de-

fenses she might have had against the two men possess-
ing her, taking her. A subconscious knowledge became
conscious, a certainty that she would never the same
again, terrifying her. She loved them. They owned a part
of her, they always had, she realized. Without her knowledge, without any effort on their part, they had already
stolen a part of her soul that she'd never be able to recover.

A part she'd never be whole without when they left.

Collapsing against Falcon's chest, wasted, satiated,
Summer drifted on those currents of realization, letting
them have her, refusing to fight them. She'd made the decision to take what she ached for. Despite Raeg's anger,
Falcon's secrets, and her own fears, she didn't fight the
realizations that came on the heels of the most explosive
pleasure she could ever imagine experiencing.

A pleasure that could become addictive.

What then when they were gone? Would memories
alone be enough?

She feared nothing would be enough once that happened.

Chapter
SEVEN

The next day, Raeg had to escape the maddening atmosphere of the Calhoun house long before Summer was ready to leave. The woman was driving him crazy, and her daddy was just pissing him off.

The son of a bitch just couldn't shut up about the men who were sometimes present for Sunday dinner, and how her *momma* had to refuse several requests from others to join them for Sunday dinner.

Her gentleman callers—Cal had called them that again that morning—were pressing her parents as well as her brothers for invitations to breakfast, dinner, or just a fucking visit?

Summer had gentlemen callers while she was home? And Summer spent the better part of the year home, Raeg told himself later that day.

According to her father, some mornings there could be up to three *socially acceptable* men from the area who would be at Sunday breakfast to charm Summer.

Damn her.

No wonder she spent so much damned time in Georgia.

And who the hell was this woman who bowed down to her family, fetched and carried for her father, and actually hand-washed dishes in a kitchen because that was how her momma liked them washed. Her momma had enough money to line the damned state in dishwashers, yet she refused to have one in her own house.

Come to think of it, there wasn't one in Summer's house either. He'd be damned if he was handwashing dishes just because he decided to dirty something. He knew what dishwashers were made for, and he damned well knew how to use one.

When he'd finally had enough of the stranger that was Summer, he'd escaped. He simply couldn't handle watching her father order her here and there every five or ten minutes. Raeg had finally had to excuse himself and leave the porch with its overhead fans and stifling heat to head back to Summer's house. Otherwise, he was going to end up telling the old bastard exactly what he thought of him.

Somehow, between the acre or so that separated the two houses, he'd wandered from the sidewalk leading through a long line of tall, heavily limbed weeping willows.

Centuries old, their branches hanging thick and heavy to the ground and intermingling from tree to tree, they created a perfect canopy, almost an umbrella effect that completely hid the clearings beneath them.

The living boundary was an exceptional privacy screen and the perfect hiding place for an enemy. With that in mind, he'd stepped beneath a few of them, just to see what he was dealing with, and found the cool, sheltered areas of comfort they held.

The whole damned farm was a security nightmare,

and her family would drive a man to drink. Brothers, sister, mother, and a father who not only treated his daughter like a maid but who saw and knew far more than he should.

Lingering beneath the thick curtain of limbs of one of the trees, Raeg fully admitted he might well be hiding from the crazy people Summer called her family.

Relaxed back on the wide, padded swing, he could understand Falcon's fascination with the shorter, narrower swing on the Calhoun's front porch.

This one was actually long enough to stretch back and nap on if a man wanted to and just wide enough for company if he had Summer's body stretched out beneath him.

Summer's body.

He throttled a groan.

All he could think about was fucking her when she was in residence at the Hampstead estate. Luckily, Falcon was rarely there at the same time she visited during those times. That was the only reason he'd held out until now.

Now, they'd already had her though, burned in her sweet heart, and he found he only craved more of her. Hell, he couldn't get enough.

He was so damned hard, so hungry for her, it was all he could do to keep his hands off her. Not that Falcon bothered to restrain his need to touch her. His brother never had. He was always pulling her into an embrace, sliding his arm around her, or holding her hand if they were moving in the same direction.

Like some fucking teenager with his first love.

When Raeg had refused his suggestion they wake her that morning, Falcon had flashed that cocky grin of his and gone to her bedroom alone. And like a fool, Raeg had stood at the bedroom doorway, dying as he watched his brother send her screaming into orgasm as Raeg held her gaze.

Had he been smart enough to join them then? Well, hell no he hadn't. He'd retreated to the shower and jacked off instead, determined to maintain as much distance as possible.

Now, all he could think about was fucking her again. But hell, that was all he'd thought about for years where Summer was concerned. He and Falcon both had lusted after her with a strength that terrified Raeg.

He was still shocked by the fact that his brother had insisted on not taking her to his bed alone for so many years. Falcon kept claiming she was a woman worth relishing, and she could never be relished properly by him alone. Taking her alone would only be an appetizer to the real thing, not the satisfaction he craved, the other man had stated.

If Falcon had just taken her when they'd first met her and gotten his hunger for her out of his system, then he'd have gone onto the next conquest and everything would have been fine.

In the past two years Falcon had hungered only for Summer instead. The time that his need could have been exorcised was long past, and Raeg knew that his hunger for her may have grown to the point that it was now an addiction as well.

She affected him on a level he couldn't quite make sense of, he admitted.

Damn, he needed a drink. Maybe a cigarette as well.

Not that he smoked. He never had, other than the occasional cigar with the senator. At this point though, he was willing to give a cigarette a try.

At that thought, the heavily leafed natural shield parted and he decided he was facing defeat in its ultimate form. He'd resisted taking her earlier, he might not be able to resist it now. Not here, wrapped in the surprisingly intimate embrace of the trees' weeping limbs.

"Daddy hides under here too sometimes." Summer sauntered across the short clearing, her hands clasped behind her back, the soft material of the white and pale cream sundress with its row of buttons down the front making her look so delicate and fragile he had no idea how she'd survived that bullet slamming into her shoulder.

"Falcon finds this, and you'll never pull him out of it," he told her, attempting a grin as she reach the swing and slid onto the cushioned seat beside him.

"Yes, he would love this," she agreed softly. "He's with Daddy right now. They're checking the gator traps along the pasture behind the house. Daddy lost one of his calves last month and he's certain a gator got it."

Her hair was loose from its ponytail, falling around her shoulders and down along her back.

Tempting his fingers.

"They have a lot of problems with alligators here then?" he asked, giving into temptation and capturing a silky curl to caress between his fingers.

The feel of it, the soft living warmth of it just made him ache to touch her more.

Ache?

Hell, he was *dying* to touch her again.

"Not a lot," she answered, gripping the edge of the swing and staring down at the ground for long moments as Raeg kept the gentle sway in motion.

"Everything okay?" Damn her. She was so beautiful, so fucking sensual it was killing him.

She exhaled heavily before turning her head to stare back at him with violet eyes that were softer, deeper than he'd ever seen them.

"I'm really sorry, Raeg," she said softly. "I know Daddy's nosiness bothers you. And I know you don't understand things." A frown marred her brow. "I'm just sorry I guess."

And now she was apologizing for her father? Son of a bitch . . .

"It's not his nosiness that bothers me," he growled, furious all over again. "It's the way you jump to play maid to him that's bothering me. 'Get me this, get me that.' 'How high, Daddy?' " he mocked her, knowing, even as the words came from his lips, that he was being an utter ass and hating himself for it.

Hurt flashed in her eyes, and this time, it wasn't a superficial twinge of her little feelings. This time, the hurt went deep, as did the disbelief. But hell, after yesterday, she could actually be surprised by his stupidity?

"Were you raised by wolves?" she snapped, her voice low, disbelief and pain filling it. "That's my daddy! Yesterday's ignorance was bad enough Raeg, but this too? You'd berate me for doin' for him?" she exclaimed angrily, her violet eyes sparking furiously. "Each busted knee, bum shoulder, knife, and bullet scar. And he'd still stand between me and Dragovich if it meant I wouldn't have suffered that bullet in my shoulder." The anger sparking in her eyes had the power to amaze him. "And how dare you even think you can share an opinion on my relationship with my daddy."

The drawl was subtle, softer, sweeter than the exaggerated sound of it she'd used for as long as he'd known her.

"Your daddy," he snorted. "Who are you here, Summer? This isn't you . . ."

Or was it? He'd known there was more to her, hated the fact that she hid it from him. But was this soft, family-devoted woman really the one she'd been keeping tucked away from the world?

"No, Raeg. The woman you knew? The one who could take the life of a traitor she believed was her friend." Her voice broke before she got control of it and went on. "Is that who you believe I am? Nothin' but a killer?" she demanded furiously.

Staring back at her, the need to harden himself, to protect both of them, to ensure she didn't get too close, that she didn't attract the notice of a monster, rushed to the forefront of his mind.

"An effective one," he snarled, and he knew better.

Something dark and bitter and filled with pain shadowed her eyes and had them suddenly gleaming with moisture.

She came off the swing with a surge of speed, almost too fast for him to catch her.

It was the tears. God help him, he couldn't keep doing this to both of them.

"Summer, wait." He grabbed her arm, pulling her back as she tried to jerk from his grip. "I'm sorry . . ." Horror filled him. "Oh God no. Baby. No tears . . ."

He couldn't stand it. No matter how fiery their arguments in the past or how filled with outrage, he'd never made her cry.

She was in his arms when he tried to pull her back. Turning her, he had her over his lap, his head lowering, her trembling lips parting beneath his kiss on a gasp. She stilled in his hold.

Raeg groaned.

The hunger he'd fought that morning, that he'd fought far too many years was free and now he had no idea how to pull it back. And he hadn't had enough of her yet, not enough that he could control the vicious, brutal surge of emotion and hunger that tore through him, and left him helpless against it.

What was she doing?

The thought was distant, too far away to really affect the instantaneous effect of Raeg's kiss to her senses. His lips slanted over hers, his tongue finding hers and, with devastating eroticism, just licking against it.

Her arms slid to his shoulders, then to his neck, her fingers sliding into his hair to clench the shortened strands.

She'd dreamed of this, of his kiss, but she'd had no idea of the pleasure until the other night, and now she found she ached for it. It was incredible. It was hot and sensual, and the feel of him holding her, bending her back to the covered mattress of the swing bed, and coming over her was . . .

Oh God . . .

He settled between her thighs, the thick, hard ridge of his erection riding between her thighs, exciting her clit more than it was already, sending moisture flooding the inner recesses of her sex.

Swollen breasts and hard nipples pressed into his chest, and despite the clothes separating them, the friction was exquisite. And oh so good.

Falcon had taken her hours ago, but Raeg hadn't. He'd watched, his gaze hot and dark with his need to join them, but he'd only watched, only hungered. And he'd left her missing him.

She tilted her hips into him, her thighs clenching on his hips, whimpering cries leaving her lips as one broad hand clenched her hip, the other sliding up her side to cup the curve of her breast. His thumb brushed over the distended peak of her nipple and the surge of sensation that tore from the sensitive tip to her clit was almost orgasmic.

Almost.

She wanted more than "almost." She wanted the dark edge of coming ecstasy to completely overtake her, to fill every particle of her and leave her sated once again. Maybe, if she were lucky, her fascination for him and his brother and their drugging kisses would go away then.

Something had to make it go away before she completely lost herself in it, because she knew there was no future in it. If she hadn't known it before, she knew it now. Knew it, and still she was helpless, mesmerized by his lips on hers, his tongue stroking against hers, his hips moving between her thighs, pushing her so close to that edge . . .

"Summer, dammit, Daddy's coming . . ." Aunjenue hissed from outside the shield of the tree. "Hurry . . ."

Raeg jumped from her as though someone had struck a fire to his ass. Before Aunjenue's warning finished, he was standing several feet from her while she struggled to sit up, to bring some order to her clothing, her hair.

Oh God, what had she done?

Lifting her gaze, she felt a flush burn from her neck to her hairline, horror filling her at the sight of her daddy glaring at Raeg from where he stood, half in and half out of the shield of willow limbs that trailed along the ground. Behind him, Falcon lifted his head to the heavens, his eyes closing momentarily before his head lowered again and he too met her gaze.

Arousal, satisfaction, and compassion mixed in the pale blue of his eyes.

Still fighting to breathe, she looked from Raeg, to Falcon, then back to her daddy in horror as she struggled to her feet, feeling as though she were coming off a drunk that made no sense.

"I . . ." she swallowed tightly.

Oh God, what could she say? How could she ever explain her total lack of control? That she'd actually let her daddy catch her . . .

She was completely mortified.

"You're a grown woman, Summer," Raeg told her softly without looking at her. "I'd think explanations aren't needed."

Her daddy just looked at him. Just gave him one of those long, disappointed looks that could make his own children feel five again.

"They aren't needed," she assured him brokenly, feeling her throat tightening with tears and regret. "But a woman should have an excuse for letting a man that's so disrespectful to her daddy actually handle her with such familiarity."

Her breathing hitched as she felt her hands shaking, felt the little girl and the woman standing in such conflict now that she had no idea how to handle it.

Her daddy just shook his head before turning his gaze to her. His look was gentle but watchful, as though he suddenly didn't quite know what to expect of her.

As though he didn't know her.

"I'm sorry, Daddy." Pushing her fingers through her hair, she glanced at Raeg's back, then at Falcon's hardening expression. "I'm very sorry. This was the wrong place . . ." She dropped her gaze, shaking her head. "I'm so sorry," she whispered, then turned and rushed from beneath the tree, unable to meet his gaze, Falcon's, or Raeg's.

Oh Lord, she just couldn't believe this. She'd never be able to face her daddy again.

The wrong place . . .

At least she hadn't said he was the wrong man, Raeg thought as he met her father's gaze again, refusing to back down in the silent war that seemed to be going on between them.

"Go after her, Falcon," Cal ordered, his voice low. "Don't let her cry."

"Yes sir." Throwing Raeg another hard glare, Falcon turned and obeyed just like some damned pup conditioned to obedience. Was there something in the damned water here? Something that made grown men and women jump to this man's command?

"Aunjenue," the elder Calhoun called out.

"Yes, Daddy?" If Raeg wasn't mistaken, there was the slightest bit of amusement in the girl's tone.

"Get your ass to the house, girl, and stop eavesdroppin'," he ordered her firmly.

"Yes, Daddy." Instant fucking obedience.

Cal leaned heavily on the walking stick he carried, clasping it with both hands, despite the fact that he stood perfectly straight and tall, his expression thoughtful.

"If you're waiting for an apology, it's not coming, Mr. Calhoun," Raeg informed the older man. "I'd say Summer just did enough groveling for the both of us."

Summer's father nodded slowly. "I didn't imagine it was," he finally said. "A man who can't see his woman's love for her family wouldn't understand why one was needed, even when it was."

The subtle insult wasn't lost on Raeg, it was just ignored.

"She's not my woman." The words were pushed out between clenched teeth. Deliberately. "I told you, I have no claim on her."

Some glint of satisfaction filled the other man's gaze

then. Whatever caused it, Raeg wasn't certain, but he could feel his gut tightening in foreboding with it.

"Good then," he declared, that satisfaction filling his voice. "That's damned good then. No hard feelings, boy. My girl has more common sense than most. You might fool her for a bit, but she'll wake up. When she does, she'll kick your ass to the curb and send you packing, I have no doubt. I'll say good evening then. See ya'll in the morning."

Turning, he let the limbs fall back in place, leaving Raeg standing in the darkened interior, confused, wondering what the hell that meant.

And the satisfaction in the older man's gaze? He was damned glad Raeg had no intention of claiming Summer. Happy even.

Raeg's fists clenched at his side, his jaw aching because his teeth were clenched so tight.

He'd be damned. Caleb Calhoun Sr. didn't think Raeg was good enough for his pretty little daughter. Now, didn't that just beat it all?

Summer left her parents' home well after dark and returned to her own house, her brother following her until she disappeared into the house and locked up. She was mortified her daddy had caught her in such a compromising position. Why, if she even thought she'd nearly caught her momma and daddy getting so personal, she'd just die.

Having her daddy actually catch her? It was so shameful she could barely face him when she'd left her sister's room to head home and met him at the bottom of the stairs.

Thankfully, he acted as though it had never happened.

No lecture. No disappointed looks. He'd kissed her cheek and called for her brother to walk her home before telling her good night.

Fog was already beginning to gather at the darkest edges of the wetlands beyond the house where swamp and marsh came together to create the unique mystery of the land she'd been born to.

Cypress dripping with moss, marsh grass growing alongside it in some areas before disappearing beneath the deeper, darker waters teaming with a variety of life. Gators bellowed into the dark, joining the other sounds of the night to create a symphony that could be found nowhere else.

Closing the door, she leaned against it for a long moment, eyes closed. Her life was simply becoming a mess, she thought, shaking her head as she straightened, her eyes opening.

She narrowed her gaze into the darkness of the living room then, her lips tightening at the knowledge of who watched her silently.

"I'm sorry, Summer." Raeg stepped from the darkness of the living room, a drink in one hand, the other rubbing at the back of his neck. He was apologizing, but there was no regret in his voice or in his eyes.

She walked in, staring back at him heavily for long moments.

It wasn't just his disrespect of her father and her relationship with him that bothered her. It was the fact that in all the years he'd known her, he hadn't even suspected that she wasn't the cold-hearted agent, the killer, and social barracuda she'd played in DC.

Even god-daddy and her dearest friend in the world, Alyssa, had known better. Hell, even Falcon knew better. But Raeg hadn't even suspected.

Because he hadn't wanted to know.

"Don't worry about it, Raeg," she finally told him, sliding her hands into the pockets hidden at the seam of her dress. "Daddy's fine. He didn't feel offended at all actually." She shrugged helplessly. "I was the one who was offended."

He frowned back at her. "How the hell did I offend you?" he demanded. "For God's sake, Summer, what we did together with Falcon in that bed upstairs didn't offend you, but kissing you under a tree did?"

His complete lack of a sense of decorum in such situations simply astounded her, she thought, staring back at him in disbelief.

"That's my daddy, Raeg," she tried to explain. Just this one time, she was going to try. "I knew that was his favorite tree, but I still let that happen. And I found it in very poor taste that you should think I shouldn't be embarrassed that my daddy caught me letting a man handle me. That was simply unacceptable from both of us."

His eyes widened for a second before he blinked and shook his head as though he couldn't believe what he'd just heard.

"Dammit, Summer. You're a grown woman, not a teenager," he cursed, which just made her mad all over again.

She wasn't going to argue with him though, she told herself again.

"In my own home, I'm a woman," she informed him, lifting her chin and glaring back at him. "What I do behind closed doors is my own damned business. But I will always be a little girl to that man who caught you bein' so intimate with me, and it's simply unacceptable that you don't understand that."

Oh, she knew him so well.

Her arms crossed over her breasts defensively at the look on his face. She so was not going to like whatever he was preparing to say.

"The same man that let some bastard nearly rape you when you were twelve?" The glass he held slapped to the sideboard next to him, his knowledge of that shocking her. "Where was he when Margot and Davis Allen flew out here and took you out of his home because he was too goddamned drunk to protect his daughter?"

Summer flinched.

The pain that struck her went clear to her soul. It burned and razed through her with a force she didn't bother to fight. Not because of what might have happened or almost happened. Or because her daddy might have been weak for a single moment during his entire life.

"Where he was doesn't matter," she cried, pointing a shaking finger back at him furiously. "Don't you ever, ever question him again. You don't have that right. You don't know him and you damned sure don't know me, and we're both well aware you have no desire to. Why don't you just go home instead of staying here, when everyone can tell you damned sure don't want to be here, Raeg? Why are you putting both of us through this?"

Turning, she rushed to the stairs and ran up them, anger and pain building inside her, pride and need warring inside her until she felt it tearing her apart inside.

Reaching the top of the stairs, she came to a hard stop at the sight of Falcon standing silently, his expression somber in the doorway of the room closest to the stairs. No doubt he'd heard every word.

"You're just as bad," she told him raggedly. "And I'm no better. Maybe both of you should just leave. I'd rather deal with Dragovich myself than to have my heart shredded like this."

Rushing past him, she promised herself she wasn't going to cry. Neither one of them deserved her tears.

Tonight, she'd never felt less like the agent, the killer Raeg thought she was, or the woman she'd showed to the political elite she socialized with.

There had been days she'd been sickened by the life she'd once thought she wanted so much. An agent, kick-ass adventures by the dozens, she thought mockingly as she slammed her bedroom door behind her.

And she hadn't been able to stand herself by the time it was over. Standing in a chapel, staring at the woman she'd killed, the woman she'd thought was a friend, Summer had known she was finished. Because she'd been so determined to be someone she wasn't, to fit into a life she'd already known wasn't hers, she hadn't been able to see the truth of who and what she was allowing to happen to herself.

And she wouldn't let it happen again.

Never again.

She wouldn't be the woman Raeg thought she was just so he and Falcon would be comfortable with her. She would not be less of a daughter, less of a sister or a friend, just because he wanted someone that didn't exist.

She was Summer Dawn Calhoun, she was not Summer Bartlett. And Raeg was just going to have to accept there wasn't a chance in hell he was going to get what he wanted. She never wanted to be Summer Bartlett ever again.

Falcon made his way downstairs, his heart heavy at the thought of the pain he'd seen in Summer's face as she raced past him. He'd be angry, he acknowledged, if he wasn't very well aware of the conflict also warring inside his brother.

"Don't start," Raeg warned him from where he stood next to the French doors leading from the living room to the wide wraparound porch.

Moving to the bar, Falcon poured a drink in the dim light, took a fortifying sip, then walked to the opposite side of the door frame, looking out onto the drifting tendrils of fog.

He'd been watching the emerging impatience Raeg was feeling where Summer was concerned for a while. It had begun coming to a head in DC the year before, while Summer had been at the Hampstead estate to help protect her friend, Alyssa, the senator's daughter.

Summer and Alyssa had been friends since they were five. Alyssa's mother Margot had actually been instrumental in Summer's training and her eventual placement in the CIA. Not that Summer had really fit in with the agency. She hadn't. In the space of eight years she'd gone from the CIA, to the FBI, the DEA, and then to the private security firm Falcon headed. But even in that less-structured atmosphere, she hadn't found what she was looking for—and hadn't realized it was the very thing she'd left behind in Georgia.

With maturity, Summer had begun missing home. Falcon had seen it, acknowledged it, despite the fact that he hadn't wanted to. It was Raeg who still couldn't see it, Raeg who hadn't yet realized the woman he was determined to protect, even from them, was the only woman who was going to complete either one of them.

But Falcon had to admit that acknowledging it didn't make it easier to accept the fact that they'd have to let her go when this was over. They simply didn't have a choice.

"You know," he murmured quietly, "her father hasn't had a drink since the night Davis Allen and Margot flew out of Georgia with Summer all those years ago." He rubbed at the back of his neck, remembering well the night Margot had told him about the fact that Summer couldn't identify who had tried to rape her. "Caleb and the boys were given a month's leave when the senator made a few calls. But when they got home, Cal was sober as a judge. He's not had a drink since."

"Fuck him," Raeg snarled. "She was a baby, and he was passed out fucking drunk, his wife out God only knows where, and Summer nearly paid the price . . ."

"Shut your fucking mouth, Raeg!" Falcon's voice never rose, it deepened, became savage in the guttural growl that filled it. "And keep your opinion of her father as well as her family damned quiet or risk destroying a woman who does not deserve it. One who will gladly force us to leave her home, and leave her undefended against Dragovich, if you continue to insult her father. Should she do that, and if anything—anything!—happened to her, I don't know that I'd survive it."

Raeg could only stare back at him in shock. No threats, no demands, simply that. The admission, finally, that she was more to Falcon than any other woman had ever been.

"I'm not going to threaten you to stay," Falcon said several minutes later, his voice still low, though not as enraged. "I know your reasons for striking out at her, I know the horror you alone faced, and nothing can change that for you. You'll always be my brother, Raeg, and I don't want to change that. But if you can't protect her without hurting her like this, then I ask you to go, and I will find someone who can help me without striking at her over what cannot be. I understand," he said softly, compassionately. "Go. No harm, no foul. I'll find someone to watch our backs. Summer has enough friends that such will not be hard to do."

As he spoke, Falcon watched as Raeg seemed to

stiffen from his heels to his hair. It was kind of amusing to watch when his brother got all worked up inside like that.

"The last time the two of you went off to save God and country alone, she almost ended up dead, and you would have died beside her if you couldn't have gotten her out of there," Raeg bit out in disgust as he pointed a finger at Falcon furiously. "I can only imagine what would happen if I leave the two of you alone here with her crazy-ass family." He gestured outside with the hand holding his drink before bringing it to his lips.

It was tearing Raeg apart inside though, and Falcon knew it. Regretted it.

"I won't have her hurt in such a way again, Raeg, I've already warned you about that. Just because you're my brother doesn't mean I'll put up with it," Falcon snapped. "Get your head out of your ass and at least give her, give us, a few memories to hold on to when this is over. Something that will ease the pain of losing her instead of making it worse."

Raeg's gaze met his, the dark, golden brown gaze reflecting the emotions and his battle against feeling anything more for Summer than he'd felt for any other woman. And Raeg simply didn't understand that it was far too late to stop it.

"She doesn't belong here—" Raeg snapped.

"Yes, she does," Falcon broke in firmly, surprised his brother hadn't realized it long before they had arrived in Georgia with her. "That's what's pissing you off so much. You're sensing what I already knew. Summer's home, and you hate it. But you refuse to see why."

Because they couldn't keep her, they couldn't stay here with her. When it was over, they'd have no choice but to walk away, and Raeg was fighting that, even though he knew it to be the truth.

"And I guess you have all the damned answers," he snarled, his rough-hewn expression angry, suspicious. "Why don't you just tell me what you think I don't know, Falcon?"

Oh, he knew exactly why his brother hated it so damned much, and why he refused to acknowledge it. So many of Raeg's emotions were trapped inside him, buried so damned deep that now that they were trying to emerge, his brother simply had no idea what to do with them.

"What do I think you don't know?" Falcon chuckled. "What I know, Raeg, is this. Each year since we first met her, the need you have for her has only grown. Just as mine has. It's because of our past, our legacy, that we can't have her, and like me, it's eating your guts alive. But I won't allow you to eat her alive because of it."

"For God's sake, could we at least keep things on the edge of reality, Falcon?" He sighed in disgust. "Just this once?"

Rather than simply telling Falcon he was right, that he ached for Summer just as desperately as his brother did, Raeg used the same line he'd been relying on for years.

She was Raeg's greatest weakness, Falcon sometimes thought. The one woman his brother ached for yet refused to allow himself.

"Reality?" Falcon asked. "Reality is, the day is swiftly approaching that we must walk away from the only woman on this earth who completes us. When we do, it will destroy us, and you know it, just as I do."

"You're reaching," Raeg snarled before slapping his

glass onto the side table close to him and plowing his fingers through his hair in frustration. "Since when did you begin mistaking lust for love, Falcon?"

"Is that what I'm doing?" Falcon asked somberly, the realization at how very far his brother intended to isolate himself now sinking in. "Perhaps you're right. I should have never tempted you to share her between us." He nodded firmly. "I can claim her for my own while we are here. I do not require your presence to pleasure her. I proved that this morning, did I not?"

Raeg actually laughed at him. A mocking, though highly amused, laugh.

"Like hell," he bit out furiously. "I'll be damned if I'll let you have her alone."

Raeg stalked from the room and up the stairs, muttering beneath his breath, causing Falcon to smile with a bit of satisfaction.

This would see their hearts destroyed when they had to leave her, but while they were with her, the opportunity to create memories to sustain them was there. And Falcon wanted those memories. If he couldn't keep Summer in his life, he wanted at least to ensure he kept the memory of her in his soul.

Chapter
EIGHT

Pond and bald cypress trees grew tall and plentiful, Spanish moss dripping from the conifer branches like ghostly beings as they shifted and waved in the eerie light of the predawn fog.

Four thirty in the morning wasn't Falcon's favored time to be out and about. He'd done far enough of that when he was younger. But Cal had a schedule, and part of his schedule was checking his gator traps before dawn.

And for the past week, he'd made a habit of inviting Falcon along on these little excursions.

Falcon had yet to see a gator trap, or watch the old man bait one. He'd seen plenty of gators though. Some a bit larger than he would have expected, all of them eyeing the flat-bottomed boat Cal either pushed through the water with an old cypress pole, or guided along the black-ish waters with one of the oars stored beneath his seat at the back of the craft.

They never used the attached trolling motor either. Even in the daylight hours.

Falcon still couldn't believe he was sitting there in

the boat with the old man rather than curled around
Summer in her comfortable bed. But he'd known when
he woke a little before four that Summer's father would
be coming to collect him. And there was Cal on the back
porch waiting, when Falcon and Raeg stepped into the
kitchen.

To give him credit, Major Calhoun invited Raeg along
each morning.

Raeg always refused. Riding an edge that bordered on
disrespect, he'd take his coffee and just turn his back on
Summer's father as he left the kitchen.

"You know," Cal commented quietly, surprising Falcon. "Leasa's daddy used to pull me out of bed 'bout this
time every morning. Made me madder than hell too." He
paused for a moment, pushing the pole along the bottom
of the water, propelling the boat further into the swamp.
"I'd bitch and rail at Leasa every morning when I came
back in. I'd order her straight up to tell her daddy to leave
me the hell alone. I was no swamp rat and I wasn't about
to become one."

Falcon's lips quirked at the amusement in the older
man's voice, as well as the acknowledgment that Cal was
rather fond of the memory.

"She'd beg and plead and order her daddy to stop in-
sistin' I go out with him, but old man Collier, he never
stopped. Then one day, we were about here"—he nodded to the area they were drifting into—"and he laughed
at me, said I was sending his sweet little girl to do a man's
job to convince him to let me laze in bed rather than gettin' out and being a man."

Falcon just listened. When Summer's father was silent
again, he just waited. There was a reason for this little
story, he knew. His own father may not have been much
on instructing or teaching his son the ways of the world,

but Falcon had been lucky enough to meet others who were.

"Summer hasn't tried to convince me to let you sleep in. And she hasn't mentioned Raeg's refusal every morning," Cal pointed out then.

Falcon flicked an amused look toward the older man's shadowed outline.

"If I didn't want to come out, sir, then you couldn't force me out." Falcon shrugged. "And it's not Summer's place to request you allow me to sleep should I decide that's what I want to do."

Neither he nor Raeg mentioned these early morning trips to Summer, though she was aware of them. He'd glimpsed her watching each morning as he and her father stepped into the wide, flat-bottomed craft Cal used to go into the murky depths of the swamp.

"You're good company out here," the other man admitted then as the boat drifted lazily through the waters. "I wonder though, if your brother would be near as well mannered."

Falcon couldn't help but chuckle as he relaxed back in the low seat, facing Summer's father.

"If he wanted to be here, then he'd only piss you off hourly—that's Raeg being nice," he grunted. "If he didn't want to be here, then he'd piss you off about every other word out of his mouth—bad enough that you'd used his body parts for those gator traps before you ever made it this far."

There was no sense in glossing over the fact that his brother could be the world's biggest prick. Especially when he resented someone as he resented Cal.

Summer's father was quiet for long moments, simply pushing the boat along the water, obviously well aware of where they were going despite the lack of light.

"You know," he said heavily when he finally spoke again. "I've heard about the two of you for the past eight years. How Raeg had taken his little jabs and pissed her off or hurt her tender heart. You'd smooth it over, get her laughing, and she'd forgive him."

Well, Falcon thought, he'd wondered how long it would take her father to work his way around to this particular conversation. It wasn't a discussion he wanted to have with the other man and he knew Summer would never appreciate her father knowing anything intimate about her life. She had a squeamishness about that he found both amusing and confusing. That was a part of what made Summer so unique though, so he didn't question it. Neither did he want to disrespect it.

Her father didn't understand their past though, or the hell Raeg had felt the night he walked in to find his lover dead only to learn his father had killed her. Because she was an agent. Because she'd been sleeping with him in an attempt to learn if he was actually Roberto Falcone's son as she suspected. It was information she would have sold to Roberto's enemies who wanted to find his son and use him to force Roberto and his lovers out into the open, so they could kill them.

"No comment?" Cal asked softly.

"Raeg doesn't try to hurt her," Falcon told him quietly. "And when he does, it actually hurts him far more deeply."

"You gonna make excuses for him like Leasa used to make for me?" Cal asked, his voice low. "Do that a lot, do you?"

Falcon gave a rueful smile at the question, knowing what the other man was trying to do and hoping he was smart enough to stay out of that trap.

"I know Raeg as no one else does," he stated carefully.

"It's not making excuses. There is no intent to hurt Summer. Making her angry places a shield between them and ensures his emotions are not affected any more than she has affected them already. You see or hear only Summer. I see and hear them both, and I see things no one else would understand."

Because he loved both of them. His love for his brother was a lifetime of shared experiences and pain. His love for Summer, just as Raeg's love for her, was just as deep, just as enduring. She was the light to their dark, and he was going to hate losing her every second after they were forced to leave.

"Your brother's in love with her." It was a statement, not a question.

It was something Falcon hadn't expected Summer's father to realize so quickly. Though he should have expected it, he realized. Cal, like his daughter, was damned good at hiding exactly how perceptive he actually was.

"He is, sir." Falcon sighed heavily. He'd fallen into the trap so fast, Raeg would be disgusted with him but hell, he respected this man. And lying to him just didn't seem right. He loved Summer as well, as no one else ever could. "As am I, before you ask. Raeg simply has yet to admit it."

This could be a mistake. This man could kill him without a single moment's guilt, Falcon guessed, but, if Cal didn't kill him, he'd at least know he showed her father the respect she would expect of him. Even if she'd kick his ass for letting out any information that would even hint that she was having sex with him and his brother.

"Two men who love her," Cal mused. "Knowing how your brother feels and how he watches her with hunger, yet refuses to claim her, why haven't you claimed her? Why bring Raeg and tempt losing her forever yourself?"

Hell of a question, wasn't it. Yes indeed, Summer was going to end up kicking his ass in the worst way.

"I'll never lose Summer to my brother, sir," Falcon assured him, ensuring his tone was far more gentle than the fierce possessiveness he felt where his and Raeg's claiming of her was concerned.

"Because both of you think you can have her?" her father charged, his voice low but echoing with anger now.

Falcon simply stared back at the shadowed outline of the outraged father. And he couldn't blame him. There was a time when such sexual acts were kept so silent that they became skeletons skulking in family closets, and never allowed to see the light of day.

"Sir, this is a conversation I'd prefer not to have at a time when you could toss me overboard and provide your friends, the gators, a bit of a predawn snack." He sighed. "Could we talk of these things when we're once again on dry land?"

With a hard push of the pole the boat turned and headed back the way they had come.

"You think you can carry on like that here in Cliffton?" Cal growled. "That Summer won't be hurt because of it?"

"Sir, I think once Summer makes up her mind about anything, then she truly does not care what others believe. I've seen her face down the worst society has to offer, and suffer nothing more than their respect when it was all said and done."

"This isn't DC, boy," the other man snapped.

Falcon remained silent.

He'd already said way too much.

He respected Summer's father and he was loathe to lie to him, but neither would he give the other man the fuel he needed to poke at Raeg. Which, Falcon suspected, was the older man's aim. Her father and Raeg were playing a very subtle, very dangerous game behind Summer's back. If she learned of it, she'd end up poking them both back. Straight into a gator nest.

If gator nests really existed.

Summer could become rather vengeful.

And a vengeful Summer was a very dangerous Summer.

"I gather we are returning early?" Falcon observed.

"Well now, aren't you the smart one this morning?" Cal sneered. "I guess—"

"I took my smart pill this morning?" Falcon asked curiously. "Now I know where Summer gets that wicked humor of hers, sir."

The other man simply grunted.

Hell.

Summer wouldn't be pleased.

Big mistake.

Probably the biggest mistake of her life.

Summer rushed from the house while Falcon and Raeg were still showering. The sun was barely up, the fog still lying heavy in the air, filling the marsh that led into the swamp below the house.

They would know where she had run, no big secret there. She'd been running every morning for the past week. And they'd been letting her do it.

There were quite intelligent when they wanted to be— they'd known she was running, and they'd followed. The overwhelming need to escape the consequences of the night before, had ensured the need to put as much time as possible between her and facing them.

She shivered as she passed the line of weeping willows, rubbing at her arms and wishing she'd taken a few seconds to grab a sweater. The thin cotton white-and-red print summer dress wasn't much defense against the moist, early morning air.

"Mornin', Daddy." Stepping on the porch, she paused to bend and place a kiss on his cheek before straightening to move into the house and help her momma with breakfast.

"Summer." His stern voice stopped her before she disappeared into the house. "Have a seat, girl."

Oh, this wasn't good. When Daddy ordered her to have a seat, that meant she really wasn't going to like the conversation at all, she thought morosely.

"Raeg and Falcon will be here in a minute, Daddy." Stepping back, she stared down at him in resignation. "If you're angry with me, could you please tell me in private?"

An argument with her daddy in front of the men she'd taken as lovers wasn't going to be a pleasant start to her morning. Especially when she suspected the argument was going to concern them.

"Did I ask to speak to you privately?" he questioned her, his tone harder now. "Now sit down there and stop tryin' to find an excuse to escape."

But she so needed to escape, she thought desperately.

"Yes, sir." She stepped up to the chair he indicated and sat herself down.

Back straight, her hands in her lap, she kept her expression calm despite the brooding look he was giving her.

The silence stretched between them until the front door opened and her momma stepped out with two mugs of coffee. She placed them on the table next to her husband.

"Remember what I told you," her momma said softly.

Her daddy rolled his eyes at the reminder.

"Get breakfast, woman," he chided her with a hint of amusement. "Summer and I are just gonna chat a minute."

Her momma shook her finger at him warningly before turning and walking back into the house.

Summer remained still and silent, only moving when her father handed her a mug.

"Thank you, Daddy," she murmured. She sat the coffee carefully on the table next to her and returned to her previous position.

Her daddy watched her for long moments before shaking his head. She couldn't figure out what he was trying to do though. It wasn't disappointment in his face, and he wasn't curious. It was like he wanted something and she had no idea what he could want that would require him ordering her to sit and talk as he had when she was a child.

"You're a grown woman, Summer Dawn . . ."

"Yes, Daddy, I am." She met his gaze squarely, remaining respectful but in no way admitting to anything. She wasn't eight anymore, and there were things her daddy simply couldn't demand of her any longer.

"Girl, you're home now," he reminded her, his voice and his expression remaining stern. "This ain't DC and it ain't Moscow or wherever else you've been. This is where people know you best, and I won't have gossip about you. Your brothers can stay in that house with you, those young men can come here and stay, or they can stay at Caleb's—"

"No, Daddy," she said firmly. She so did not like the way this conversation was going.

"Then you can—"

"No, Daddy," she repeated in the same tone, determined to remain firm now.

His deep blue eyes narrowed on her warningly. "Summer, this arrangement is unacceptable." For all its softness, his tone was a stern, unyielding demand. "You should know better than this."

Yes, she should.

Come to think of it, she did.

"Very well." She nodded abruptly, narrowing her eyes back at her father. "When this is over and I have the option of leaving, I'll give the house to Caleb and find a place closer to Atlanta," she informed him. "But, until this is finished and I know ya'll are safe, then things will remain as they are."

She'd actually expected this the day after their arrival. It wouldn't have hurt near as bad then.

"Summer, girl, think of what you're doin'," he demanded though his voice was gentle. "I'm not sayin' they're not good men. Davis Allen assures me they are, even that Raeg. But I know now the things my old friend refused to mention—"

She tried to stop him. "Daddy—"

"Men that allow other men, especially their brothers, the liberties of touchin' their women can't love themselves or their woman."

Liberties? Oh. My. God. He was going to try to discuss her sex life?

She was going to lose her ever-lovin' mind. She could not handle this.

Summer jumped to her feet.

Outrage and sheer disbelief vied with the ultimate embarrassment. This was not a discussion she could have with him, not even in a million and one years.

"I am so not discussin' this with you," she burst out, horrified.

Her daddy hadn't even mentioned the birds and the

bees back when she'd started dating. Daddy did not mention such things in front of his daughters.

"Girl, you sit back down there," he demanded, his expression fierce as he pointed to the chair. "Right now."

No way in hell. She absolutely could not sit back down there and listen to this. She'd burn alive with mortification.

"Daddy, I love you and I respect you tremendously . . ." She wrung her hands, certain she was going to burn in hell now that her daddy had to attempt such a conversation with her.

"Then act like it," he barked, glowering back at her. "And listen to me. Certain liberties, proper young ladies don't allow—"

"Daddy, I won't hear this." She was going to cover her ears with her hands if she had to. She couldn't bear it. "This is goin' too far."

"Summer, you tell me right now," he ordered firmly. "Are you givin' yourself—"

Oh God, no! She could not listen to this.

"La la la la la . . ." She covered her ears. "Stop this, Daddy."

"Tell me that's not what's goin' on in that house then," he snapped.

"Oh my Lord . . ." she muttered, looking around desperately for a means of escape. She could feel shame curling through her, and she was certain she was going to hyperventilate.

"Summer, girl, I'm no fool," he sighed. "I know you've had lovers."

"Oh my God, Daddy . . . stop . . ." Scandalized, she couldn't bear to hear anymore.

This simply was not done.

Her daddy did not talk about such things to her.

"Now, Summer . . ."

"No, Daddy. Does Momma discuss Caleb's friend-ships with him? Oh my God, you know she never would." Momma would die of embarrassment first.

"Friendships?" he glared at her. "Is that what you're callin' it now?"

She stomped her feet, the heel of her shoe cracking against the boards of the porch, to get his attention.

"Daddy, I am appalled at this." She stared back at him in disbelief, her hands settling on her hot cheeks. This was too embarrassing.

"And you should be," he agreed fiercely. "Those two scoundrels bringin' their wild ways to your home and to your bed like that."

"Daddy . . . please, I'm beggin you," she cried out des-perately. "Please stop sayin' these things."

Something akin to satisfaction and pure devilry sparked in his gaze as he stared back at her. Something that simply had her heart sinking.

"Summer . . . ?" Raeg spoke behind her, and she knew then exactly why her daddy was so satisfied.

"Oh Lord," she whispered, panic tightening her chest. "Where's Momma? This is simply too much."

Her daddy turned and looked to his side where Raeg and Falcon stood, his expression disgusted. "Boys, it's rude to eavesdrop on a man's conversation with his own daughter," he informed them in his best drill ser-geant voice. "Where's your manners?"

She turned to Raeg and Falcon, staring at them, beg-ging them silently even as she shook her head desper-ately. They could not let this conversation happen. They couldn't.

Raeg crossed his arms over his chest, the black shirt,

sleeves rolled back to his elbows, and eagle-colored eyes giving him a piratical air.

"Damn, Falcon, you were right about the rules in the South being different from those at home," he sneered. "At least there we take up our disagreements with any 'friends' our sister has with the men themselves rather than with her."

Momma . . . Summer wailed silently.

"The two of you are a disgrace," her daddy snapped, glaring at them with disapproval. "Especially you." He pointed at Raeg imperiously. "You're damned disrespectful to boot. Summer's not one of your city girls to be used like you think you can use her."

Use her? She was going to be sick.

And it was so obvious her momma wasn't going to help her out here.

"Summer, perhaps you should go inside and help your mother," Falcon suggested gently, his expression as hard as his eyes. "We would speak to your father about this privately."

Her eyes widened, her heart suddenly racing.

Falcon might have spoken gently, but his expression was savage, his gaze icy. He was furious. Completely furious. That was never a good thing.

"I will not—" she began to object.

"Now." Raeg directed the full force of a gaze so demanding and fierce she stared back at him in shock.

"Go on, little girl," her daddy drawled. "Go on back in the house with the women. I'll just discuss this myself with these two."

Little girl? Her daddy called her little girl?

No, he had not!

"Daddy, I won't have this," she informed him, pressing

the fingers of one hand to her temple. She could feel that migraine coming for sure now. "Stop it this instant."

His smile was slow, anticipatory.

"Now how do you think you can enforce that, little girl?" he drawled, that vein of satisfaction deepening in his tone.

She thought fast. It wasn't the best plan. But maybe . . .

"I can do exactly what I should have done when I first got here," she informed him furiously. "I'll stay a night in town and tell everyone I meet my daddy disowned me and I'm moving back to DC. Dragovich's men will definitely follow me then."

She put her hands on her hips to keep from wringing them in pure approaching hysteria. Her daddy was up to something, she knew he was. She just wasn't certain what or why. But what he was doing was simply not good for her peace of mind.

"The hell you will," he snapped, frowning down at her.

"Daddy, you just don't want to bet on that." Her voice rose, her panic along with it.

"Little girl . . ."

"I have a name, Daddy!" she yelled. "You should know it. Momma let you choose it, and that name was not 'little girl.' I've not been a little girl for many years now."

"Well now, a grown woman would understand the she-nanigans these two are up to." He waved toward Raeg and Falcon.

"That's enough out of both of you." Raeg was suddenly beside her, yelling at the two of them.

"He started it." She stabbed her finger in her daddy's direction furiously.

Oh, she was so mad at both of them now, the reason to her father's behavior suddenly clear. "My personal business is just that. Mine. And he's just set to provoke

me because you're so ugly with him." She turned on
Raeg, pushing his arm away as he reached for her. "Get
the hell over it right now or you're gonna be sleepin' in
Caleb's barn instead of my home. You will not continue
to cause all this trouble, Raeg."

Raeg stared down at her incredulously. "You're
joking?"

"Raeg." Falcon stepped onto the porch then. "We do
not need Summer in this discussion. Let her go inside
first—"

Raeg's bark of laughter wasn't a comfortable sound.

"She's joking, isn't she?" he snapped, his gaze filled
with incredulity and anger. "Damn, Falcon, what good
would letting her escape accomplish? All you want to do is
kiss his ass anyway. You're just as bad as she is to ask how
high, when he says jump. I'll be damned if I'll do it too."

"That's my daddy," Summer protested, staring back
at him in shock. "You cannot be so rude to him in his
own home."

"I can't be rude to him?" Furious, mocking amusement filled his face. "Summer, he all but called you a
whore to your face—"

Before the last word left his mouth, her daddy moved.
His arm flashed past her face, the solid, powerful whack
sounding before she could even follow the move and
swing around to Raeg . . .

. . . who went down.

Backward.

Sprawled out on his back, eyes closed.

Lights out.

"Oh my God," she whispered, staring down at Raeg,
then at Falcon's incredulous expression. "Oh my God . . .
Daddy?" She turned to her father in disbelief. "What
have you done?"

He snorted at the question as she gripped his arm desperately.

"Taught him a manner or two I hope," he informed her, satisfaction filling his expression as well as his voice. "He'll live." He grinned down at her. "Your momma surely has breakfast on the table by now, sweetheart," he declared jovially. "Ya'll come in. He'll rest just fine there for a minute." He gave Falcon a firm look. "Come on, son, don't baby him now, you'll undo all my fine work here if you do. Get in the house with Summer." He urged her toward the door. "Go on now. Get."

And in she went, she assured herself, simply because she was in shock. But that didn't explain why Falcon gave his brother a long, thoughtful look before following her.

This was not going to be good.

Still in shock, she looked up at Falcon, met his laughing gaze, and knew it was going to be bad. Really, really bad.

"He'll leave," she whispered.

Falcon bent his head to hers. "I'll call Lucien Connor if he leaves. That will bring him back quickly, I promise."

She could only shake her head and let him lead her to the table where her family as well as Caleb's foreman and several ranch hands waited patiently, amusement filling all their faces. Bowe and Brody were choking on their laughter.

This was so horrible. It was simply horrible.

Her momma waited in her seat opposite her daddy's, her expression serene, as Summer stared back at her desperately.

This just wasn't good at all . . .

He'd be damned if he was going to let that old bastard run him off. And he damned sure wasn't going to be shamed from Summer's side.

Thankfully though, he didn't come to in time for breakfast. Hell, he still hadn't figured out what half of what he was eating, actually was. Or how to eat it.

Sitting on the porch steps, Raeg worked his jaw gingerly. The bastard damned sure packed a punch. Then again, the former Delta Force commander had been known for his punches.

Still battling the gremlins playing bury-the-axe in his brain, Raeg tensed further at the sound of the front door opening.

The subtle spice of her scent was like a balm to his senses. The coffee she placed next to him almost brought a groan from his chest.

"Thanks," he muttered, picking up the cup and lifting it to his lips.

He swore the first sip was ambrosia.

"You're welcome." Lowering herself to sit on the step below him, she turned sideways and smoothed the tea-length skirt of her sundress over her knees.

Four-inch heels graced her small feet, making them look even tinier while making her legs look a mile long.

"Ready to go home?" he asked, feeling the coffee sinking inside his senses.

He might be able to walk now.

"Everyone's still on the back porch discussin' politics or somethin'. Falcon said he'd be out in a bit though."

She clasped her hands together and propped them on her knees. Violet eyes stared back at him, those thick, black lashes making her eyes appear more mysterious and exotic when combined with the shadowed emotions he could glimpse behind them.

The long, thick waves and curls of her hair flowed down her back, almost to her waist. She'd pulled it back from the front of her face and secured it with a jeweled clip at the crown of her head.

Damn her.

She was so pretty he could barely believe it at times. Not gorgeous in the accepted sense of the word. Uniquely pretty, her features delicate and radiating with some soft inner glow that he couldn't put a name to or fully understand exactly what looking at her did to him.

Besides making him hard, that was.

"Waiting on an apology?" he asked curiously, noting she'd yet to mention the earlier confrontation.

No doubt she deserved an apology. She hadn't deserved her father's lecture or his deliberate bating. But, maybe, his own final comment hadn't exactly been fair to her.

"I've never known you to apologize to anyone," she finally answered, the subtle drawl of her voice resigned. "I'm not the one you need to apologize to anyway."

Oh, he knew that tone and he knew exactly who she was suggesting he needed to apologize to. And there simply wasn't a chance in hell. Like she said, he did not do apologies well at all.

"I have no reason to apologize to your father," he told her firmly. "As you said earlier, he started it."

The bastard had known Raeg and Falcon would be right behind her. Just as he'd known that chastising her over their desire for her, and her response to it, would not be acceptable.

Turning her head, she stared out along the front of the house. Pasture stretched out on one side of it, extending to the east and north of the house.

"That's my daddy, Raeg," she said without looking back at him again. "All my life he's loved me and done his absolute best for me. If he blinked one night, then that's between me and Daddy. But I will tell you, from the time we could walk, Daddy taught Aunjenue and me both how to defend ourselves if we had to. And that's what saved me from something worse than a beating." Her expression hardened, the gaze she turned on him resolute. "I don't care if you like him or not any more. I know you won't stay here once the danger Dragovich represents is over, so the situation between the two of you doesn't have to be fixed. From here on out, you can keep your distance from him with my blessing. And I will tell you what I just told Daddy. The next blow thrown by either of you, no matter the reason, and both of you will pay for it." She rose, stepped to the cement walk, and stared back at him with chilling regard. "Now. Finish your coffee. I have things to do at home. And I prefer to do them alone. I think you, Daddy, and Falcon need to do some serious thinking where I'm concerned though. Because at the moment, all of you are showing me just how little my feelings, my wishes, or my heart, matter to any of you." She paused, pain flashing in her eyes then. "But then, I don't think any of that has ever mattered to you anyway. Has it?"

She turned and walked away from him unhurriedly, the breeze playing through her hair and the thin material of her dress. She looked like a damned princess or something with her head held high, her shoulders straight, and that aristocratic little nose lifting with such disdain.

It just made him just want to fuck her even more.

And she terrified the hell out of him.

He couldn't stay, claiming her was out of the question. Once Dragovich was taken care of, it would be time for him and Falcon to leave, if they wanted to keep her safe.

Her safety mattered. It mattered more to him than his own.

But he'd realized in the last week that the thought of

leaving her gave rise to other thoughts. What she would do, what her future would hold. And those thoughts just pissed him the hell off.

She'd probably end up marrying some dumbass who would give her weak-chinned babies or something. Not that he could imagine a child of Summer's ever being weak.

A child.

He rubbed at his bruised jaw gingerly. God help him, he'd have to kill the son of a bitch who gave her a baby, who marked her heart and her mind to that extent. The thought of it was so damned infuriating that he shot a glare in the direction she'd taken toward the house.

The thought of making amends with her father just made his pride cringe though.

Yeah, he had quite a bit of thinking to do.

Chapter
NINE

Summer knew the moment she stepped into the house that something wasn't right. It was her home, her personal space in the most intimate sense of the word.

And something, someone, had invaded it.

She could feel the danger in the air, the sense of dark malevolence waiting for her. Her eyes went around the room slowly, finally landing on a shadow that shouldn't be spreading out next to the doorway leading into the kitchen-dining area across from the living area.

It took every ounce of control to keep her hand out of the pocket of her dress, away from the little .22-caliber mini-pistol she kept there. Just in case, she didn't want an intruder to know she was armed before she could actually use the weapon.

Within seconds, she knew standing and fighting wasn't going to be an option as another shadow shifted at the doorway to her side that led into the formal dining room.

She swung around quickly, intending to run for the still-open front door even as she shoved her hand into the pocket, her fingers curling around the tiny gun, her finger sliding against the trigger. Before she could pull it free, the sudden, agonizing burn that latched onto her shoulder blades and dug deep inside her nerve endings taking her to her knees.

By luck, chance, or training—she couldn't be certain which—her finger tightened on the trigger as she toppled to the floor, the sound of the weapon's discharge shattering the stillness of the house.

The electrical charge that shot through her had her shaking, gasping for breath as it began overloading her system.

This was fucked up. It shouldn't be happening. It was the middle of the day for God's sake on a farm filled with employees and former tough badasses who were still badass, only smarter.

The middle of the day? How the hell had they gotten into her house in the middle of the day without being seen?

Darkness edged at her mind, the sound of voices filled with panic, two male voices, though there were no accents, Russian or otherwise. She had expected Russian accents. After all, their boss was Russian and he didn't care much for outsiders even on a good day.

Hard male hands gripped her around the waist, lifting her as she fought the sickening crash of her system and the darkness swirling at the edges of her mind.

The voltage was a little high. Higher than she'd been trained to endure and overcome. The body could only endure so much though. She might like to think she was bullet proof and weather resistant, but reality was another matter.

She couldn't fight it when she felt the world tilt drunkenly and wondered if she'd throw up. They were shaking her around like a mixed drink on a Saturday night and if they weren't careful, Momma's breakfast was going to make an appearance none of them wanted.

That darkness was moving closer too.

God, if she passed out, she wouldn't have a hope in hell of escaping. They'd have her trussed up like a Christmas turkey before she ever woke.

Where was help?

Surely someone heard the gunshot.

Surely someone knew something was wrong . . .

The sound of the gunshot, distant though it was, had Raeg jerking to his feet. Before he could sprint for the line of trees, the front door flew open and Summer's father came running from the house, a compact assault rifle gripped in his hands.

He jumped from the porch to the walkway, never breaking stride, and ran for the tree line even as Raeg was moving.

Raeg was only distantly aware of Cal running next to him. As he jerked his weapon from the holster at his back, his only thought was reaching Summer.

Violet eyes and masses of long black hair. Smart-ass attitude. Far too much courage filling a too-delicate, too-fragile package that drove him crazy on a good day.

As he raced for the house he could see Falcon and Summer's brothers running silently from the back of the house and hitting the tree line just as he did.

Raeg paused only long enough to check the front yard and porch before he tensed to sprint the rest of the distance to the front door. Just as he began to move, Cal grabbed his shoulder, jerking him back before he could push past the thick fall of weeping branches he was looking through.

"Sniper. Right there." The older man pointed out the

barest shadow within the marsh on the south side of the house.

Falcon and Summer's brothers hadn't run for the back of the house either.

"Leasa has overwatch, give her and the boys a sec to get eyes on anyone waiting to pick us off. I'm going to say we have two shooters," Cal told him softly. "There will be two inside. It would take two of them to get the upper hand on Summer. That was her twenty-two that went off. Nothing since. They've managed to incapacitate her."

The trill of a whip-poor-will sounded through the trees.

"That's Caleb," his father reported softly. "He has eyes on the second shooter." A second call sounded from somewhere behind them. "That's Leasa. She has the one to the south. Now, we get sight on those inside, or give them enough time to come to us."

"Or kill her," Raeg growled.

"Naw, that Russian wants her alive," Cal said coolly. "She busted his pride. The only way he can get it back, is to bust hers. They'll try to take her alive. If they can't, then he's going to want to kill her himself, face-to-face."

They stood there, watching the house carefully, for what seemed like hours but couldn't possibly have been that long.

Finally, the front door eased open an inch or so.

"They're just checkin'," Cal whispered. "Just want to know if anyone's out here. They'll go out the back when they don't see anyone. That's what we want. They'll head for the marsh or the swamp itself. Probably poled in on an airboat. That would be the only way to get her out of here fast. They're not dumb enough to go out the front door."

"And they weren't intelligent enough to stay the hell away from here," Raeg stated.

"No, they sure as hell weren't," Summer's father agreed. "Now get ready, they'll move soon. When they go, they'll try to be wily. Let's see how fast we can outsmart them."

Moving quick and silent, Cal led the way to a spot along the line of trees where they could see the back door.

And the old son of a bitch was right. No more than seconds later the back door opened. Two black-garbed figures and one unconscious Summer bouncing on a shoulder, were quickly out the back door.

Just as quickly, as they cleared the porch and began running, four shots were fired. The two runners went down immediately. Not even a heartbeat later, movement within the marsh and just within the shadowed depths of the swamp revealed the two snipers falling out of shelters, lifeless.

"Summer." Raeg whispered her name, darted from cover and, using the various yard ornaments placed in a sheltered line to the back porch, made his way quickly to where she laid silently beneath the heat of the late morning sun.

Reaching the back porch he sprinted for the silent form of the woman he feared was going to be the death of him. He was already on the verge of a stroke. The fact that she wasn't moving terrified him.

"Cover, cover!" Cal yelled behind him just as a volley of gunfire began spatting around them.

Raeg threw himself over Summer, aware of Falcon sliding in front of them and Cal right beside him, firing into the swamp.

From the second floor of the main house, a rifle fired

in half a dozen slower bursts before the sound of an air-boat could be heard racing from the area.

At the sound of the airboat Raeg picked her up in his arms and ran for the house as Falcon and Cal covered him.

She felt boneless, almost lifeless. Breathing though, he'd made certain of that first thing. But Summer had not just passed out. She wasn't the passing-out type, and he knew it.

"Momma and Aunjenue are coming through the front!" Caleb yelled. "Lay her on the couch. Bowe's calling Doc."

Falcon had the back door open, allowing Raeg to rush inside with her. Crossing the kitchen and breakfast area into the large living room, he laid her on the couch gently, aware of the others rushing in behind him.

She was paper white.

Pulse was strong.

No obvious head trauma or bullet wounds.

"Move, Raeg, let me in there." Summer's mother pushed at his shoulder firmly. "Let me see her."

Raeg moved away from her slowly and allowed her mother to begin checking her, feeling as though he'd been holding his breath far too long.

Behind the couch, Falcon, Summer's father, and her brothers stood silently. Raeg looked his brother over quickly, making certain he was unharmed. Falcon's pale blue gaze was icy, his expression savage, as he watched Summer's mother check her for wounds.

"They used an electrical charge," Leasa snapped as she lifted one shoulder and revealed the raw burn mark hidden by the strap of her dress.

Raeg eased Summer to her side, revealing the second wound the electrical prongs had made. Easing her back,

Raeg watched as her mother brushed Summer's long, tangled hair away from her face, her lips trembling for the barest moment.

"We were almost too late," she whispered tearfully, looking up at her husband as he stood next to Falcon. "Almost too late, Cal."

"Almost doesn't count," he answered, his own voice hoarse, his eyes damp. "Remember that. It doesn't count."

They'd all nearly failed her, Raeg acknowledged. He intended to make certain that never happened again.

More than an hour later Raeg stood in the dining area of the kitchen, looking into the swamp where the body of one of the snipers had dropped, not far from where Cal said the airboat had been hidden.

The shooters had a direct line to the back of the house, and no one could figure out how they'd gotten past the safeguards in place to alert the family of any intruders.

"Someone's helpin' them," Cal breathed out roughly from where he sat at the table, nursing another cup of coffee. "They couldn't have gotten past the alerts we have in place without someone here on the farm helping them."

"Bowe and I will slip out this evening and change the alerts locations," Brody told his father. "Caleb can shift the hands out of sight of the house for some reason and give us time to do it with no one the wiser. We leave the ones that're out there currently in place and spread word around the farm that we believe water damage caused them to malfunction. No one will know any better."

That could work, Raeg agreed silently, glaring into the swamp.

"It's not the first time some dumbass thought they could get the jump on us," Bowe spoke up. "It's just the first time they got so close to actually succeeding."

Because Summer had been alone, Raeg thought wearily.

"She was distracted," her father said, drawing Raeg's attention to the images reflected in the window. Cal raked his fingers through his hair on a heavy sigh. "My fault. I should have just let things go."

He should just let the old bastard take the blame for it, Raeg thought. It would get Cal off his back and keep it that way. If Summer's father took the blame for her distraction and loss of attention to her safety, then it would ensure the older man never demanded Raeg's respect again. Summer's father would know for a fact he didn't deserve it.

And it would be a lie.

As much as Raeg wanted to find a way to maintain his emotional distance, he couldn't do it at the expense of Summer's life or possibly her father's, because he was plagued by guilt. And losing her father would destroy Summer.

"This wasn't your fault, it was mine." Keeping his back to the room, his arms crossed firmly over his chest, Raeg glared at the images of the men behind him.

Complete silence descended behind him. A patient, waiting kind of silence.

"How is any of this your fault, son?" Cal finally asked heavily.

Son. Hell, even his own father had never addressed him like that.

"My mother and I were at the Hampsteads the night Davis Allen and Margot flew here and took Summer." He waited.

He was certain Summer's father would have an excuse. When nothing came, he turned back to stare at the other man.

Cal just stared back, his eyes damp, his expression creased with grief.

Why didn't my daddy help me? He'd heard Summer ask Margot that question the next day, and it still haunted him. So why wasn't he using it to drive the nail deeper into that man's soul?

Summer's father finally nodded. "I understand then," he said hoarsely. "You have every right to hate me."

The son of a bitch. Where the hell were his excuses? His desperation to make Raeg accept that somehow it wasn't his fault?

"It's not my place to hate you," Raeg finally sighed wearily. "Summer said the two of you had already settled it, and her understanding is all that's required. Summer was distracted and alone because of my insistent anger toward you. This one was my fault."

"Yes it was." Aunjenue stepped into the kitchen, her expression, her voice so like Summer's that they could be twins. "Daddy, Summer needs you upstairs." She turned to her father with a little wink. "Ya know how she gets when she thinks she's been weak. Daddy has to tell her what a brave little girl she's been. It's so pathetic."

Pride flashed across Cal's face.

"Like he does when you break a nail?" Bowe snorted, laughter filling his expression.

"Boy," his father growled sternly. "I warned you. Stop now while you're ahead."

Aunjenue threw her brother a gloating look before turning back to her father. "Go tell her how brave she was, Daddy. I need to get home. Momma's gonna be running me ninety miles a minute to have dinner ready as it is." She propped her hand on her denim-clad hip with a sigh. "So try to hurry."

Her father nodded quickly, pausing only long enough

to lay a kiss on his youngest daughter's forehead before heading upstairs.

When he was out of earshot, she turned back to Raeg.

"Daddy might not shoot you, and my brothers might be too damned amused to stop your stupidity, but if you ever disrespect my daddy again, I will. And Momma will skin you out for it. So put a sock in it, mister, or take your ass back to where you came from. Your choice."

Turning on her heel, she followed after her daddy, that nose lifted, anger shimmering on the air around her.

The brothers in question looked at each other before they chuckled, a sound they kept quiet enough that she wouldn't hear, Raeg noticed.

"Welcome to the family," Caleb snorted. "Momma only threatens to skin us daily. And according to Auna, her gun stays loaded to shoot one of us." He indicated himself as well as his brothers. "Now, let's see if we can figure out how to draw Dragovich out into the open to keep him and his men from striking out at her again. 'Cause I'm tellin' you, he sure is about to piss me off . . ."

They were all fucking crazy, Raeg decided hours later when Summer's family finally left the house. It was an effective crazy though, the kind of crazy that he hoped Dragovich could never anticipate.

Chapter
TEN

Too close.

God help him, they'd come too close to losing her.

The next morning, Raeg was still trying to recover from the almost successful attempt Dragovich's men had made to take Summer.

He knew the terrifying sight of those bastards running from the house with an unconscious Summer would live in his nightmares for the rest of his life. They'd managed to incapacitate her and actually get her out of the house. Within seconds they would have had her in the airboat and out of sight, and there wouldn't have been a damned thing he could do to stop it.

Even worse, it would have been his fault. Because he'd let her retreat as she'd asked him to. Because he'd taken his eyes from her and given the enemy the chance to strike. It was a mistake he had no intention of making again, he told himself later that afternoon.

Sitting at the dining room table, positioned with a direct line of sight to where Summer and Aunjenue sat in the sheltered corner of the back porch talking, he realized there was more than just protectiveness rising inside him. He could feel the possessiveness brewing in his mind as well.

Strange that he knew what that feeling was, because he'd never felt it before, not for any woman. And he'd felt that dark sense of ownership toward her for a long time, he realized.

He turned his attention back to the laptop and the program connected to the cameras the Calhoun family used to monitor the swamp bordering their home. The four surveillance devices were good, good enough that the programmed motion activation should have worked when the airboat invaded the vicinity.

Even if Dragovich's men were using jamming technology, an alert should have gone out that the devices were offline or unable to connect.

Caleb had been right the day before when he said someone on the farm had to have helped the men who came after Summer. There was simply no other answer. Only someone who knew the location of the cameras and security alerts could have gotten past them. And only an employee or family member would know that information.

Pulling up a file he and Falcon had been putting together, he once again began going over the information on the men who had been on the farm the day before.

He put aside those of the friends who had visited with Summer's brothers. Joel Wyman, a man Cal described as his eldest son's best friend since childhood. The beer-drinking, loud-mouthed prick wouldn't have been Raeg's first choice as Caleb Calhoun's best friend.

Then there were Bowe and Brody's friends, Luke Jagger and Drew Stilman. Luke was Special Forces, home on leave after an injury, while Stilman was an investigative agent for the Bureau. There were no alarms going off there, so that left employees. Especially the foreman, Clay Tucker, and his assistant, Whitt Grayson.

Clay was a career farmer, Whitt a former Army Ranger with a dishonorable discharge haunting him. The Ranger was a little too obvious to suit Raeg, but he'd sent the information on to the team now parked in Cliffton.

Hopefully, Falcon's agents could find something on one of them. The fact that Dragovich had to have a mole on the farm was apparent. Finding them would be the challenge.

Lifting his head from the screen of the laptop as his brother entered the front door, Raeg watched Falcon reset the security before pushing his fingers wearily through his hair. Catching sight of Raeg, he stalked across the living area into the dining room.

"Problems?"

Falcon's lips pursed consideringly. "I'm not entirely certain."

His brother's expression was a bit thoughtful, maybe brooding, but Raeg couldn't see any indication of coming danger. Going back to the files, he waited, knowing Falcon would tell him whatever was on his mind whenever he was ready.

The fact that it was taking the other man so long to give vent to whatever had the irritation gleaming in his eyes assured Raeg that it definitely had something to do with Summer.

Over the years, Raeg had learned his brother had definite telltale signs whenever Summer had done something, or was doing something, that confused Falcon. It wasn't often women confused his brother, was how Raeg always rationalized it. He seemed to be able to see straight into their hearts, detect their feminine secrets and ways, and adapt in dealing with them.

Only Summer had ever put that particular look of frustrated confusion on Falcon's face. Just as she was the only woman who had ever managed to break Raeg's control. But was he smart enough to run as far away from her as quickly as possible? Evidently not, because right there he sat, his gaze moving to her every few minutes to make certain she was still on the porch with her sister.

"Has Summer mentioned any parties to you?" Falcon finally asked, his voice clipped as Raeg lifted his gaze to his brother's with a bit of surprise.

"I haven't heard anything about any parties. She'd know better than to try to attend one with Dragovich gunning for her. Why?" Surely she would know that now was not the time to attend any parties.

Falcon leaned forward and braced his folded arms on the table.

"Her aunts are currently at her parents' house, and I could have sworn I heard something about parties this weekend, and Caleb sent a crew to open the guesthouses. They're obviously expecting company."

Saving the work he'd done on each of the files, Raeg closed them out, shut the laptop down, and closed it before giving Falcon his full attention.

"They have family reunions or something," he recalled aloud.

"Family reunions are at the end of summer, not late spring." Falcon shook his head. "The dates are always at the same time of the year, so that's not what's going on. And when I questioned Caleb about it, he became evasive."

"What makes you think it has anything to do with a party then? The family's well aware of the danger Dragovich represents, and they have enough situational awareness to know the danger any parties would represent. I don't think they'd take that chance."

Falcon's lips thinned, his irritation increasing. "I considered that, until I learned the closest guesthouse was being outfitted with a hair dressing station and that Steven McGillan is arriving late, day after tomorrow. Steven's her favorite hairdresser. I've heard of her having him flown in from DC to Paris just to fix her hair for an important event. The man's weird as hell, but he only comes out for Summer when she's preparing for some big event."

Raeg turned his gaze to the glass doors and the two women still talking, their expressions intent as they stared down at the tablet Summer held to allow both of them to see it.

Surely to God she'd know better, he thought again. Summer wasn't a stupid woman and she didn't seem to have a death wish. Parties right now would be both stupid and suicidal.

"Why haven't you asked Summer?" Raeg questioned his brother, turning his gaze back to meet Falcon's frowning expression as it flickered with surprise.

"We both know Summer quite well, Raeg," his brother pointed out. "Until we know what's going on, questioning her isn't something I'd advise."

Raeg lifted his brow mockingly. "You're just afraid she'll get angry with you." He snorted at the thought. "When are you going to start standing up to her, Falcon?"

Amusement, a hint of chagrin, and a whole lot of pleased male idiocy filled his brother's expression.

"Because, spoiling her gives me pleasure as well, Raeg. I'm surprised you haven't figured that out yet." He chuckled. "But I also know Summer far better than you do, something you don't seem to want to admit. If she's planning something, it's better to learn the details oneself than to depend upon her to give you everything you need to know. She's far too independent for that."

"You mean she's far too secretive and contrary?" Raeg growled.

Falcon's brow lifted in surprise. "Is there a difference?"

Raeg stared back at his brother, exasperation rising inside him.

Unfortunately, Falcon was right. Before confronting Summer over anything, it was better to have one's facts in hand if they wanted to take her to task. Still, it didn't change the fact that the woman was damned difficult to figure out—or do anything with.

"Independent," Falcon liked to call it.

There were times Raeg thought she delighted in being just as difficult as possible instead.

Staring out at her again, he wondered if she had any idea the havoc she caused in men's lives, in his and Falcon's lives definitely. Still, Summer might be difficult, impulsive, secretive, but she wasn't stupid. Besides, she'd know there was no way to hide her intention to attend any sort of party of the like that she'd need her favorite hairdresser, Steven McGillan, for.

"When are you meeting with the team?" Raeg asked his brother thoughtfully.

"In about two hours." Leaning back in his chair, Falcon stared back at him with dark impatience. "I don't like how easily we were surprised by that attempt to grab her yesterday. There's just something off about it, Raeg. It shouldn't have been possible."

"As Cal said, they had help," Raeg reminded him.

"The cameras weren't defective. I just finished going over the software. The warning alerts were taken offline and rerouted I suspect. That would require access to this laptop." He flicked his fingers to the device Summer's brother had brought to him earlier. "Which her brother Caleb assures me is always locked in Cal's office. It could have been done at any time before Summer even returned home, there's no way to be certain." He shrugged. "Until now. I adjusted the programming and laid in a few safeguards no one should expect. They attempt it again, and I'll know who it is."

The webcam would go online covertly, snap a picture of whoever thought they were reprogramming the software, and instantly upload it to a secured cloud drive Raeg kept. The software would also alert Raeg through the sat phone he carried.

"Mother always did say you were the smart one," Falcon snorted, amusement flickering in his gaze.

"My mother always said you were the pretty one," Raeg pointed out mockingly, the brotherly insult bringing fond memories rather than crashing fury.

The smile that touched Falcon's lips was bittersweet.

They shared a father, but their lives had been separated even before birth until after they were grown and knowledge of the legacy they shared had been revealed. They'd learned, even from those early years, to always be on guard though, to always protect anything they cared about and to hide the fact that they might care about anyone.

"Okay then, smart-ass," Falcon sighed, rising to his feet. "I'll get ready to head out, but"—a warning flashed in his gaze—"I'm telling you, we may see a party as idiotic, or somehow far too dangerous, but that doesn't mean Summer will. If Steven's heading out here, then it's a major event. That means Dragovich's ability to access it increases."

"I'll talk to Summer first." He held up his hand as Falcon began to protest. "I'm not nearly as frightened of her as you are," he assured his brother. "And I can see through those innocent acts of hers far easier than you can. She leads you around by your dick."

Falcon arched a brow knowingly. "Jealous, brother?"

"Of your escape to town," he snorted, knowing better.

Maybe in a way he was a little jealous of his brother's ability to play with Summer, to pull that warmth and sweetness free that she kept hidden inside her.

"Keep telling yourself that," Falcon advised him with a grin. "And keep your eye on that one." He nodded to where Summer and Aunjenue were laughing on the porch. "I think we'd regret losing her."

They both knew it would kill them to lose her.

His gaze slid to her then, lingering on the rioting waves of black hair as it fell from where she'd gathered it at the top of her head and secured it with a large clip. One heavy ringlet had fallen from the gathered waves and caressed her creamy cheek before she brushed it back absently.

She'd painted her nails the night before, he realized, glimpsing the dark red color against the peachy complexion of her cheek.

Today, rather than a dress, she wore a long, incredibly soft beige and cream pleated skirt paired with a thin vestlike top secured with tiny buttons. She wore no makeup, no jewelry. Hell, she wasn't even wearing shoes today.

"I always knew she was the prettiest woman I'm ever going to see," Falcon stated softly, pulling Raeg's gaze back to him. "Tell me, Raeg, will you leave a part of your soul with her when we leave, as I will?"

His brother didn't wait for an answer, not that Raeg had one to give him. Admitting that he suspected Summer owned the most important parts of him already was incredibly difficult. Hell, he was having trouble admitting it to himself. Admitting it meant he had to make a decision, and he knew it. A decision he'd never wanted to face. Just as he'd never wanted to face exactly what the woman meant to him, and why he'd become so damned furious every time he saw her, spoke to her.

How else was a man supposed to feel when he was faced with the woman his soul recognized as that one in a million who could accept him as he was, only to know he couldn't have her? Not safely, not with any assurance that the darkness that waited just out of sight wouldn't reach out and snatch her away.

Summer's laughter drew his gaze to her again.

She and Aunjenue were out there giggling like schoolgirls, their expressions animated, their nearly identical faces side by side as they watched something on the tablet.

He'd learned they watched cute animal videos together, painted each other's nails, and teased each other unmercifully. Aunjenue was a wicked child though. Summer could not countenance any sort of sexual references from her parents nor about her parents. She'd blush from her breasts to her hairline and stare back at the offender with scandalized anger.

Just as she had with her father the morning before when Raeg and Falcon interrupted them on the back porch.

The fact that Cal had orchestrated that little argument concerning Summer's relationship with him and Falcon, was a "no-brainer," as Summer called the obvious. But

Raeg had seen her genuine inability to accept any sort of conversation of the like with her father.

It was kind of sweet though. Almost innocent. And he realized, very Summer.

"Daddy," she called him, and in her love for her father Raeg saw all the innocence and warmth he'd never known Summer possessed. With her father, she was that little girl filled with wonder and a sense of invincibility. And Raeg realized her father could have never accepted that life had jaded one of his daughters.

Whatever happened that long-ago night when Summer was barely thirteen, he still wasn't certain. What he did know was that it had to have been so completely out of Cal Calhoun's control that there could have been no stopping it. Because Cal loved his children, all five of them, but he frankly adored his daughters, cherished them. The only thing the man could love with the same dedication and soul depth was his wife.

How did a man take that kind of chance with his soul, Raeg wondered? To love so completely was to ask for fate to reach out and strike at what he cherished so deeply.

Especially wives and daughters.

Enemies always seemed to know a man's greatest weakness. The destruction of a wife, a child, especially a daughter could destroy a man faster than anything, and Cal Calhoun had taken three chances, standing tall and daring fate to take any of them.

The other man was far more courageous than Raeg knew himself to be. More courageous than he could ever allow himself to be, he reminded himself.

The regret that slammed inside him was like a wrecking ball to his chest. Sharp, resonating with agony, it tightened his chest and had him jerking his gaze from Summer concentrating on the laptop once again.

If he didn't get the hell away from her, then he was going to do something stupid like try to keep her. That would be the height of idiocy, because he wouldn't be resigning just himself to a coming hell, but his brother as well.

Sharing their women was far more than just a sexual desire neither wanted to walk away from. They could walk away from it if they had to, Raeg knew, they would simply prefer not to have to, if the situation of their lives had ever changed.

The fact was, sharing their women ensured no one ever suspected that any of those women were important to either of them. After all, what man would share the woman he loved? There were many who did, he knew, but they kept that fact quiet, kept the sharing hidden for the most part. A forbidden pleasure that the world wouldn't necessarily understand.

An enemy wouldn't see that woman as important to him and Falcon. Their hunger for their lover's ultimate pleasure served as the perfect smokescreen to hide any fondness they felt for their lover. It gave them a respite from the knowledge that they could ultimately be the reason a lover died.

And that one Raeg was well acquainted with. He'd smelled the horrific scent of his lover's blood, seen the death that filled her eyes, and knew he'd been the cause of it. And he knew he could never face that again.

Chapter
ELEVEN

Summer was running out of time and she knew it. The parties would begin at the end of the week. That Friday day and Saturday night her momma's sisters were hosting the informal barbeque and evening dancing. The week after, her momma's best friend would host the event. The third weekend, her parents were hosting the formal ball on Friday night, and another barbeque that Saturday day and evening.

With the exception of the one formal ball held at her parents' home, the parties were informal house parties that would spill out to the patios and lawns once the cooking started.

All but Summer's ball gown was ready for the three weeks of socials her momma and aunts had planned. One of the most beautiful dresses she'd ever seen, she admitted. She couldn't wait to wear it.

"Trina's comin' to the house to finish the final touches on your gown," Aunjenue told her as they looked at the detailed drawing of the gown once again. "Tomorrow, then next Wednesday for the final fitting."

The gown was exquisite. Antique ivory lace peeking from beneath sapphire chiffon.

"I still can't believe Trina was hidin' that design on the rest of us," Aunjenue protested with a rueful wrinkle of her nose. "I would have snapped it up before you even had a chance to see it."

The playful teasing in her sister's voice didn't hide the fact that she was completely serious. She and Aunjenue made a game of trying to find the prettiest gowns. While Summer did often allow her sister to snag the best ones, this particular gown was just her. Whimsical, feminine; not frilly, but soft.

She adored it.

"You hussy." Summer shot her sister a mock frown. "You get the benefit of her talents all year long. I haven't had a single dress in forever. I deserved that dress."

"I'm just tellin' you, it's a good thing she had it hid deep, else you'd have missed out big time and I would have been wearin' it myself." Aunjenue shrugged, shooting Summer an arched look. "Count yourself lucky."

Her sister was all grown up, Summer thought with a bit of regret. She was a woman now rather than the too-skinny kid with scratched knees and eyes that looked far too big for her childish face.

Her features weren't childish anymore. The graceful arch of her cheekbones, the playful tilt of her nose, and her stubborn chin were almost identical to Summer's. She was independent and sometimes reckless as hell, and though she loved training to fight and shoot, she had no desire to leave home. At least, not yet. Truthfully though, Summer couldn't see her sister ever joining law enforcement or a federal agency. Racing four wheelers in old man Pritchard's bog, definitely; being in the middle of a firefight, not so much.

"Your hairdresser called by the way." Aunjenue sat back in her chair and picked up her cup of coffee once again. "Momma's havin' the guesthouse at the end of the road prepared. He sent her a list of everything he needed. Where in this world did you find him anyway?"

Summer couldn't help but grin at the question. "You wouldn't believe me even if I told you," she promised. "You'll love him though. He's been doin' my hair for the past five years in DC. He's a sweetheart."

Middle-aged and gruff, Steven McGillan loved his single-malt Scotch and swore that taking care of Summer's hair was the highlight of his advancing years. He'd actually come out of retirement for her that first year she'd met him.

"Well, Momma was just pantin' over his accent. She told Daddy she thought she was gonna swoon while she was talkin' to him." She fanned her face with one hand. "Then she and Daddy disappeared upstairs, like forever. And I swear, I heard Momma gigglin' like a teenager."

Summer winced at the information, that part of her that refused to accept such things as sex between her parents cringing in dismay.

"I didn't need to know all that," she informed her sister, frowning back at her.

Aunjenue only laughed.

"Anyway, your Mr. Steven McGillan will be here day after tomorrow. He asked that you come see him Thursday morning but not a moment before because he has to unpack and recover from his jetlag."

Steven swore jetlag hated him and that it took a full twenty-four hours for his still remarkably fit body to acclimate to a new time zone. She swore he just liked to get to see the sights and get his freak on whenever he traveled.

"Have Caleb take a bottle of Daddy's best single-malt to the house. Just leave it on the counter. He'll look for that first." She had a habit of leaving him a bottle whenever he traveled to do her hair.

Aunjenue snorted at the order. "Momma will take care of it, I'm sure," her sister giggled. "She likes getting flirty because then Daddy gets all frisky on her. I swear, I came in last week and they were on the couch swappin' tongues like newlyweds."

No!

Outrage, horror, amazed denial exploded in her mind.

"Oh my God!" Summer all but all screeched before covering her ears, a little late. She so did not need that image in her head. "Do not be tellin' me that stuff, Auna. I swear, I'll throw your ass in the swamp and let the gators have you for breakfast. You know Momma and Daddy would never act that way."

Aunjenue was cackling with laughter, the hussy.

"You are so funny. Do you really think the gators left us on the doorstep when we were babies, Summer? You do know Daddy was just joking right? You know all about the birds and the bees, like you should?" Aunjenue was beside herself with amusement.

"Daddy would not lie to me," Summer assured her sister with a fierce glare. "And if you don't stop bein' ugly with me right now, then I'll refuse to let Steven fix your hair. You'll be fixin' your own."

Aunjenue narrowed her gaze back at Summer, though the laughter was threatening to bubble up and explode once again.

"Oh yeah, Daddy would never lie to us," Aunjenue agreed with mocking disbelief. "We're all just gator babies conceived in the swamp and birthed in the marsh."

When she'd been five and asked him where babies

came from, her daddy had sworn that gators had left his and Momma's babies on the back porch. That the momma gator had made them with spit and mud, then laid them in the marsh to dry out in the sun until they looked like real babies just before Jesus breathed life into them. And he'd kept that story going for as long as she could remember. Never, not at any time, did her daddy, or she, mention sexual relations until just the day before when her daddy had simply horrified her by implying things about her sex life.

Still, while *she* could have such a life, her parents simply could not. The very thought of it was too embarrassing to even contemplate.

"Summer." Propping her elbow on the side of the chair and cupping her chin in her hand, Aunjenue grinned back at her mischievously. "You do know that if you marry, Daddy is gonna know you're doin' the nasty. Right?"

"I would never," Summer gasped, blinking back at her sister as though aghast that such a thing would even be considered. "Daddy knows I'd never do that."

At least, that was the pretense she intended to keep at all times. Even she was often amused by her reaction to anything intimate where her parents were concerned. She couldn't help it though. It was all her daddy's fault. If he hadn't blushed and stammered and been so uncomfortable when she asked him where babies came from, then she herself might not be nearly so reticent about it.

"Oh Lord." Aunjenue tried to smother her laughter. "You are a basket case. And I guess you think he was jokin' yesterday when he implied he knows you're doing the nasty times two with those two hunks you brought home with you?"

Summer blinked back at her sister in surprise. She denied the charge, probably a little too vehemently. "I am not! Not with either of them. Definitely not with both of them."

And she was so lying through her teeth. She just hadn't done it last night. Or this morning come to think of it.

She clamped her lips shut. She could feel the heat burning from her breasts straight to her hairline as the most awful blush in the world began sizzling over her skin.

Damn her sister.

Aunjenue just watched her, her expression filled with wicked amusement.

Her lips tightened. "Stop bein' mean to me or I'm going to throw your ass in the swamp."

Her sister shook her head back at her in disbelief, the ponytail she'd pulled her hair into falling over her shoulder.

"Have you told them about the parties yet? Or why we're havin' them?" she asked, glancing toward the glass doors as she kept her head lowered, ensuring whoever was in the kitchen couldn't read her lips.

Yeah, Raeg was still in there watching them. She doubted she'd been out of his or Falcon's sight since Dragovich's men had attacked the day before.

"No," Summer sighed. "And I'm not talkin' about it right now. They're sneaky. They eavesdrop better than I do."

Her sister snorted at the claim.

"Raeg won't give a damn either way why we're havin' the parties, he'll just be pissed that we can't cancel them. Falcon won't handle the reason for them well though." She stared down at her fingers for a moment. "It's not that he loves me or anything. He just won't understand it."

Smoothing her thumb over a newly polished nail, she

lifted her gaze to Aunjenue's then, hearing the laughter retreat beneath a silent understanding.

"And you love both of them," Aunjenue said quietly. She'd been swearing for over a year that Summer was in love with the two men.

"It's not that . . ." she began.

"Lie to Momma and Daddy if you have to. Lie to Falcon and Raeg if you need to. But don't lie to me. I'd never do that to you," Aunjenue protested.

It wasn't a lie, Summer assured herself. She cared for them. She cared for them deeply, that was all.

"If I loved them, then I wouldn't be considering a life with any other man, little sister," she assured her.

But, was it the truth?

She was scared to death of letting either of them know about the parties or the fact that they were being thrown to allow Summer to meet the men her momma, daddy, and aunts thought would suit her. She hadn't done a very good job finding a man she found interesting herself, so they were going to give it a try.

Falcon, always the more easygoing of the two brothers, had his limits to what he called her "shenanigans," and he would definitely see these parties as shenanigans. He'd be pure pissed off. Raeg just stayed angry anyway but she'd been known to push him to that anger as well.

"Daddy always has said you like lyin' to yourself." Aunjenue shook her head, though her expression wasn't in the least accusatory.

"Oh be quiet now," Summer demanded, unable to hold back another grin. "I just have to figure out the right words to use, that's all. They didn't know about the parties—that will be the part that pisses them off the most."

They didn't know because her family hadn't invited

them. They had always received invitations whenever her mother threw a party for whatever reason. They'd be instantly suspicious when they learned they hadn't received an invitation to these particular parties.

"Momma did notice when we saw their names on the list of men *not* to invite," Aunjenue told her. "Momma was very amused and I believe Daddy called Davis Allen to see why such eligible men were bein' blacklisted by you." She rolled her eyes in amusement.

Oh, that was just wonderful. No doubt her daddy knew everything there was to know about Raeg and Falcon now. Especially the fact that they were prone to share their lovers. She couldn't see her daddy liking that much. And she knew he'd have something to say about it. And sooner rather than later, no doubt.

"What did Davis Allen tell him?" she asked, almost afraid to know.

"Daddy didn't tell me. He *wouldn't* tell me," she amended. "But he told Momma he should have locked you in your bedroom the first time you mentioned Raeg."

There were times she wished he had, Summer thought whimsically. Raeg and Falcon were going to break her heart, she could feel it coming. And that was one of the reasons she'd run from DC as she did.

She was so weak, it was pathetic.

"I do still have friends in DC myself though, big sis," Aunjenue said just when Summer thought she was safe. "And I know those boys have an intriguing little habit where their lovers are concerned." She wagged her brows suggestively. "No wonder you can't make up your mind which one you love. It's one for all and all for one."

Summer groaned, dropping her head before shooting her sister a look of retaliation.

"I said—"

"Oh phooey on what you said." Aunjenue rose from her chair, obviously laughing at her. "I know you better than you think I do, sweetie. Now, I'm gonna go get ready. Aunt Mary and Calista will be at the house in a couple of hours, and Calista is bringin' that little baby of hers. I can't wait to just snuggle her."

Their cousin's newborn was only six weeks old, a black-haired, blue-eyed little darling Summer had been dying to hold herself.

"I'll be there in a bit," Summer promised. "I want to get my tablet and the notes I made."

"Well, take your time," Aunjenue suggested. "Mike Taggart was at the house when I left. I think he's still tryin' to convince Caleb and Daddy to sell him that piece of land he's been after. Hopefully, he'll be gone soon."

Great. Mike Taggart wasn't her favorite person. How the man had managed to remain friends with her brothers she couldn't figure out.

"I'll slip in the back," Summer told her. "Just be watchin' for me."

Aunjenue gave a low laugh before walking quickly from the porch and along the walk to her parents' back porch.

Gathering up the coffee tray, Summer carried it to the door and pushed into the kitchen to place it in the sink. Two cups were drying in the dish rack, and she could see that several pastries along with a good bit of the fruit had been eaten.

Raeg and Falcon weren't really all about breakfast. Lunch and supper, yes; a heavy breakfast, not so much. Falcon did love his sweets though.

Washing the coffeepot and cups quickly, she dried her hands and headed upstairs to collect her tablet. She hadn't heard Falcon or Raeg in the house, and she was sincerely hoping they were with her daddy as they'd planned the night before to check out the property's security.

Having them there in her home was a bit problematic for her, she admitted. She hadn't wanted memories of them there, nor had she wanted the temptation. Once she'd made up her mind about the course of her future, she'd put the fantasy of having the two men as lovers behind her as well.

There could never be anything more than that between them, she told herself. Raeg had already warned her once in the past that he would take her as a lover for a night or two but never as a wife.

She was a one-night stand, Raeg had decided years ago. And Falcon would never be truly happy with any woman he didn't share with his brother, she'd known that. They did not take their lovers separately, and she hadn't wanted to accept being nothing more than a single night of fun and games for the two men who meant far more to her than she was comfortable admitting.

The question now was whether she wanted to throw away the chance to pretend for just a little while that she had what she couldn't seem to stop fantasizing about. They were here, and they were determined to stick around long enough to take Dragovich down, which would at least give her a little more time with them.

She could hold them, love them while they were here, and then she'd let them go when the time came. It would destroy her, break her heart, and leave her wounded forever, but she would let them go.

And she had a really bad feeling that the reason for these parties was pretty much in vain. Once Raeg and Falcon were gone, she wouldn't want another man or another man's baby. She'd be alone, and that had always been Summer's own vision of hell. Old and alone, with no one of her own to love her.

As bleak as such a future would be, and she knew "bleak" was a mild description, she also knew she couldn't resist them. She'd already had a taste of them, their touch, their possession.

They were already a part of her.

Raeg watched Summer enter the house from the shadowed doorway leading to the hall at the other side of the kitchen. With the lights out and the shades closed, the hall was the darkest part of the house. Not that that was why he was there. He was there because it was the best place in the house to install one of the cameras he was using to monitor the place.

Still, he didn't let her know he was standing there. He just watched her. The long beige print skirt she wore swished around her ankles, making her look more delicate, more fragile than ever. The thin top she wore emphasized her surprisingly full breasts, the rounded shape a perfect handful and topped with the prettiest nipples.

His cock, already hard and aching, swelled further, throbbing its reminder that he hadn't touched her since the other night. He hadn't tasted her kiss, hadn't felt the glove-tight heat of her pussy milking at his erection.

He grimaced as she finished washing the coffee service she and Aunjenue had used and left the kitchen. And of course, he followed her, knowing where she was heading, knowing he didn't think he could go much longer without taking her.

He was worse than a moth to a flame, he thought with a heavy breath before following her, drawn to her by a hunger he simply did not want to ignore any longer.

Letting her escape into her room before following her up the stairs, Raeg came to a stop at her open bedroom door and watched her as he leaned against the doorframe, a grin edging at his lips. She had her back to the doorway, but he had no doubt she knew he was standing there watching her.

She sat on the side of the bed, all those long, black waves and curls falling to just above her hips. She looked sweet and innocent. Her head was bent to allow her to see the screen of her tablet, the slightest turn of her body allowing him to glimpse her profile.

"Stop starin' at me," she finally ordered him, tossing a querulous look over her shoulder. "What are you doin' here anyway? I thought you and Falcon were goin' out with Daddy to see the security protocols."

Ah yes, that reminded him.

"Why is this place more secure than some presidential retreats I've seen? Hell, you have working cameras just inside the swamp and some of the most cleverly disguised shelters Falcon swears he's ever seen submerged in the water. And that's not counting the security measures we only suspect are in place." Raeg grumbled, remembering how impressed Falcon had been.

Her lips twitched. "And once you're gone, every bit of it will be taken down and moved."

Standard procedure, he thought. If you can't move the safe house, then change the security used for the safe house.

"Or just what Falcon has been shown will be taken down?" he grunted, straightening and walking across the room so he could better see her expression.

"Well now, anything's possible when you're dealin' with a former CIA intelligence analyst and her Delta Force husband. Momma was with the CIA when she and

Daddy met on a mission somewhere in Asia. Then there's
Caleb, he's former Special Forces." She laid aside her tablet to count off fingers. "Bowe's a sniper with the best
eyes I've ever heard tell of and Brody spent his life in the
swamp learnin' everything my uncle David, Momma's
brother, knew about native warfare. You could say all that
trainin' and subsequent war stories builds a bit of paranoia in a man's mind. Not to mention a woman's."

That was possible, he thought. Perhaps not probable,
but possible.

"Six guesthouses?" He lifted a brow with the question.

Summer's eyes widened. "There's a lot of relations
that come in during family reunions, weddings, funer-
als." The innocence in her expression would have been
believable if he didn't know her so damned well.

"So why did Caleb send men out to get those guesthouses ready for occupation?" he asked, watching her
carefully. If he hadn't been watching her so closely he
would have missed the little telltale sign of deception so
unique to Summer it always amazed him.

She didn't blink, her gaze didn't change, her lips didn't
thin. When Summer was hiding something from him or
Falcon, she had the oddest reaction, something that never
happened if she lied to anyone else or when she was on
a mission. When she was deceiving them though, she always made the mistake of giving the cutest little twitch
of her nose. Just like she just did.

"Momma has some family coming in. You know my
cousin just had that pretty baby of hers?" She grinned as
though that said it all. "She's six weeks old now, plenty
old enough to show off to family. We're all very close you
know."

Ingenious. He had to give it to her, but her nose
twitched again. Just a little bit. Nothing others would

catch onto very quickly. And then there was the fact that she didn't exactly lie. No doubt family was coming, he was just curious as to why. And yes, her cousin just had a baby, the infant was six weeks old. And she no doubt felt six weeks was old enough for family to be viewing it. Each sentence stood on its own and created a perfect cover without actually lying.

Moving across the room until he stood in front of her, he couldn't help but marvel at the quickness of her response as well.

"And you're sticking to that story?" he asked, staring down at her and seeing the latent amusement lingering in her gaze.

Leaning back, she propped her hands on the mattress behind her hips and gave him a look of sweet surprise.

It wasn't a look he found comforting.

"Of course I am, sugar. It's always best to stick to the truth, ya know." The playful smile edging at her lips only made his dick harder, only made him hungrier for her.

Damn her, he wanted to push her to the bed, slide between her thighs and pound inside her with animal lust. That was what she did to him. Made him so desperate to come, his balls ached.

As she stared up at him, the laughter in her eyes slowly faded and a flush began to heat the skin of her face.

"Well, I best hurry." She cleared her throat, watching him warily. "Momma and Aunjenue are expecting me at the house soon. I of course get to see Calista's baby today."

The smile she flashed him was meant to be teasing, but he saw the hunger that flared in her eyes.

"Are you running again, Summer?" he asked. "I think we've all learned that running isn't going to work."

As long as they were together like this, in the same

house, there was no ignoring it, no denying a lust that simply refused to be sated.

"And you think breaking my heart will?" she asked him, causing him to still, to stare back at her intently.

"Is that what you think I want to do?" He allowed her to maintain the distance between them for the time being, to let her think there was a way to avoid what he knew was coming.

"Just because you don't want to, doesn't mean you won't," she warned him. "You forget how well I know you, Raeg. Both of you. Neither of you have more than that fling you talked about years ago in mind. Taking me separately is only going to make all this more real to me and when the time comes to accept the fact that it's been a fling, I'll only be hurt."

No, she wasn't into flings. Summer had never really been into relationships, period, he realized. She'd had a few lovers, but only a few and that had been years ago. And he remembered each of the lovers she'd chosen those few times.

Summer didn't want what other women wanted, what other women searched for in a lover. She'd never gone the conventional route in anything she'd ever done. Summer had always done things the hard way. It was simply part of her nature. And she was nothing if not stubborn as hell.

As long as they took her together, did she really think she could ignore what he was beginning to realize himself? That there would be no walking away from this without all of them suffering for it?

"Only taking you together isn't going to change the outcome for any of us," he warned her. "And just because I very much enjoy seeing the heights Falcon and I can take you to together, I still intend to part those pretty legs and eat that sweet pussy until you're screaming to come before you leave this room."

Before she could jump away from the bed and run, Raeg came over her, lowering her to the mattress instead, allowing her to feel the iron-hard width of his erection against her lower stomach.

"Raeg . . ." her voice was low, the sound of helpless, feminine need filling it. "Please."

"Please, Summer?" he growled, one hand tangling in the hair at the back of her neck to tug her head back and allow him to stare into the violet depths of her gaze. "Please let me lick all that sweet cream I know is gathering between your thighs. Please let me fuck you with my tongue until I feel you coming on it."

A man didn't beg Summer—she only saw it as a weakness. She was an incredibly strong-willed woman, he thought with sudden insight. She would never again give into a weak man.

"Go ahead," he demanded. "Tell me this isn't what you want. Lie to me Summer as easily as you lie to yourself."

Chapter
TWELVE

What happened?

Where had this come from?

Even as the thoughts raced through her mind, her senses imploded. Raeg's lips covered hers, his tongue pushing past, tasting her, setting fire to her senses.

She should say no.

He would let her go if she demanded it, if she lied to him. Instead, a moan whispered past her lips, her fingers fisted in the shirt covering his chest, and her response to him overwhelmed her.

His fingers tightened in her hair, tugging her head back further, sending pleasure raking through her. Little zaps of sensation raced from the heated tugging along her scalp to shiver through her body.

And his kiss wasn't gentle. His lips possessed hers, his teeth nipped at her lips, his tongue owned her mouth. She didn't have the will to fight him.

She didn't want to fight him. This pleasure was incredible, fiery. It didn't matter, together or apart, Raeg and Falcon both could throw her senses into complete chaos.

Feminine weakness washed through her, her strength sapped by the pure dominance suddenly pouring from him.

This wasn't supposed to happen.

A whimper escaped her as the intensity and the pleasure only rose. With each stroke of his tongue past her lips, with each beat of her heart, her need for more only rose. It was like striking a match to a hunger she hadn't realized lurked inside her.

Pulling at the material of his shirt, lifting against him, she tried to get closer, tried to sate the suddenly greedy and overwhelming need tearing through her. And Raeg was determined to stoke that hunger.

The arm locked around her waist loosened, his hand stroking over her hip to her thigh, his fingers bunching in the loose material of her skirt, pulling it up and out of the way to allow him access to the sensitive flesh of her upper leg.

He nipped at her lips, a growl rumbling in his chest as she shuddered helplessly against him just before his kisses trailed lower, to her neck. His fingers moved higher, from her thigh to her blouse, the buttons releasing beneath them while Summer tore at the buttons of his shirt.

She wanted him naked, wanted them both naked, and she knew she was crazy for the inability to push them out of her life, out of her bed. Realistically, she knew it was too late to do either. As Raeg hurriedly stripped her, then himself—his lips and hands always touching her, stroking her, kissing her—she knew there was no avoiding the coming pain.

"Damn, how pretty you are," he growled, lifting her until she was stretched across the bed, staring up at him in dazed lust-filled need as he stretched out beside her.

He didn't waste any more time on words.

His head lowered, lips parting, to cover the painfully sensitive tip of her breast, sucking it inside the heat of his mouth.

"Oh God, Raeg . . ." The pleasure was so extreme, so incredibly erotic, her womb clenched in impending release.

Each firm draw on the nerve-laden nipple sent forked pulses of fiery sensation to attack her womb, her clit. She arched into the intense draws, her head tossing against the mattress as her nails bit into the hard muscles of his shoulders, clenching against his flesh.

Releasing her reddened nipple, he began moving down her body. Kisses to her stomach, her abdomen, as he slid between her thighs, pushing her legs apart to wedge his shoulders between them.

"Raeg," she whispered his name, watching as he lifted her legs until her knees bent, the soles of her feet resting on the mattress.

Then his head lowered, his lips devouring her saturated flesh, his tongue licking through the narrow slit with hungry demand.

Her clit was swollen, pulsing with the need to orgasm, as his tongue worked around it, below it. He licked and tasted her, humming his approval against the too sensitive flesh.

Sliding his hands beneath her rear, he lifted her, lips lowering, his tongue spearing inside the clenching opening of her pussy.

Her juices spilled to his waiting tongue, rushing along the channel as his tongue stroked and rasped against the delicate inner tissue. Thrusting in, retreating, he fucked her with his tongue in rapid strokes, pushing her so close,

so high, she could barely breathe for the sensations whipping through her.

"Raeg, you're killing me!" she cried out, wanting to
scream in frustration each time he pulled her back from
the release waiting for her.

Her hands clenched in the blankets beneath her, pulling at them, wanting to claw at them as the sensations
only intensified, the pleasure becoming agonizing, so intense, so hot that perspiration gathered on her skin and
it felt as though flames licked across her nerve endings.

"Please . . ." She all but wailed the plea. "Raeg,
please . . ."

His tongue pushed inside her again, retreated, then
traveled back to her clit in flickering, teasing little licks
that had her muscles tensing further, already so tight they
ached as she fought to catch that wave of release held just
out of reach.

"Damn you, fuck me," she demanded, shuddering as
another wave came closer, so very close, only to escape
at that last heartbeat. "Now Raeg. Please, fuck me."

He jackknifed between her thighs, his lips damp from
her juices, his face stained brick red, as his fingers
wrapped around the base of his thick, erect cock.

Darkly flushed and broad, the flared crest gleamed
with moisture and the promise of pleasure as he came
over her, guiding his erection to press against the entrance of her pussy.

She couldn't help but watch, and Raeg held himself
above her, allowing her to see the wide head part the
swollen folds of her pussy before he began pushing inside her.

The heavy, stretching invasion stole her breath just
as the sight of his penetration parting her flesh destroyed

her senses. Pulling back, her juices clung to the thick shaft, slick and shining, easing his way as he thrust inside her again, shuttling deeper with each inward movement and stretching her with such delicious waves of pleasure-pain that she felt the wave rising, growing more intense.

"Like that, do you, baby?" he whispered, his voice hoarse. "Like watching me take you? Filling you up with each stroke?"

Like it? She loved it. She'd fantasized about it.

"That's what it's like for me and Falcon, watching the other take you, stretch you. Knowing how fucking good you feel wrapped around our dicks, but we get to see your pleasure at the same time," he groaned.

His cock jerked inside her, seeming to thicken as it throbbed in her grip.

"I love fucking you," he swore, his voice hoarse, more strained as his thrusts became heavier, quicker. "Pushing inside your tight little pussy—" His voice broke as he forged in to the hilt, and Summer wailed at the pleasure racing through her now.

"Move. Move!" she demanded. "Please Raeg, I can't stand it. Please fuck me."

"Tell me how good it is, Summer," he groaned, his hips shifting, stroking inside her. "Tell me why you love it, baby."

Why? Why she loved it?

"It hurts so good," she moaned. "Oh God, Raeg, I love it because it hurts so good. Because you make my pussy burn for more . . ."

He lost it.

She said "pussy." Saying "fuck" was bad enough. Whenever she said "fuck," it tempted the leash on his control but didn't break it. But she said "pussy". She said he made her "pussy burn."

The snarl that tore from his throat was a sound he'd never made before, and he wasn't certain why he was making it now except that it happened the second he lost his mind. The feel of her pussy clenched so tight around his cock, so slick and hot, rippling and milking his flesh, was simply too much when combined with that husky drawl whispering those naughty words. Just way too damned much.

Levering back, kneeling between her thighs, he pushed her knees back, holding her in place, tilting her pussy to him. He began rocking inside her furiously. Short, furious thrusts, stroking her inner flesh with a friction certain to destroy both of them.

His balls drew tight to the base of his cock, her pussy tightened even further, sucking at the head of his dick, clenching and rippling until he heard her cries change from pleading to ecstatic.

She jerked in his hold, her body shuddering with each hard explosion as it tightened her further around his cock, had her pussy sucking at it harder, tearing the last of his sanity free and sending him hurtling into a release that rocked his soul.

Gathering her to him and groaning at each hard pulse of semen jetting from his cock inside the brutally tight confines of her pussy, Raeg knew there would never be anything this good in his life again.

Not just the complete, overwhelming pleasure, but the feeling racing through him as he held her to him in the aftermath. The melting, softening feeling in his chest that he'd never felt in his life until this moment.

"Hold me, just for a minute," she whispered when he would have pulled from her. "Let me hold you . . ."

The words broke off just as her voice seemed to echo with emotion. An emotion that intensified that feeling radiating through his senses.

"I have you, baby," he whispered, rolling to his side and holding her close to his chest, feeling her hand press against his heart as he cupped the back of her head and held her to him.

"This is so dangerous." Her voice was so soft he could barely make out the words. "You know it is, just as Falcon knows."

"I know it is." Still, he stroked her back with his other hand, luxuriating in the softness of her skin. "We both know it is."

He felt her breathing hitch before she controlled it, breathing in deep as a tremor shook her.

"You can't stay, can you?" she asked. "When this is over, when Dragovich is gone, you and Falcon won't stay, will you?"

He stared into the sun-drenched room, fighting the past, wanting nothing more than to hold onto this moment and knowing it simply wasn't possible.

"No," he finally answered, hating it, hating himself and everything he hadn't known he wanted until this moment. "We can't stay, Summer."

She didn't stiffen in his arms, didn't pull away or become angry. A sense of resignation settled over her instead as she nodded against his chest.

"We can have this right now though." Tilting her head, she stared up at him as he turned his head to meet her gaze. "Until Dragovich is taken care of. We can have this, without questions or recriminations?"

The vulnerability in her gaze caused his chest to ache.

"No questions, no recriminations," he agreed. "But

only here, in your home. What the world doesn't know can't hurt any of us."

Especially her. If no one knew how much she meant to him and Falcon, then she couldn't be hurt because of it, because of them. That was all that mattered. That was all he cared about, nothing else. Protecting her as much as possible.

What the world didn't know couldn't hurt them.

Laying her head against his chest once again, Summer fought to hold back her tears, to keep from sobbing in despair. She pushed it back, swallowed against the pain, and promised herself there would be a time to cry later.

Later.

When she was alone and they were gone. She could cry then. When she was looking at life without them, then she could give into the pain.

"Summer . . ."

She shook her head, fighting the trembling of her lips, the emotion clogging her throat.

"Just hold me, Raeg," she whispered. "Just for a few more minutes. It feels good to know you're not angry." She forced a facsimile of a teasing little laugh past her lips. "We fought for so long, this feels really good."

His lips pressed to her temple, but she told herself he couldn't possibly know the pain shredding her heart.

"Why do you think we fought?" he asked, his voice soft, gentle at her ear, the husky pitch a bit thick. "I ached for you until all I could do was push you away to keep from taking you. And you knew it, didn't you? Both of us have known . . ."

That they could never have more than this, Summer finished silently.

"When it's over, and you leave, will you do me one favor, Raeg?" she asked.

"If I can." She could feel his fingers playing in her hair, tugging at the strands gently, rubbing them between his fingers.

She swallowed against the tears again—"don't come back, no matter what. Don't do that to me, and don't let Falcon do it."

Falcon was always the wild card. He was the one who'd refused to give up, refused to let the hunger growing between the three of them be.

"As long as you're safe," he promised cautiously. "But get another Russian after that cute little ass of yours, and all bets are off. Agreed?"

"Agreed," she answered, a single tear slipping past one eye.

She wouldn't have enough time with them. Dragovich moved slowly, but he didn't move that damned slow. But she didn't have to push him to move any faster either. She just wanted to hold onto this a little longer.

"You know, it was Falcon who convinced the senator to push you into working with him," he told her, his voice soft, his fingers still moving through her hair. "You were going to come home then, and I swear he spent three days cussing in three different languages when you told him you were thinking about leaving DC. He swore you'd never return if you did. You'd marry and start having babies, and we'd never see you again."

She let her fingers curl slowly into a fist.

"I was getting tired," she whispered.

She was so tired. She was too young to be this tired, she thought, to realize she was going to lose so much and there was nothing she could do about it, there was no way she could stop it.

"When this is over, you can rest, baby," he promised her. "When you wake up, you can put the past behind you. Find what you're looking for."

She nodded, but she knew she'd already found what she wanted with Raeg and Falcon.

Silence descended between them then, each immersed in their own thoughts, their own regrets.

She had Raeg and Falcon for this moment in time, she told herself, for the here and now, and she wasn't going to spoil it by being angry because tomorrow would see it all taken away. Nothing lasted forever, she reminded herself. Well, nothing but the pain she feared, once they were gone.

Several hours later Summer sat in the heavily padded rocking chair on the back porch, its gentle motion having lulled her cousin's infant back to sleep as she rested in Summer's arms.

Her little rosebud lips were parted, her tiny button nose wrinkling at times to some noise from inside the house threatening to disturb her. Long black lashes rested above her rosy cheeks, fragile lids hiding bright blue eyes. A light covering of raven black hair grew over her little scalp, with the slightest hint of gold at the tips.

Her cousin Calista had dressed the baby in a frilly white dress adorned with little pink rosebuds and matching socks. A pale pink, ultrasoft blanket was wrapped snuggly around the tiny baby, keeping her warm and feeling secure.

She was a perfectly formed little angel, Summer thought whimsically as she brushed the back of a finger over the little darling's black hair.

Calista had fed the baby, changed her, then placed her in the antique cradle in the living room to allow her to sleep. Summer had given her cousin enough time to join the others in the kitchen before promptly making away with the infant and escaping to the back-porch rocker. There, holding the baby in her arms, she marveled over the little miracle her cousin had given birth to.

The gentle rocking motion of the chair, the baby's easy, dreamless sleep, and the warmth of the spring day all combined to calm the pain radiating through her when she had left the bed earlier and showered while Raeg went to his own room to do the same.

There were few things that had the power to bother her too much when she had a baby in her arms. Babies were calming, reminders that innocence existed in the world. A baby was also a reminder of what Summer ached for.

Raeg's and Falcon's babies.

She would have loved having their babies, watching the two men raise the children they gave her. This would be worth fighting for, she thought. A home, someone who loved them, children. Surely men weren't so different from women in that regard?

Or perhaps it was Raeg and Falcon who were different.

What could be so terrible that they couldn't risk taking a chance on happiness? Taking a chance on her.

They wanted to. She'd heard it in Raeg's voice, and she'd seen it more than once in Falcon's eyes. They wanted to take that chance, wanted things they wouldn't allow themselves to have, and they refused to reach out for it.

Was it her? They could care about her, but not love her? Men regretted leaving women who loved them, women they knew would be hurt worse because their lovers didn't love them as well. At least, that was what Caleb had told her years ago. He'd warned her that trying to hold onto a man who didn't love her enough to push past his own shortcomings was only asking for more pain.

Had he somehow known what she felt for Raeg and Falcon and knew that they wouldn't love her? What did he know about them that she didn't, she suddenly wondered? Her brothers weren't upset with Raeg and Falcon, even knowing their sister was sleeping with both men—even her father wasn't really as outraged as he should have been.

She frowned at that realization, wondering why she hadn't picked up on it before. They knew her. They knew she wouldn't be taking this risk with them if she wasn't in far too deep emotionally. And she was definitely in far too deep.

She might even be drowning in it.

Closing her eyes, she continued to hum the familiar lullaby she remembered from her childhood.

Little Dawn Rose was lucky, she thought. Just as lucky as any other child who had been born into the family.

Summer's parents, her momma's sisters and her momma's two best friends since childhood all lived close to one another, and sometimes it seemed everyone in the family was raising each other's children. Babysitters were always plentiful; watching eyes and steady hands were always there as protection.

Her momma's family came from a long line of paranoid government agents and Special Forces soldiers with a few less-than-savory relations thrown in. Somehow, that paranoia worked for them though, and over the generations had honed rowdy, fun-loving, ready-to-fight-or-play individuals who may not be easy to live with but were always easy to love.

A grin tugged at her lips at that thought.

Well, she herself might not be so easy to love, except

for her family. She'd grown to be too independent, her momma and daddy both complained. And they were probably right. They seemed to know their children rather well after all.

She wanted to look back one day and realize that she knew her own children that way, knew they were rowdy, independent, fun-loving, and compassionate. She wanted to know that when that day came, she wouldn't be alone in that realization, or in her memories. She wanted to share them with the father of her children and know she wasn't alone in the world or in the protection of her babies.

The world wasn't a kind place now, not that it had ever been, she knew, but children shouldn't ever have to know that.

She'd considered telling her momma that she wouldn't be attending the parties, that she couldn't possibly consider life with another man at this point, but as she held her cousin's child, that desperate ache building inside her overrode the decision.

It wouldn't happen soon—that she knew. It would take a while to stop hurting with the ragged, sharp pain of losing someone she loved. She'd find a way though. She didn't want to live her life alone. She didn't want to be alone. And damn it, if they didn't want to give her babies, then she would find someone who would.

She might not marry—that part was harder to consider. Her baby would have uncles though, cousins, family. Her child wouldn't lack love, she'd see to that.

Just a father.

As that thought went through her mind, the sound of the back door opening quietly had her fighting back tears that otherwise might have fallen.

"There you are, you baby snatcher." The amused

accusation had her eyes opening as she blinked back the tears and stared up at her cousin with a mock glare.

"You go have another one, and I'll just keep this li'l bit," Summer informed her. "You can have her back when she's so completely spoiled she's ruined."

Which would be just about never, Summer thought.

"Well, that's already happened." Calista rolled her eyes in amusement. "I knew I should have never moved in with my parents while Luther's overseas. They sneak her out of her crib and sleep with her between them. I swear, Luther's gonna have a fit when he comes home on leave and learns his little girl can't sleep in that crib he special made for her."

Summer could only shake her head at her cousin. "Calista, sweetie, Luther won't let this little angel sleep outside his sight, I have news for you. She'll be sleeping between her own parents then."

Relenting, she let the baby's mother ease her into her own arms where she cuddled the sleeping infant against her breasts.

"You need one of your own," Calista pointed out. "As much as you love babies, Summer, you'd make a wonderful mother."

She wanted that. She'd always wanted to be a mother, she'd just always imagined a father in there somewhere. Fathers. For years, she realized, she'd imagined Raeg and Falcon as the fathers her children would have.

"Just one?" Summer laughed. "I want a houseful. At least five and every one of them driving me crazy with their wild ways."

Calista's eyes widened. "Lord help you, you're as crazy as your momma," her cousin informed her. "I want one more, maybe in a few years. I want time with this one first." She laid a gentle kiss against Dawn's downy head before grinning back at Summer. "Maybe you'll find the love of your life at one of these parties. I know our mommas have invited every man they believe would suit you from three states. You could be married and ready to have one of your own before this time next year."

Not this time next year, but maybe, in a few years, she thought.

"It might take a little longer than that," she assured her cousin quietly. "But it won't hurt to know my options, right?"

Calista stared down at her somberly. "Are you okay, Summer? Are you reconsidering the parties? You're not committed to choosin' a husband at all if you don't want to, you know that."

Summer nodded. "I know, Calista, but I am committed to getting my butt out of this chair since you stole that baby right out of my arms."

Rising from the chair, Summer looked at the baby fondly, hoping she'd get a chance to steal away with her again before Calista and her mother left.

"Does Momma need help in the kitchen?" she asked, reaching out and opening the back door for the new mother.

Calista snorted at the question. "Your momma needs her head examined, is what she needs. You will not believe what popped out her mouth about those bodyguards of yours. Do you know she's quite convinced those two would just share your favors forever and ever amen?"

Heat flooded her face. Geeze, her momma was determined to completely mortify her. Her mother's habit of mentioning risqué things lately had to be Aunjenue's fault, she decided. Her younger sister was just being a bad influence on their parents.

"She's getting weird in her old age," Summer muttered. "Just ignore her."

"I don't know," Calista laughed. "I saw those hunky devils standing in the tree line together while we were on the porch and you were holdin' Dawn earlier." Wicked amusement filled her eyes. "Personally, I'm convinced your momma might be right."

"I'm convinced you're both insane."

She was going to have to have a talk with her momma about these things. Later. God only knew what would pop out of her mouth if her daughter tried to lecture her about her impure thoughts. Summer was far too amused at that possible scenario.

Her mother had a wicked sense of humor after all.

Chapter
THIRTEEN

Falcon could feel the pure, raw fury gathering in his gut, threatening to explode and erupt in a way he'd never experienced in his life. Fists clenching, his muscles tightening painfully, it was all he could do to hold onto his control. He could feel the fiery tempter that went hand in hand with his Spanish nature threatening to overwhelm him.

He couldn't believe what he'd just heard.

He couldn't believe Summer would even consider such a thing. He knew she'd been dissatisfied with life, that she was searching for more than she'd had in the past, but he'd never imagined she'd consider marriage and children.

She'd once said that if she wanted to hear the pitter-patter of little feet, she'd put shoes on her cat. And she'd sounded incredibly serious at the time.

Fuck.

Turning on his heel he stalked back the way he'd come, returning to the office in the barn where Summer's father and brothers were still going over security for both houses with Raeg.

Of course, the male members of the Calhoun family knew exactly what the hell was going on, just as they knew about the damned parties Summer and her cousin were discussing. There was no way they could not know.

This was why the guesthouses were being prepared, why Summer's hairdresser was being flown in from New York. This was why his agents had such a hard time finding a fucking hotel room in town. Summer's potential suitors were taking up all the rooms, no doubt.

Damn her.

Gripping the doorknob, he pushed open the door with a bit more force than he intended—okay, a lot more force. The panel crashed against the wall behind it.

Raeg, Cal and his sons, the farm's foreman, and one of the men who had served with Caleb in Special Forces all stared back at him in shock.

"Falcon?" Raeg straightened from where he'd been leaning over the long table going over a map of the Calhoun property. "Is everything okay?"

"What is it Summer says?" he snarled furiously. "Everything's just peachy?"

Cal's brows lifted as Caleb glanced at his brother worriedly, wariness filling his expression.

"Yeah well, it's never a good thing when Summer says that either," Raeg snorted. "So why are you so pissed?"

His brother frowned back him as he crossed his arms over his chest, watching him warily.

Falcon's gaze turned to Summer's father. "You couldn't tell us about these parties beginning this weekend? Did you think we wouldn't notice Summer preparing to leave? That we wouldn't object to such exposure. Especially"—

he snapped, his fury growing to the point that he only barely realized how the words were coming out, each sentence a different language, and he didn't give a damn— "considering these fucking parties are no more than a venue to find a willing stud to father her children on. Have all of you lost your fucking minds?"

"English, Falcon," Raeg growled, though Falcon knew he understood every damned word of it. No matter how many different languages he used.

"Oh, I understood him." Cal's smile was tight and hard as he leaned back in his chair, his dark blue gaze assessing. "Spanish, Italian, and I'm certain that was some near-perfect Hebrew," he mused before turning to Raeg. "Your brother seems a mite upset, Raeg."

Falcon saw the darkening of his brother's eyes as well as the flash of resignation, and he knew Raeg had no intentions of fighting this.

"Parties are too dangerous right now, Cal," Raeg said then, his tone a hell of a lot milder than Falcon's was. "You know this is the wrong time for that kind of exposure."

Cal's lips quirked, whether in mockery or acknowledgement Falcon wasn't certain. "It had been too late to cancel them even back when you showed up to inform Caleb of the danger stalking Summer. These have been in the works for nearly six months, Raeg, and the women involved would have our heads if we even try to cancel them."

Raeg actually seemed to be considering the argument. How could he even consider such fucking insanity? Stepping forward, Falcon's lips parted to tell the old bastard just what he thought of it when he caught the subtle warning in his brother's sharp look.

"Stand down, Falcon," Raeg suggested mildly. "We're

just here to protect her. Remember?" He turned back to Cal and Summer's brothers as they watched him broodingly now. "I'll need a full briefing on the venues, guest lists, caterers, et cetera," he told them. "If the parties begin Friday, then I'll need all that immediately."

Caleb gave a mocking snort of amusement while his two brothers chuckled, obviously amused for some reason.

"Summer has everything you need." Cal shrugged. "She's worked on every step of the parties with her momma and her aunts. Just ask her for whatever you need."

Summer had it all?

This was what she spent so many hours doing on her tablet? Planning these parties to find a stud for her babies?

"This is ridiculous," Falcon snapped, pushing his fingers through his hair before glaring at all of them in amazement. "Since when does a woman such as Summer need to do such a thing to find a husband?"

Since when had Summer decided she even wanted a husband, let alone children?

"Since the woman is a highly trained agent capable of killing a man with a toothpick, and needs to meet men just as strong as she is," Caleb informed both of them caustically. "She doesn't want to leave the area to do that though and hasn't been home during the social season enough to know the men available who would suit her temperament and her skill sets. That's what the parties are for, to introduce her to the gene pool, so to speak." He chuckled, obviously amused by his lack of wit.

"Like hell—" Falcon began.

"Falcon, enough already," Raeg ordered, that cool,

assessing expression the same one he used to face down senators and the DC elite he dealt with on a daily basis as Senator Davis Allen Hampstead's chief of staff.

"Invitations were sent out?" Raeg turned back to Cal.

"Six months ago." Cal nodded, lacing his fingers and propping his hands on his abdomen as he leaned back in his chair. "Everyone has sent in their RSVP and they've already begun arriving in town for Friday's and Saturday night's parties. A new crowd will begin arriving next week, then another group the week after that."

"You receive an invitation, Falcon?" Raeg asked.

"I did not." He glared at Cal now.

The other man chuckled lightly. "Leasa did add you to the invitation list, but Summer marked your names off. Seems she didn't want either of you to be invited for some reason." He tipped his head to the side and watched them curiously. "Wonder why that was."

She had marked their names off the invitation list? Not that they could have been in the running as husbands, but still, to not invite them, period? Even worse, to not inform them now that they were there, sharing her bed?

"I'm wondering why the two of you would even think you would get an invitation," Brody interjected, his tone far too amused as he tucked his hands in the back pockets of his jeans and watched Falcon with smug satisfaction. "If either of you were considered husband and father material by her, then she would already know it, wouldn't she?"

Father material?

Falcon felt a punch of reaction to his abdomen, the sharp sensation causing him to grit his teeth furiously. Because the bastard was right.

But still, father material? The man who would give

Summer a child, who would watch her carry that child, give birth and nurture it. The man that would forever mark her heart and soul in the most intimate of ways?

There was no sex act, no touch that could ever mark a woman as a man marked the mother of his children. That bond was one that was never broken, no matter the circumstances. His body would forever be a part of that woman's for his child having rested inside her.

And another man would give her those children.

He cursed.

First in Spanish, then as his anger only grew, in all five languages he knew with a fluency usually reserved for the natives of those lands.

Turning, he stalked from the office, slammed the door closed, and fought the need to go straight to her parents' home and drag her back to her own. As he neared the exit to the barn he found himself ramming his fist into the wall with enough force that the resulting crack echoed through the barn.

"Dammit, Falcon . . ." Raeg cursed.

He ignored his brother.

Teeth clenched, brutal fury ripping through him, he strode quickly from the barn and headed for Summer's home. It was peaceful there. Her presence filled it even when she wasn't there, the scent of her infusing the house, washing over a man with a subtle warmth he wasn't aware of at first.

And she would choose another man to share that home with? To share her bed with?

Because he and Raeg were not worthy . . . because they could not stay and share that life, those children she so wanted, and the peace she filled her home with. Because they had no choice but to walk away when this was over, and they all knew it.

She had somehow known it even before she had left DC.

Summer would have never done something so outrageous unless she had resigned herself to being unable to love any man she might marry in the future. She wouldn't meet so many men believing in love at first sight. No, Summer had known her connection to him and Raeg was too deep, no matter her battles with his brother. She had known that finding a man to share her life with, to be the father of her children, wouldn't be an emotional choice.

They had already lost her even before she left DC, he realized as he stepped into the home she had created for herself and closed the door silently.

This was the legacy he and Raeg shared, he thought wearily. A legacy of always being alone, of always fearing that what they would love the most would be taken from them. Because of their father's overpowering love for two women he had endangered, he refused to trust his sons to keep the secret of their location and their new identities. And because of that lack of trust, he would murder any woman his sons claimed if he considered her a threat. Especially a woman who had been part of the CIA.

This was their legacy, he thought, staring around the sun-dappled rooms and knowing the day would soon come when he and Raeg would be forced to walk away.

"I will never forgive any of you," he whispered bleakly, thinking of his mother, of Raeg's mother, and of the father who always seemed to be watching no matter the safeguards they used. "Do you hear me?" he snarled into the silence. "I did not hate until this moment. I could have forgiven . . ." He would have forgiven, if that was what it took to have a chance at a future, at a family that he and his brother could share.

He shook his head at the thought. There could be no forgiveness for this, for the loss of the woman Falcon was realizing owned so much of his spirit.

He would never completely leave her. He could never do so. His heart would always linger with her, it would never desert the woman who had given him so much in the past two years.

Wiping his hands over his face he stalked to the bar, pulled free the decanter of whisky, and poured one of the short glasses nearly full before taking a healthy drink of the fiery liquid.

"Summer-shine," he said on a heavy breath, that bleak, burning bitterness that always lurked in the darkest corners of his mind encroaching closer now. "How I wish . . ."

But wishing was futile, he told himself, taking another drink and making his way upstairs to the room Summer directed him to when he and Raeg had first arrived. They'd slept in her bed though. He and his brother, one on each side of her, surrounding her with their warmth, with their protection.

God help him, would he survive when he'd learn that she had married? He had a feeling survival would be the least of his worries if he ever learned she carried another man's child. There would be nothing inside him but fury once that occurred, a fury he knew would destroy him.

Raeg stared at the empty exit from the barn for long minutes after his brother had stalked away from it. His gaze slid then to the cracked plank of wood where Falcon's fist had slammed into it and wondered if his brother had finally managed to break a bone.

"You know he loves her, don't you?" Cal turned to Raeg then, his dark blue eyes filled with censure. "Says you love her too, though you won't admit to it. Yet, I have a feeling the two of you will walk right away from her once you kill Dragovich, won't you?"

Raeg rubbed at the back of his neck before dropping his hand to his side, knowing he should just walk away from this conversation as well. He should check on Falcon, make certain he hadn't broken his hand.

"I knew your mother," Cal said. "Lot of years ago. You were probably about three or four."

Before his mother had nearly died, before Roberto had been forced to hide them all. Before Roberto had murdered the lover Raeg had taken when he was barely twenty.

He wasn't talking about his mother. Selena Raegent was, as far as he was concerned, as much a part of the past as his father. Her mother's love had contributed to the death of a woman who hadn't deserved to die, just as Falcon's mother had.

He and his brother had walked away from them years ago, and they had stayed away. Roberto would stain his hands with the blood of the women his sons loved and never look back; they knew that, their mothers knew that. And their mothers agreed with it because, as they had argued, loving a woman came with trust and men could never understand nor accept that their love could be flawed, and they would trust those women even with secrets that could see other lives destroyed.

Lives such as that of the sister their parents protected now. It wasn't just their lives, their mothers had reminded him and Falcon, it was their sister's life as well.

"Raeg, there's no canceling this," Cal reiterated. "Summer would have canceled it if it was possible. She wouldn't have chanced you knowing her plans once the two of you left if she could have kept it from you."

"For God's sake, why are you pampering his poor

little feelings?" Brody sneered, the youngest son obviously less than pleased with his father. "You know what the hell is going on in that house. Those two can't take a woman without the other helping. They're disrespectin' Summer every time they crawl into her bed with her."

Raeg wasn't a violent person. He'd been known to keep his calm even when staring down at the lover he hadn't been able to protect so very long ago. He'd learned young that losing his temper, to allow others to see his pain, was the worst mistake he could possibly make.

There was something about the words though, the sneering, smug-ass tone of voice that exploded through his head and had him moving before he realized what he was doing.

He swung around, grabbed Brody by the neck with a well-practiced grip that the younger man would have no idea how to break. And he tightened his fingers just enough to make breathing difficult, to assure the bastard that he could kill him in a heartbeat if that was what he wanted to do.

He could hear Bowe and Caleb yelling at him, and each time they thought to get too close, he tightened his grip on the other man's neck until they backed off.

"I could kill you between one heartbeat and the next," his voice was low, guttural, as he stared into Brody's eyes. "And trust me I will if I ever hear you say something like that in regards to your sister again."

"Fuck . . . you . . ." Brody gasped, anger filling his expression, pure stubbornness tightening his jaw.

"Let him go, Raeg," Cal ordered from behind him. "Brody doesn't know your secrets, he only knows you're rippin' his sister's heart from her chest. How else is he supposed to feel? Yet, all three of her brothers have held back for her sake. I'm sure she'd expect you to do the same."

Yeah, she would. That didn't mean he should, but he knew he couldn't kill the jackass, no matter how badly he wanted to.

He loosened his hold slowly, finger by finger, until he was stepping away, staring at the other man warningly. This would be a very, very bad time for Brody to keep pushing him.

Turning to follow his brother, Raeg found himself facing Cal instead and the compassion that filled the older man's eyes.

"The heart wants what it wants," Cal stated gently. "And her heart's been set on the two of you for years. All of us have known it. And when you leave, her heart will no doubt go with you. Would you really deny her a little happiness after that? A husband that can stand by her side, give her the children she's always dreamed of having, and grow old beside her? Or is that love selfish, Raeg? Does she have to be just as lonely and as alone as you and Falcon will be?"

Not alone or lonely. She should be with him and Falcon. She shouldn't have to worry about her heart following them, they should be there, they should have the choice of being there with her. A choice that would only endanger her.

"Dragovich is a saint compared to what could strike out at her because of us," he rasped, realizing his heart was racing, his breathing was hard, heavy. "Staying isn't an option. It would show we care . . ."

It would show she was a weakness, a possible confidante. Someone who could one day learn their secrets, or be used against Raeg and Falcon to force them to reveal their secrets. Either way, it placed her in a monster's crosshairs.

"Then you should have been man enough to stay out of her bed," Cal stated softly. Understanding flickered across his expression. "Either way," he breathed out heavily, "it's too late to worry about it now, just as it's too late to cancel these parties. And once she marries, it will be too late to come back. Summer will always honor her vows, no matter the temptation to do otherwise, and you know that. So be sure when you walk away, that you're going to be able to keep from walkin' back."

"Go to hell," Raeg snapped, his lip lifting in a snarl of fury before he pushed past the other man and left the barn.

It might be too late to cancel the party, but it wasn't too late to cancel Summer's role in that party, he decided furiously. Summer would have to see that. She was an intelligent, logical woman. She'd understand that this party simply couldn't happen. God only knew who Dragovich had working for him. It would be someone the family trusted, and from what he'd seen that was damned near everyone they'd introduced him to in the past week he and Falcon had been there.

And it wouldn't be just one person. The Russian mobster knew how to hedge his bets and how to plan for contingencies. When the first attack against Summer hadn't succeeded, he would have already known how and where he was attacking the second time. Dragovich was just waiting for that time to arrive.

Stepping onto the porch leading to the front door of the Calhouns' home, he ignored the two armed men who sat with all apparent laziness in the chairs positioned close to the door. They didn't speak and neither did he.

He pulled open the storm door and stepped inside, his gaze moving automatically to the living room where Summer sat in a padded rocker, watching the tiny face of the child she slowly rocked and hummed to.

The sight of it was like a punch to the gut and a fist to his heart. This was what he and Falcon could have had if life had been different. The woman both of them loved and a child conceived by one of them.

God, how he ached to give her that child, he thought painfully. To see her growing round, the love she felt for that child and for the men she shared her life with glowing within her face.

Moving silently across the room, he stopped just in front of her and waited as her head lifted, her expression causing that inner darkness he always lived with to howl silently in protest of ever letting her go.

"We need to go home, now," he told her softly, loath to disturb the babe sleeping in her arms.

Indecision and wariness flickered over her face. "I wasn't finished . . ."

"Now," he repeated. The almost silent anger that burned inside was an alien sensation to him.

He never burned with fury. Everything stayed contained, controlled, carefully restrained. Nothing else was acceptable. He couldn't allow himself to let his anger free. He never allowed that. If he did, he may go hunting and commit a sin so unpardonable that . . . He cringed at the thought of it.

The sin of murdering his father.

Moving carefully, Summer rose to her feet, her gaze wary as she glanced at him a final time before walking slowly from the living room to the kitchen.

Raeg waited for her by the front door, listening to her

as she told her family good-bye and tried to ignore her mother's protest that they had plans to finalize.

Plans to finalize. Plans for the damned parties geared to finding her a husband and a father for the children she would one day have. He wanted to curse it, rail over it and declare it would only happen over his dead body. Unfortunately, he couldn't stop it and he knew it. That didn't mean he could allow her to risk herself by attending any of the damned events, until Dragovich was stopped. That he would definitely keep from happening.

One way or the other.

Chapter
FOURTEEN

She could tell they knew about the parties.

The second Summer saw Raeg's expression, saw the emotions roiling in his eyes and darkening them, she knew her secret was out.

There was a strange sense of relief in the knowledge that she no longer had to worry about telling them. Her time had been running out and she'd known it. The first party was in just days, the afternoon barbeque and social to allow everyone to meet and become familiar with one another would have been impossible to attend without them being aware she was gone, she'd kept telling herself mockingly.

Now, they knew. Now there was just the battle of wills to get through, and hadn't she battled with them enough in the past years over one thing or another to know what to expect? The only difference was that she'd never had to battle both of them at once.

Raeg didn't speak as they walked to the house and neither did she. Her chest ached with the knowledge that they could no longer ignore the fact that life would go on if they survived this battle with Dragovich.

Life would go on, they would leave and return to DC, and she'd be left here with nothing more than the memories of them to haunt her home.

Stepping into the house with Raeg, she winced as he slammed the door behind them, then stalked past her to the bar.

Falcon sat on the couch, his elbows resting on his knees, a half-filled glass of whisky held in one hand, his pale blue eyes like chips of ice glowing in the savage features of his face.

He didn't speak as she walked into the room, her gaze going between him and Raeg, the silence between them so thick she felt as though she were trying to swim through it.

God, it hurt, she thought. She'd had no idea how much this would actually hurt. Facing them, knowing they knew that she had every intention of living, of building a life after they were gone. Though, that wasn't exactly true. The plan had been to build a life period, to ignore what she wanted and go after what she could have.

That was before they'd touched her, before they'd shown her how good it was being a part of them, being their lover as well as their friend.

"The two of you act as though I've betrayed you," she said when neither of them spoke.

Falcon lifted his drink and took a healthy swallow, not even grimacing at the sharp burn of the whisky, never taking his eyes off her.

She'd never seen him look so cold, so hard. Despite his fiery nature, the pale blue color of his eyes always gave the impression of implacable emotionlessness that had always fooled the casual observer.

She'd never been fooled though, but neither had she ever seen that ice encompass even his whole expression. She would have expected him to be cursing in every language he knew, railing at her, demanding. The fact that he wasn't caused her throat to thicken with tears. The only time she'd ever seen him not give into that temper was the night she'd been forced to kill Gia.

"You can't go to these parties, Summer." It was Raeg who spoke, but he wasn't ordering her, he wasn't commanding her. His voice was hoarse, his expression tormented, as he stood at the bar staring into the glass he'd just drank from. "You know it's too dangerous."

She couldn't do this.

It hurt so bad. They weren't screaming at her, they weren't being confrontational, they weren't giving her a fight. There was no place to expend all the emotion building inside her, ripping her apart.

She couldn't cry. She wouldn't let herself cry because it would only hurt all of them more, and none of them deserved that.

"It's too—"

"Late to cancel," Raeg pointed out, appearing reasonable, even sounding reasonable. "It's not too late to make the decision not to attend."

That was Raeg, she thought, no matter the situation, he managed to remain logical. If only she could do the same.

She'd actually thought of not attending, actually discussed it with her family, but eventually rejected the idea.

"It won't make a difference," she breathed out, her voice rough as she pulled her hair over her shoulder and slowly began braiding the long length.

That calmed her. It was a crutch, one she rarely used, but the act of concentrating on the intricate mermaid braid kept her focused, kept her from giving into whatever tormented her, whatever hurt her.

She was aware of Falcon following the movements of her fingers, his gaze brooding, his expression never shifting from the hard, granite lines they were composed in.

"Why not?" The snap in Raeg's voice caused her to flinch. It was like a lash of dark, bitter emotion slapping against her senses.

"Dragovich isn't going to attack a crowd, it's too risky. Especially a crowd of military and law enforcement personnel. It would be suicide," she pointed out. "He'll strike when I least expect it instead."

"You wouldn't expect it at one of those parties," Raeg argued before tossing back the rest of his drink, then pouring another.

"Actually, everyone has been alerted to the fact that I've been targeted. I wouldn't allow anyone to walk in unknowing, Raeg. I'm not that cruel nor am I that stupid."

No one had backed out of the invitation though, most of the men had actually informed her family that they'd be coming armed, just in case.

"Don't do this, Summer." It was Falcon who spoke, the Spanish flavor of his voice actually more pronounced now.

Like Raeg, he stared at his drink rather than at her, his expression hardening further despite the fact that she hadn't imagined it could get harder.

She worked at the braid desperately now, the tightness in her chest agonizing as she stared between them. She couldn't remember a time when they had avoided looking at her while they disagreed. Falcon always yelled in several different languages, while Raeg became insulting and sarcastic in one. They weren't displaying either characteristic at the moment. They were so self-contained it was frightening.

"This isn't about Dragovich," she finally stated, abandoning the braid when it was only half-finished. "It's not about the potential of him attacking, because all three of us know the chances of that happening are practically nonexistent. This is about the reason for the parties. Let's admit it."

If they knew about the parties, then they knew about the reason for them. Everyone knew about the reason for them—to introduce Summer to the men her family considered a suitable match for her.

She wasn't the only woman that would be there. The guest list was evenly matched between the sexes, with no expectations where Summer was concerned. It was simply an opportunity for her and the other unmarried male and female guests to meet and get to know one another. It wasn't the first time such events had been arranged, it was actually quite common among the social set her parents were a part of.

Raeg and Falcon weren't speaking now, they were concentrating on their drinks, glaring into their glasses after sipping at the liquor, the tension practically humming around them.

"Friday's barbeque is Aunt Bee's," she informed them quietly. "It's about an hour from here. We'll need to leave about three in the afternoon and we'll be there until around midnight. When we return, Caleb, Bowe, and Brody will come to the house with us and make certain it's still secure, though several of the men Caleb once fought with will be watching the house while we're gone. Everything's going to be fine."

At least, that was what she kept telling herself. Everything would be fine. And if Dragovich did decide to make a move, they'd be alerted before they returned to the house.

Either way, it would be dealt with and Dragovich would be neutralized.

Falcon lifted his head, his gaze meeting hers then, and Summer barely smothered the cry that lay trapped in her throat. The agony she felt ripping her heart apart lay in his expression, in that deceptively icy gaze.

"Don't do this, Belle," he asked, his voice low, deeper than normal. "Not while Dragovich is still a threat."

Not while they were there, not while they had to watch her socialize with a potential future husband. She understood that far more than they knew.

"Would the timing matter?" she asked painfully. "It wouldn't, Falcon. And I'll hate being there, I'll hate knowing you're there, hate knowing you're aware of why I'm there. This way though, I can't fool myself. I won't have the option of believing the fantasy could be reality or that you'll stick around once Dragovich isn't a threat any longer. This way, we can't hide from the truth. Right?"

Raeg tossed back the rest of his drink and slapped the glass down on the bar, the crack of sound causing her to flinch again. Raeg didn't normally show his temper, she reminded herself. Just as Falcon didn't remain quiet and aloof when *he* was pissed. None of this was normal, none of it was how she'd imagined it would be at all.

He was shattering on the inside. Falcon had never felt himself breaking apart, piece by piece, before. Not even the night he'd believed his and Raeg's mothers had been murdered, and not when he'd learned years later that they hadn't been. None of the betrayals in his life had ever shattered him, but this . . . this was killing him. Ripping at his guts and slicing into his chest with agonizing realization.

And all he could do was sit there, desperately searching for an argument, a way to keep this from happening, all the while knowing the only way to stop it wasn't a choice he could make.

He'd known walking away from her was going to feel like splitting himself in half, but he hadn't expected the tearing sensation to begin even before it was time to leave her.

He finished his drink, not even feeling the burn he knew should be tearing its way to his belly. Hell, it was his third drink—he should be nearing that point where everything felt numb. Nothing felt numb though. Each pulse of blood through his body was a lash of agony resonating through his senses, and he wasn't quite certain how to handle it.

If he was hurting, Summer was hurting worse. The second she pulled her hair over her shoulder and began to form the intricate braid, the knowledge of her pain struck at his chest.

Her eyes were like wounded violets in the stark features of her face, and she seemed unable to hide the pain that filled her features.

The conflict she felt more than matched his own and made him murderous. It made him dream of ripping apart the man who would make Summer pay for the fact that he and Raeg loved her.

"It won't work," he told her. "I know you, baby, like no one but Raeg knows you, and I know this isn't going to work. Just as you do."

He and Raeg would go insane watching a bunch of

bastards socialize with her, the knowledge that she would eventually be choosing a husband, possibly from one of the men she met at the arranged parties, uppermost in their mind. The men in attendance would be men who knew their own minds, their own strengths, and the very nature of those chosen for Summer to consider would ensure they went after what they wanted, what they thought they could have.

Seeing that in the men, knowing that once he and his brother left, Summer had every intention of building a life without them, was killing him, even though he knew he couldn't blame her. No one could blame her, least of all him and Raeg.

They blamed themselves, or the past—a monster without remorse. That was who they blamed, that and the very things they couldn't eliminate.

"I'll kill the bastard who touches you within my sight." The savage, naked fury brewing in Raeg shocked Falcon.

Summer's face whitened, her breath hitching audibly as her gaze swung to his brother.

Falcon glanced at Raeg, then rubbed at the back of his neck in resignation. He had only said what Falcon felt as well.

"Raeg . . ." She whispered his name, regret filling the sound as tears gleamed in her eyes. "This wasn't what I wanted. It wasn't what I planned."

"But you knew I'd fucking lose my goddamned mind with it, didn't you?" Raeg wanted to throw something.

Son of a bitch, he clearly understood why Falcon had slammed his fist into the barn wall earlier. Better the pain of a shattered hand than a shattered soul.

She shook her head, her lips parting to deny the charge.

"Of course you did," he bit out furiously. "You knew or you wouldn't have taken our names off the invitation list. You would have made damned sure we knew what you were doing if you hadn't known what it would do to us."

She blinked furiously, her fingers linking together nervously as she shook her head, her expression stark white and filled with shock.

"I didn't want to know you didn't care," she said, her voice resonating with so many pain-filled emotions that he hated hearing it. "That's why I took your names off the list. The thought of you showing up, amused . . ." Her voice broke, a hand lifting to cover her lips, but not quite quick enough. He caught the subtle trembling, the sound of tears that thickened her voice. "I couldn't bear it."

"You knew I would care," Falcon objected, and regret filled Summer's expression.

"And I knew you wouldn't do anything even if you did," she stated, that knowledge stamped on her face, filling her eyes. "I've always known the two of you would never commit to a woman separately. It's simply who you are and I was too frightened that Raeg wouldn't care. That he didn't care."

"Don't fucking do this while we're here, Summer." Raeg wanted to make it an order, he wanted to demand she have mercy on all of them, and he couldn't.

"I'm sorry," her voice broke again, lips trembling before she fought back her tears, breaking his heart with the knowledge that like them, she was holding back the pain tearing her apart. "If I do what you want, Raeg, then it will break me when you leave. Is that what you want?

Is that really what you want to see as you walk away?"
Her lips trembled and Falcon swore the tears filling her
eyes would fall. "That's not what I want for you. For
whatever reason, you feel you have to go. But I don't want
you to be alone when you leave. I want you to find
love . . ." A sob almost escaped, and Falcon's throat tightened, the agony trapped inside him threatening to escape
in a howl of pain. "I want you to be happy, even if you
can't be happy with me."

Turning, she all but ran for the stairs then, reaching
for the banister as Falcon jumped to his feet to run to her.

Raeg beat him to her. He gripped her upper arm, pulling her around and against his chest, one hand pressing
her head to him as his arm wrapped around her fragile
body.

He bent his head over hers, and Falcon watched his
expression twist painfully, eyes closing as Summer's fingers clenched in his shirt and her body bowed into the
pain he knew was exploding through her.

She wanted them to find love, wanted for them what
she wanted so desperately to give to them, and she had
no idea the depth of love they felt for her, Falcon thought.
She couldn't know, or the betrayal she would feel later
would only be deeper than it would already be.

Standing several feet from his brother and the woman
both of them treasured, Falcon could feel the murderous
fury threatening to steal his control, and the veil he'd
kept between him and that fury was torn away. Hatred
crept from the darkness where it had hidden, pure, bitter,
complete hatred for the man who caused this, a father
who would strip their souls without remorse.

"I will kill, Summer," Raeg whispered against the top
of her head, holding her, vowing what Falcon knew both

of them felt. "Understand that, baby, believe it. If even one man dares to lay his hands on you in my sight, I will kill . . ."

Because she belonged to them. She was theirs, and they were far more possessive than even they'd suspected. They might share her with each other, but never, not at any time, would they'd willingly allow another to touch her. Not and keep their sanity.

Chapter
FIFTEEN

Friday came far too quickly, yet time seemed to drag in slow motion, each second filled with so much emotion, so much pain, that she didn't know how she survived it.

The fitting for her dress was quiet, absent of the laughter and teasing she, her sister, and their friend and dressmaker, Trina had shared during the other meetings. The beautiful gown no longer filled her with excitement, or with a sense of beauty.

Steven arrived, and that afternoon she sat in the beautician's chair, staring blankly at the mirror as the older man slowly, methodically straightened the curls and waves of her hair.

Steven was a little older than her father, she guessed, at least in his early sixties, though like her father, he carried his age very well. Easily six two, his shoulders still broad, his body toned, he was the least likely beautician in the world. Yet, he was a master. She rarely allowed anyone else to fix her hair.

"So much hair," Steven stated, his voice a bit hesitant

as he spoke. "You are the belle of whatever ball you arrive at, my dear."

There was a curious, questioning gentleness to his voice as his hazel eyes met hers in the mirror.

Summer stared at her hair, knowing it wouldn't be this long once Raeg and Falcon left.

"I'm thinking about cutting it," she said hollowly. "It doesn't seem worth the effort anymore to keep it so long."

Steven paused, his expression reflecting his surprise.

"Why would you do such thing my dear?" he asked softly as he sectioned off another portion of her hair, combing it carefully, then laying the straight iron to it before drawing the iron slowly down the long strands.

"It would be better short," she answered, fighting the trembling of her lips, the pain that was only building.

Raeg and Falcon had barely spoken to her since the day before. And they hadn't slept with her. They'd stayed in the guest rooms, though like her, she doubted they'd slept much.

"Shall I assume this has something to do with those two young men waiting outside?" he asked somberly. "Have they broken your heart, sweetheart?"

The gentleness in his voice was filled with fondness and years of friendship. He knew things about her that no one else was aware of, secrets he'd never revealed nor gossiped about. He was one of the nicest men she knew, and sometimes he seemed to understand so much more than his words ever said.

"I must say," he continued when she didn't answer him. "I'm not really surprised to see them here. I had the pleasure of shaping Alyssa's hair just after you left. Raeg seemed rather put out when I inquired about you at the time, more so than usual. Shall I assume he and Falcon are the reason for all that pain filling your eyes? Should

I take them to task for wounding your tender heart, sweetheart?"

Tears filled her eyes, because she knew he was serious. He was very protective of his clients, and he always swore she and Alyssa were his favorites.

"No," she whispered as he continued to work on her hair. "It's complicated."

"Love is very simple my dear," he disagreed. "It's the reasons we fight it that can become complicated. Usually far more complicated than they need be if I know those two."

There was a question in his voice. Of course he'd want to know why they found it complicated. She did as well.

Summer could only shrug. "They won't tell me why."

"Do you ask?" he questioned her curiously.

"Falcon would tell me if he could," she admitted. "I think it's complicated." She frowned. "Maybe it's me, Steven," she whispered. "Maybe it's like Caleb said about the heart he broke. Maybe they just care so much that it hurts, but they know they don't love me the way they should and it will hurt me less if they walk away." She stared at his reflection in the mirror, needing someone to explain this to her, needing some way to make sense of why they would walk away from her.

His brow furrowed, his hazel eyes meeting hers before he turned his gaze back to his task, perhaps considering what she'd just asked him.

"I've known Raeg and Falcon, albeit distantly, for many years now," he finally answered. "You know when Raeg was about twenty, there was a young woman he was enamored of, one who preferred not to have his brother in their bed. The brothers went their separate ways for a while. The young woman was murdered in their bed while he was meeting his brother for drinks one night."

She stared back at him in shock.

"That's not in his CIA file," she said, not in the least worried about revealing her status as an agent. Steven had been referred to her by Margot Hampstead, the senator's first wife, just before her death. He was an agent himself, though he claimed to be retired.

"Of course it isn't." He waved the comment away. "His parents were agents for the company as well. His father and mother, Falcon's mother too. They made an incredible team. It was his father who killed the young woman actually. She was an agent herself, determined to prove a suspicion that Raeg's and Falcon's mothers were alive and reveal where they were hiding. Some governments simply refuse to accept that enemies don't live forever," he snorted, rueful amusement crossing his face. "From what I understand, Raeg trusted her implicitly but the information she wanted didn't exist. There's rumors that while he was meeting with his brother she was making plans to kill him on his return. I gather his father was rather put out over that, and killed her instead."

She'd known Raeg's parents were CIA, she hadn't known about this, though.

No wonder he refused to love anyone, she thought.

"He really loved her then?" she asked, the pain only growing inside her. "That's why he's willing to walk away from me?"

"Men can be stubborn," he advised her. "We're not exactly logical where our hearts are concerned. And we'll often fight real love with the same determined force that we would any enemy."

"He won't stay, will he?" she asked the other man then, knowing the answer even before he paused and stared back at her.

"I doubt it," he sighed heavily, compassion filling his gaze. "Raeg will always remember that first mistake, that trust he gave to someone planning to betray him. That's a powerful memory for a man."

A powerful enemy for a woman to have to face, she thought.

"I love them," she whispered, saying it out loud, needing someone to hear the words.

"Yes, you have for a long time." He nodded. "Just remember, my dear, whether returned or not, love is never wasted. And they may be angry over the parties at the moment, angry that you're making plans to continue on without them, but remember this. There is nothing more powerful than the challenge of realizing a woman is strong enough to live without you. Never, never allow them to realize any different. If you have any chance of keeping them, then that's it."

There was no chance of keeping them, she already knew that. Her pride wouldn't let her fall in front of them though. A terrible thing, her pride—she knew that. She would easily cut her own nose off to spite her face, as her mother was prone say.

"Cheer up, Summer," he ordered her gently, the Scot's accent a soothing burr. "True love can never be defeated. It's invincible, I promise you this."

She stared back at him, hoping she hid her disbelief. Hell, she'd never imagined Steven was more naïve than her little sister, but it appeared he might very well be.

She was fucking beautiful.

Steven had straightened every strand of her long black hair before pulling the front of it back to the crown of her head in a ponytail that trailed strands of tiny, silver bells whose muted sounds were heard only occasionally and so softly at first that he wasn't even certain what he was hearing.

She wore one of those soft, feminine skirts that looked so damned good on her. This one fell to her ankles in muted shades of gold and pale blue, the loose material swaying around her seductively. It was paired with a soft bronze camisole top and strappy flat sandals.

She looked like a gypsy as she drifted about the crowd gathered in her aunt's backyard, her sister and her mother at her side.

They stopped and talked to damned near every man there but just long enough for introductions before Summer just drifted away, sometimes in the middle of a conversation.

"We're killing her," Falcon said from beside him, his voice rough with fury, with pain. "It's like watching her bleed out slowly."

Raeg just watched her, his arms crossed over his chest, tight. The need to hold back that ache centered beneath them imperatively.

"Fuck," Falcon cursed when Raeg didn't answer. "I'm getting a drink."

He broke his silence. "Get me one. A double."

The drink was neutral. It didn't take thought, it didn't take restraint, or an awareness of his control to deal with. It was just a drink.

They'd been there for hours. The barbeque, the meal, and hours of watching Summer float around the yard from table to table, that facsimile of a smile on her lips, killing him with a knowledge of the pain she was holding back.

"That woman," Mike Taggart, Caleb's boyhood friend, commented as he stepped to Raeg, "is not Summer Calhoun." His expression, his gaze, was filled with dislike as Raeg met his gaze. "What the hell have ya'll done to her?"

Loved her, Raeg answered silently. They had been ambushed by the one emotion they'd sworn they wouldn't let themselves feel.

"Find somewhere else to be, Mike," Raeg suggested coldly. "I'm not in the mood for your bullshit."

He'd only met the man twice, and each time, the bastard had done something to piss him off.

Mike grunted at the order. "It could be Caleb standin' here instead. He's ready to kill you and your brother, you know. Him and his daddy both. That look in Summer's eyes is about to kill everyone who knows her."

It was killing him and Falcon as well.

Raeg kept watching her.

She stopped and said something to her mother and Aunjenue, shaking her head at her mother's response. She didn't smile, she didn't flit around from group to group, flirting and driving him insane with jealousy. She was just there, physically.

Mike's muttered curse was ignored just as his warning was, and finally he turned and stalked off, returning to the table where the Calhoun men sat. Thankfully, Summer's brothers all remained at the table with their father.

No one approached him and Falcon, though Raeg recognized damned near every man there. The intelligence community was actually rather small in some circles and mingled with certain law enforcement and military groups closely.

Those were the men who chatted and socialized with the multitude of women flirting and chatting willingly with them. Still, there were far too many whose eyes followed Summer, who watched her with male interest and speculation.

"Here." Falcon shoved the drink at him before turning to watch Summer again, his body tight with tension as he sipped at his drink.

This had to end soon, Raeg thought wearily. They couldn't continue like this. It was killing all of them.

"How much longer do we have to do this?" Falcon growled, the low, guttural tone of his voice at odds with his brother's normally fiery nature. "I'm not going to deal with these bastards much longer."

"No one's touching her," he reminded his brother.

"They're undressing her with their eyes and being fucking lewd in their thoughts and it's pissing me the hell off," Falcon informed him.

That possessiveness would be the death of all of them, Raeg thought, because it was no different than how he felt. When he and Falcon began agreeing on who needed to die, then there could be problems.

Summer chose that moment to turn and meet his gaze.

Her expression was still and composed, but he could see the pain she was holding back.

"She's trying to let us go," Falcon breathed out roughly from beside him. "You know that, don't you? She's trying to take on all that hurt herself and just let us go."

There was no letting them go, Raeg thought. They would walk away, because they had no other choice if they wanted to ensure her safety. But they wouldn't let her go.

"Do you think she'll actually marry one of the bastards she meets at one of these parties?" Falcon asked when Raeg didn't say anything. "You know that's not going to go over well with me, don't you?"

Raeg breathed out heavily. Yeah, it wasn't going to go over well with him either.

Lifting the glass to his lips, he finished his drink before placing his glass on the high table next to where he and Falcon stood, partially in shadow beneath the vine-covered arbor growing next to the two-story historic house.

The brick patio and the paths leading around the back gardens were huge, with dozens of benches and tables scattered around for the guests.

He wasn't going to make it until midnight.

Each time Summer was stopped by one of the men invited to meet her, he stiffened, recalled what he knew on the bastard and discarded any chance that he'd allow Summer to actually marry that individual. No one here was good enough for her it seemed. Not a single one of the hard-eyed killing machines her father seemed to think so highly of was good enough for her in his opinion.

And not a single damned one of them was going to have her.

Summer could feel them watching her.

For hours upon hours they watched her, their gazes never wavering, never leaving her.

Summer's nerves were stretched thin and, surprisingly enough, she was so damned aroused she was about to go crazy. Every inch of her body was so sensitive that even the breeze was a caress.

"Darling, you're wearing your heart on your sleeve," the Scot's soft brogue sounded just behind her, a whisper of sympathy and of warning.

"I hate men," she muttered, keeping her back turned to Falcon and Raeg and forcing Steven to move around her to face her.

As he did, Summer caught the thoughtful look he slid her way, as well as a gleam of playful amusement.

"I have heard you spent a brief amount of time playing same-sex games," he assured her with a subtle wink. "Thinking of returning to bat for the home team, my dear?"

Summer snorted, unable to stop the laugh that bubbled up in her throat.

"You are a wicked, wicked man, Steven." She could feel the blush staining her cheeks, as well as the abashed amusement she couldn't quite help. "You are older than my daddy. You shouldn't be thinking that way."

He looked heavenward as though seeking guidance. "Lass, you such have strange ideas about those of us over the age of fifty, I'm curious where you came by them." He slid a look to his side, settling briefly on her momma. "And I'm certain that fine young lady who birthed you had no hand in such beliefs. That is a woman that could inspire wars for the chance to love fully."

Summer's eyes widened, abashment turning to full-fledged disbelief that he'd said something so outrageous.

"Be quiet, you!" she demanded. "Don't be thinking about my momma like that."

He directed a doubtful look her way, his expression a little too knowing. "My dear, tell me you are not one of those young ladies that believes her mother is still a virgin and her father completely ignorant of sexual urges."

"Steven," she huffed, glaring back at him. "We do not talk about my momma and daddy in that manner. Now be good or go find someone else to torment."

He slid a look her momma's way again.

"Stop it," she hissed, realizing his gaze was directed far lower than her momma's face. "My daddy will shoot you."

Gripping his arm, she all but dragged him away from

all possible views of her momma before her daddy decided to feed him to the gators.

"You have a suicide wish," she informed him in exasperation.

"No, my dear." He smiled down at her fondly then. "Merely a wish to take that look of haunted pain from your face for a moment." He patted her hand before covering it when she would have moved it from his arm. "Walk with me for a bit and give your young men a chance to breathe. They've been absorbing the pain on your face like a towel gathers moisture. I don't believe I've ever seen Raeg affected quite so deeply over anything."

She gave herself a pat on her back for not turning to look at them.

"You're a good man, Steven," she sighed, laying her head briefly against his broad forearm. "I count myself lucky to have your friendship."

"Perhaps I'm the lucky one," he told her as he guided her slowly along the brick walk. "You've been a joy each time I've seen you. And it's been a pleasure to get to know you over the years. You know, I actually resisted meeting you when Margot first suggested you?"

"Really? And me being such a sweet thing?" she asked with a fond laugh.

The first time she'd seen him, long before they were introduced, she'd had her finger in Raeg's face informing him how hell was going to freeze over before she'd ever follow whatever order he'd tried to give her.

Steven chuckled at her observation. "I'm actually very fond of young John Raegent," he informed her. "The boy hasn't had it easy, you know. Neither has Falcon, come to think of it." He sighed heavily. "But, they rose above the challenges and despite their stubborn ways, they've turned into fine men. Just as you turned into a woman of such depth and with such a sense of honor, that I count myself lucky to know you. There are few women with your qualities."

"Oh, they're around," she promised him quietly. "They just have better sense than to join the agency and chase adventure as naïvely as I did. We think we know it all at that age," she observed sadly. "And I realized almost too late how it was chipping away at my own soul."

And it had been. The slow, bitter realization that she wasn't furthering democracy, or being a patriot, so much as she'd become a disposable pawn had been painful.

"But you didn't let it steal your soul," he pointed out, pausing to stare down at her, his hazel eyes watching her quietly as they stepped to the side to allow others to move past them. "That's what sets you apart, Summer, and that's why those two young men can't let you out of their sight." His gaze flicked over her head before returning to her. "Now, let me give you a piece of advice that will serve you far better than any other where they're concerned."

"Steven . . ."

"Quiet now," he commanded, his voice low but firm. "I've been giving this a tremendous amount of thought. They've shied from committing to a woman because of their father's retaliation against a double agent out to destroy those he loved. Roberto wasn't known for his forgiving nature, I have to say. Now, that being true"—he smiled down at her with affection—"why would a father who loves his sons, as Roberto truly does love them I believe, strike out at a young woman who so obviously loves them? You're no double agent, and clearly unable to hurt either of them, even in your anger. So what reason would Roberto have to harm you? Before you allow them to walk away, ask them that question, then open your hands and without tears, without recriminations, let them go." He smiled once more, his hazel eyes filled with some amusement she couldn't quite make sense of. "Don't allow them to see your tears, and never beg." He wagged his finger at her. "Strong men require a stronger woman. Ask your mother, she'll tell you."

"Thank you, Steven," she said softly. "I appreciate your advice more than I can say."

He sighed at the thought. "But, you will simply let them go, won't you?" he asked knowingly. "What will I do about you, Summer?"

"They're grown men," she whispered, that tightness in her throat filling her voice now. "Logical, intelligent men. They should know that already, shouldn't need me to point it out."

He shook his graying head, his expression tightening, reminding her of how Falcon would so often make flash decisions when he got that look on his face. Decisions that invariably got him into trouble.

"I'm a grown woman, Uncle Steven," she teased him, using the title he'd used himself so often when advising her. "And as you said, one who knows her own mind. I don't want them if I have to use games, or point out the obvious to them in something so important. Please, allow me to make or break my own heart if you don't mind."

Amusement gleamed in his gaze once again.

"Make or break your own heart?" he asked.

"Men don't break women's hearts, Steven. We're perceptive creatures and we usually know when something isn't good for us. I knew what I was walking into, and I might not have known the reasons why they wouldn't stay, but I knew they wouldn't stay," she revealed. "Still, I loved them."

"Why?" Tilting his head to the side he watched her now as though she were some amusing experiment. "Explain that to me."

"They're mine." She spread her hands helplessly as she fought to make him understand. "Even furious with them, I need their touch. They comfort me, calm me, *and* infuriate me. They balance me, when no one else in my life has ever been able to do that. I loved them before I was even aware of the meaning of my reactions to them. But, the damage to my heart was my doing, because I knew the odds were stacked against me, and I chose to experience every second I could have with them rather than never knowing what could have been."

Her decision.

Summer felt something loosen inside her at the admission, felt the anger dissolve. The pain was still there, just as sharp, just as deep as ever before, but that dark undercurrent of growing anger eased away.

"Thank you, Steven," she said then, reaching out to grip his arm and stare up at him with eyes that blurred for a moment with her tears. "For helping me to see something I'd missed."

The confusion on his expression deepened. "I am at a loss." He shook his head in bemusement.

"The forest for the trees," she said. "Sometimes, we don't always see what's right there, plain as day, until someone who's important to us says just the right words or helps us to say them. The pain is worth what I've had with them. I'd make the trade again, every single time. And how can I be angry when it was a decision I made myself."

His features softened more than she'd ever known them to ease. Steven was never really relaxed, he was always on guard, always prepared.

"You are a woman wise beyond your years," he said then. "Now, I must be going. I see that pretty little blonde who promised to rock my world tonight." He wagged his brows and as if on cue, Summer felt heat blaze in her face as he chuckled in delight. "Come along." Holding his hand to his arm once again, he led her back the way they'd come. "Come to the house early tomorrow, I have something extra beautiful planned for your hair and I want your approval before I begin. I believe I might have a gift hidden in the house for you as well."

"A gift?" Steven rarely gave anyone gifts.

"A special gift," he promised her. "So be early."

He left her with her momma and sister once again, winked at her momma, then with a chuckle hurried away as her daddy moved toward them.

She looked around at the still full crowd and knew she couldn't bear being away from Falcon and Raeg any longer. Bidding her parents good night and letting them know she was heading home, she caught Falcon and Raeg's gazes and moved toward them.

They met her halfway. Flanking her, they led her from the party to the limo two of the agents from DC had arrived in earlier.

There, they slid into the back with her, keeping her securely between them. If only, she thought, she could stay between them forever.

Chapter
SIXTEEN

Her aunt lived nearly an hour from the Calhoun property, the reason why Falcon had ordered two of the agents from town as added security to and from the party. They'd left her house, one in the SUV Raeg and Falcon had driven in, and the other security agent had driven the limo in later.

She was completely alone with them in the back of the limo, the privacy window securely locked.

They hadn't spoken since leaving, nor had they spoken during the party unless they'd been given no other choice. They sat there too still, too silent—characteristics that were nothing like them.

She hated it.

Breathing in deep she tossed her small purse to the seat opposite them, lifted herself from her seat, then turned and slid between Falcon's thighs as he stared back at her in surprise.

"Shh," she whispered, lifting a finger to her lips.

Lowering her hands, she gripped the hem of the camisole top she wore and pulled it over her head, dropping it carelessly on the seat behind her. She toed her sandals off, hooked her thumbs in the elastic waist of her skirt, and shimmied out of it before tossing it behind her and kneeling once again between Falcon's legs.

Clad only in her pale peach balconette bra and matching thong, she held Falcon's gaze, seeing the hunger burning in his eyes though he kept his hands carefully at his side.

"Did I undress for nothing?" she asked him softly before glancing at Raeg for a moment.

Turning back to Falcon, she felt uncertainty beginning to fill her, discomfort edging at the arousal that burned inside her.

Just when she was certain the rejection was coming he moved, his hands going to his belt, jerking the leather loose before his fingers tore at the metal tab and zipper holding them closed.

A second later, his cock was free, the broad, flushed head moist from pre-cum and throbbing imperatively as his fingers gripped the base, a pulse of moisture spilling from the slit at the crest as he gripped the shaft tight.

Quickly leaning forward she licked over the head, gathered the salty male essence to her tongue, let the taste of him infused her senses.

No sooner than her tongue licked over him, his hand flashed out, fingers burying in the hair at the back of her head and clenching in the straightened strands of hair, holding her still until her gaze lifted to his once again.

"I won't be easy," he warned her, his breathing hard and heavy. "Do you hear me, Summer?"

"I have never asked you for easy, Falcon. Not from either of you," she assured him.

As he held her before him, he slid his fingers from the base to the tip of his cock, palmed the head, then stroked down again. Following the action her lips parted and she fought to drag in enough oxygen to at least remain half-way intelligent.

She was distantly aware of Raeg releasing his slacks as well, and drawing free the heavy length of his erection.

Both of them. She was so greedy, she thought. She had to have both of them to be complete.

"Come up here between us," he ordered. "On your knees. Let me fuck those pouty lips, baby. And remember, you didn't ask for easy."

No, she hadn't; she didn't want easy. She wanted them as they were now, wanted to still the agony burning in all of them, and ease the wild need that was only growing inside her.

Moving slowly she eased back onto the seat between them, following the demand of his hand in her hair until she was on her knees, her torso bending as he guided her head down, her lips parting for the wide, engorged crest.

He didn't tease her before pushing into her mouth. He pulled her head down as his hips pushed up, pushing past her lips and filling her mouth as deep as possible in one, dominant thrust.

At the same time, Raeg hooked his fingers in the band of her panties and ripped them from her hips. Immediately, his teeth raked over the curve of her rear, his hands gripping the rounded cheeks and parting them erotically.

"Fuck, I love your mouth," Falcon growled, holding her head in place as the head of his cock throbbed at the back of her tongue, refusing to allow her do more than close her mouth around the flared head and suck it. "That's it, baby, work your mouth around my cock. Show me how hungry you are for it."

She cried out around the intrusion, shock tearing through her as she felt Raeg's tongue swipe along the cleft of her rear, raking over the puckered entrance hidden there.

"I felt that little jerk," he panted, his fingers kneading her hair as she drew on the flesh filling her mouth despite her shock and uncertainty. "Do you have any idea how good fucking your tight little ass is? Parting those pretty cheeks and watching that tiny, tiny entrance flaring open to milk one of our dicks inside it?"

The explicit words should shock her, scandalize her. Instead, they sent moisture spilling from her pussy, gathering on the folds beyond and coating her clit.

At the same time, Raeg's tongue eased along the shallow cleft again, paused at the forbidden entrance, and had her crying around Falcon's cock as shock and lust built to a critical level.

"Does it feel good, baby?" Falcon groaned. "He's tonguing your tight little ass, isn't he? Want to know what that means?"

Her hands clenched the material of his slacks as she swallowed around the thick intruder throbbing inside her mouth.

"He's going to fuck that pretty ass first. Fill it with his cock and ride it until you're begging to come, screaming around my dick, desperate for just the right touch to throw you into that storm."

He was drugging her senses. Drugging her mind even as she bucked at the sudden, quick thrust of Raeg's tongue past the puckered little entrance, stroking nerve endings that were far too sensitive.

"That's it, baby," Falcon groaned. "Hum around my cock just like that." He moved, drawing back no more than an inch before pushing to the back of her tongue again. "Ah hell yeah, tongue my dick, baby and Raeg will tongue that tight little ass . . ."

Falcon was dying. He could feel his balls drawing tight to the base of his cock, semen building, desperate to spill into the silky heat of her mouth. It was too damned good to let it end though. He couldn't come, not yet. Not until Falcon was finished getting her ready to take them both.

"Her pussy's so wet," Raeg groaned as he retrieved the black nylon bag they carried in every vehicle they used.

Inside was a tube of lubrication that they kept for far more than just sexual acts. They hadn't expected to take Summer in the back of the limo. If they had, they would have brought more than just the lube.

Dragging the tube from the bag, he quickly zipped it up and tossed it to the floor. His lips lowered once again then, his caresses causing shocked gasps and cries to vibrate around Falcon's cock, the sound heightening the lust already tearing him apart.

Staring down at her he tightened his hold on her hair, watching her cheeks hollow, feeling her mouth and tongue working around the sensitive head of his dick. Eyes closed, her face flushed, her pouty lips stretched around his shaft, she was the most erotic sight he'd ever laid his eyes on.

She jerked again, harder this time, dazed pleasure filling her face as what would have been a scream of pleasure raced around the throbbing crest filling her mouth.

"Ahh, pretty baby," he groaned. "What's he doing to you? Filling your sweet pussy with his fingers?"

Her fingers were clawing at the material of his slacks,

her body drawn tight as Falcon looked over at his brother kneeling on the floor behind Summer. From the position of his arm, he could see his brother wasn't thrusting into the wet depths of her pussy. Hell no. His expression rapt with lust, Raeg was working his fingers between the cheeks of her rear, easing the flared length of the butt plug Falcon had forgotten buying while in Cliffton. Evidently his brother had found it and stored it in his ready bag.

"Ah, baby, you get to have fun tonight," he groaned, his body tightening as Raeg continued to work the toy inside her rear.

It was equipped with a vibrator and a wireless remote. They were going to drive her crazy, and destroy themselves in the process.

The muscles of Summer's rear were bunching, tightening as Raeg worked the toy inside her, obviously enjoying the sight of the plug stretching her open, penetrating, before he finally lodged the anchoring base inside her.

Mewling cries spilled from Summer's throat, torturing the head of Falcon's dick, and once the toy was securely inside her, shudders raced up her back.

Easing back on the hold he had on her hair to allow her to move her head, he watched his brother lift Summer's knee until he had one foot bracing on the edge of the seat, allowing his lips and tongue to reach the folds of her pussy.

Her mouth tightened on his cock, moving up and down, taking it to the back of her mouth, working her tongue beneath it, then sucking heatedly as she moved on it again. The fingers of one hand gripped the shaft, stroking it, the moisture from her mouth making the heavy stalk slick.

"That's so pretty," he groaned, watching her lips move

on him, seeing the hunger burning on her face. "I hate to make you stop, darling, but you have to."

He wasn't coming yet. Not yet.

Forcing her head up Falcon watched her lashes lift, her gaze dazed, almost unseeing as she whispered his name, her lips swollen and red.

"Falcon," she whispered again, shuddering as Raeg eased back from her, his lips gleaming with the thick excess of her juices. "I don't know . . ." She shook as Raeg touched the remote he held in his hand, flinching as a ragged cry tore from her lips.

"Like that, Summer?" he asked her, helping Raeg turn her until she was kneeling in the seat facing forward, her hands gripping the back cushion desperately.

The next cry was almost a scream, her eyes widening, hips pressing back into the seat as Raeg played with the remote. One of the options increased the width of the toy marginally, just enough to burn the sensitive ring of muscles gripping it.

"Spread your knees," Falcon ordered, kneeling in front of her as Raeg continued to play with the device. "Wider, baby." Pressing against her inner thigh he guided her until her legs were spread wide enough to part the swollen folds.

Her clit was engorged, flushed a dark pink and gleaming with her juices. The flushed, naked folds dripped with her juices as she shuddered in front of them, her head tossing as Raeg used the remote.

"Fuck," Raeg groaned, one hand wrapped around his cock as he stroked it, the other holding the remote. "Every time I change the setting it's like laying a lash to her."

He pressed the button that caused the toy to thicken again and vibrate harder inside her.

"Oh God . . ." she wailed, nearly sobbing as Falcon increased the low light in the back of the limo, watching as perspiration gathered on her skin and her nipples swelled harder than before.

"Fuck her," Falcon groaned.

Raeg shook his head. "I want to watch her as you fuck her. Watch her as I change the settings of this toy and watch you stretch her until she's begging."

Raeg's gaze met Falcon's. "She's going to scream for you when you push inside her. She's stretched tight, Falcon. So tight that her pussy's going to be like a vise clamped around your dick.

Raeg had his own kinks, Falcon thought, not in the least surprised that his brother wanted to push Summer's sexual boundaries and endurance first.

"She can ride me," Falcon decided, moving to sit in the seat once again. Then he and Raeg drew her slowly from the position she was fighting to remain upright in.

She was dazed, following their hands as they moved her.

Easing her legs over his, her back to his chest to allow Raeg to suck her swollen nipples, Falcon gripped his cock and eased it between the hot, slick petals guarding her pussy.

"Tell me if it's too much, Summer," he ordered as she began bearing down on his cock, her juices spilling over the head. "Take what you can but let me know if it's too much."

She worked her hips as she bore down further, shuddering, those desperate cries that escaped her lips filled with both pleasure as well as pain.

Summer was lost in a place where nothing but sensation existed. Where ecstasy and agony were striking at her senses, her body, while destroying her mind as Falcon pushed slowly inside her.

He was killing her.

The vibration in her rear kept her senses focused on the alternating sensations, the razing sensation causing her to take more and more of him, her senses becoming high on the mix of pleasure and pain.

It seemed to take forever for him to thrust fully inside her, his cock throbbing along with the vibration of the toy, as she sobbed in pleasure, her body shuddering with the sharpened sensations racing through it.

Before she could adjust, before she could get used to the dual penetrations, Raeg's lips covered the painfully hard tip of a breast, sucked her nipple into the heat of his mouth, and destroyed her as Falcon began thrusting beneath her.

Summer's head fell back to Falcon's shoulder, lifting her breasts to Raeg, shaking, flying, as he drew on first one, then the other, sucking it deep, letting his teeth rake them, his tongue lash over them. As Raeg tortured her nipples, Falcon's thrusts grew faster, pushing her closer to the edge of an explosion she knew she couldn't possibility survive.

She was racing closer, so much closer, sensations increasing, becoming sharper, hotter, blazing through her until she shuddered violently, fighting to scream, fighting to save herself as she felt her senses unraveling with the explosions of ecstasy suddenly ripping through her.

Falcon kept thrusting harder, faster, pushing her through the violence of her orgasm as he groaned beneath her and the heat of his release ejaculating inside her only fed the inferno.

She couldn't bear more. She couldn't live with more.

Shaking in his arms, shivering through the smaller explosions, she cried out again as Falcon pushed in to the hilt, the final pulses of his release jetting inside her as she fought to catch her breath.

Nothing could have prepared her for this, she assured herself. Nothing or no one could have convinced her that sensations so extreme could actually become addicting.

"Summer, sweet sweet baby," Falcon whispered at her ear, his voice hoarse as she felt them lifting her, lowering her to the opposite seat.

"Can you take me, Summer?" Raeg whispered, his lips brushing against hers. "Tell me if you can't."

She forced her eyes opened, forced herself to focus on him.

"Please." Her body was humming again, the vibration in her rear igniting the flames inside her again. "Take me Raeg. Hard. Take me hard."

Raeg dropped the remote to the erotic toy as he lost all sense of control.

Hard. Take me hard . . .

Lifting her legs to his hips, he positioned the head of his cock and thrust inside her. An inch. Maybe an inch.

The vibration of the toy attacked the head of his dick, her muscles locked around it, and he knew if he didn't get inside her he was going to come just like that.

Thighs bunching, he forged inside her, working his stiff flesh inside the clenching, brutally tight confines of her channel, and knew, fucking knew, she owned him. Heart, soul, body, and mind.

Owned him.

Groaning with each push inside her, his hips rolling,

thrusting against the hot grip, he swore it took forever to bury his full length inside her.

Her pussy was so tight around him, he felt sweat pop out on his forehead, felt his mind dissolving with lust.

Her legs wrapped around his hips, broken cries escaping her, shaking, shuddering as Falcon now played with that damned remote.

He couldn't stay still. Lingering to relish the feel of her was impossible. Holding her hip with one hand he braced his weight with an elbow on the seat next to her and began working inside her. Hard, plunging strokes that pushed through flesh clamped tight around his cock, rippling over the sensitive head, stroking the throbbing shaft.

Her head tossed on the seat, turning back and forth, her lashes slitted, the violet color of her eyes glowing like gems within the passion-drugged features of her face.

He was dying. Ah God, he was dying for her.

When the already tight grip of her pussy began clenching further, milking at him, Raeg pushed her harder, thrusting faster inside her, the sound of wet flesh, of lust crazed thrusts and feminine cries filling the cabin as she stiffened in his arms and he felt her coming for him. Felt each explosion around his pounding erection, the rush of her juices and his own senses detonating with a release that he swore tore his soul from his body for fragile seconds.

His semen exploded from his cock, filled her, spilling inside her.

Groaning, shuddering, his hips jerked, tiny thrusts that extended the pleasure, uncontrollable, a reflex to the agonizing pleasure overtaking him.

His Summer.

His heart.

God, he loved her. Loved her until he was dying with it, dying for it.

She was his heart and his soul, and it was destroying him.

Chapter
SEVENTEEN

Saturday was dinner and dancing.

Summer had lost her appetite before the barbeque the day before and it hadn't returned.

Steven had done a wonderful job with her hair, just as he'd promised, and the gift he'd had for her was absolutely exquisite.

His mother's, he'd told her. It had been meant to go to any son he might have. Some men, he'd stated then, weren't blessed with sons. He'd secured the bracelet around her wrist, declared it the perfect accessory to go with the tea-length emerald and cream chiffon dress with its slender straps and sweetheart bodice. The back ties held the dress snug around her breasts to her hips, where it then flared out in folds of weightless material that fell to her calves.

Flat sandals rather than her normal heels, her hair a lush, long skein of masterful ringlets that glistened with dozens of fragile silver chains dripping with emerald crystals threaded through them.

The front of her hair was pulled back from her face

and secured at the crown of her head, the style flirty and
playful, but casual enough for the setting.

Once Falcon and Raeg were gone, Steven had promised to cut her hair. They'd discussed various styles and
settled on a layered cut that would end at her shoulders.

There was no sense in dealing with it for her own pleasure. She hadn't kept it long for herself anyway. She'd
kept it long because Falcon had so loved the length. She
hadn't known how much Raeg had found pleasure in it
as well.

Now, standing beneath the garden lights, music drifting around her, Summer let her gaze find Falcon and
Raeg once again where they stood, always watching her.

They hadn't talked when they had reached the house.
She'd barely had time to put her clothes on once she could
move again, and after they helped her into the house and
up to her room, once again Falcon and Raeg had left her
to sleep alone.

She hadn't protested it. It was what they wanted, and
she hadn't pushed it.

She'd already turned down just about everyone there,
she figured. She loved to dance, but she couldn't find any
joy in the thought of dancing with another man. Especially as Raeg and Falcon watched.

"Summer, this is ridiculous," Aunjenue hissed as she
moved to her side. "Not a single dance . . ."

"Don't." Summer shook her head, afraid to discuss it,
to hear a lecture on it.

She didn't want to cry, and she could feel the tears
building, tightening in her throat and dampening her
eyes.

"I think I hate them," Aunjenue muttered, the warm
weight of her hand settling against Summer's shoulders
for a moment. "They're killing you."

She shook her head again. "It's the only way to let go, Auna," she told her sister.

She understood what they were doing, and why they were doing it. She had been so determined to find a husband, a family, that she had agreed to these parties. They weren't going to interfere, they were letting her go instead. And now, that husband, those children who weren't theirs . . . she couldn't do it. She knew she'd never be able to do it.

"Daddy's so mad he's threatenin' to start to find a chew," Aunjenue told her. "That's bad, sis."

That was very bad. Her father hadn't practiced the disgusting habit of chewing tobacco since he'd been discharged from the military. To her knowledge, there were only a few times in the years since that he'd threatened to pick it back up.

"Everything will be okay," she promised her sister. "I promise. Daddy won't start chewing again, Momma won't let him."

"Momma's threatenin' to smoke, Summer," Aunjenue sighed.

Summer blinked back tears that almost refused to go away.

If her momma was threatening to smoke, then it really was bad.

"I'm sorry." She rubbed at the chill in her arms, hating what she was doing to herself and to those who loved her. "I'll get a handle on it, I promise."

"No one else probably knows," Aunjenue assured her. "They're all used to you bein' distant anyway. Momma and Daddy know you though. As do Caleb, Bowe, and Brody. We hate seeing you hurting like this."

She hated hurting, but she was going to have to find

some way to bury it deeper than she was obviously burying it.

"I'll be okay, I promise." She found Raeg and Falcon
again, her gaze meeting theirs, their expressions just as
implacable as they'd been the night before.

"You should dance," Aunjenue snapped, her lips thinning as Summer faced her, anger gleaming in her deep
blue eyes. "You should have fun. Show them they're not
going to kill you."

"But it's killing them as well, Auna," she told her sister
softly, her lips curving with a weary smile. "They just
hide it better, that's all."

Her sister rolled her eyes, anger flashing in them as
she shot Raeg and Falcon a fierce glare.

"If this is love, count my cute little ass out," her sister
declared with a little wave of her hand. "Because I'm sure
it just ain't worth the headache."

It *was* worth it, but that was something Aunjenue
would have to learn for herself, she decided.

"Go find a dancing partner," Summer ordered her
sister as she glanced at the large brick circle laid just for
summer parties. "I'm having fun watching, I promise."

"And you are such a liar," Aunjenue accused her. "But
Momma's demandin' my presence again." She rolled her
eyes. "God save me, but that woman is makin' me crazy.
I told her already I don't need a damned husband . . ."

Summer watched her sister stalk away, turned back,
and started in surprise to see Falcon standing in front
of her.

He held his hand out to her as a slow, incredibly sensual tune began filling the air.

"Dance with me, Belle," he demanded, his voice low.

Reaching out, she took his hand and let him lead her

to the patio. Stepping into his arms, her breath caught at the sensation of belonging as he pulled her against him.

Summer rested her forehead against his chest, following his lead, swaying against him and feeling warm for the first time since they'd stepped from the limo the night before.

"We have to stop this," she told him as he bent his head to hers, his lips against her ear, his hand caressing her back beneath the cover of her hair. "You know we do."

The silence, the refusal to speak, the pain-filled nights they were spending alone all had to stop.

"Shh," he whispered, his hand stroking down her back again. "Just let me hold you, Summer. I need to hold you for a minute."

"I need to hold both of you," she objected. "And I'm tired of sleeping alone. This isn't over yet. I was supposed to have this time until Dragovich was dealt with, and you're cheating me out of my time, Falcon."

Don't beg, Steven had advised her. Summer wasn't very good at begging and she knew it. But she damned sure knew how to demand.

"This is the final night of this week's parties," he said, his voice remaining low. "The nights you're attending them there's no other choice. These men are here for you, we've heard it over and over again, Summer. And I swear to you, if I hear one more time how some son of a bitch wants to keep you barefoot and pregnant, I'm going to haul out my gun and shoot him in the dick."

Her lips twitched.

It really wasn't funny, she knew. He was actually mostly serious. He was furious over it. But he was also so dramatic when he was pissed off.

"You'll sleep with me tonight then?" she asked, feeling lighter, the shadow of agony easing enough to allow her to relax against him.

"*We'll* sleep with you," he promised, his lips brushing against her air. "Stop making me want to cry with those big, shadowed eyes of yours, and I promise we will hold you between us until this hell begins again."

Until the next party, that is, a week away.

She could do that.

The tension slowly eased away from her, part of the pain easing back, sliding from her senses, allowing her to breathe again.

"My sweet Summer," he sighed. "I would trade the world and all that is in it to take the pain from you."

She smiled, remembering another time he'd said that. In Russia, when she'd burned with fever from the bullet Dragovich had put in her shoulder.

He stopped moving.

Looking up, she saw he'd led her to the table where her family sat. Stepping back, his fingers stroked down her arm before he released her, nodded to her parents, then returned to stand next to his brother.

"Hey, Summer." Mike Taggart nodded to her as he stepped to the table. "Mr. McGillan asked me to find you and tell you he's getting ready to leave. He wanted to see you first though. He was in the foyer when I saw him."

He turned to Caleb then with some comment about one of the women bemoaning the fact that Caleb wasn't dancing.

"I'll be right back," she told her parents. "Steven has to leave and I want to make certain to tell him good-bye."

She strode away from the table and headed inside, weaving through the guests and navigating the crowded dining room before moving through the rest of the house.

The dimly lit rooms past the dining room were silent

and empty, the house quiet after the loud chatter from outside.

It took several minutes for her to reach the marble foyer, only to find it empty as well.

Frowning, she stared around, waiting impatiently, certain Steven would show up any minute. Glancing behind her she expected to see Raeg or Falcon, only to realize they hadn't followed her.

That was odd. They hadn't taken their eyes off her at any other time, but now they were nowhere to be seen?

Two more minutes, she thought silently, that was as long as she'd wait.

If she waited that long.

A chill eased down her spine. The hairs at the back of her neck lifted in primal warning and she swung around, determined to hurry back to the party, to Raeg and Falcon.

She hadn't taken two steps when the first broad male form stepped from the dark shadow of the curved staircase. In the next heartbeat, two more blocked her way, weapons gleaming dully in their hands.

"Dragovich is waiting for you," the heavily accented voice of the taller Russian stated malevolently. "We can take you to him as you are, or bleeding and weak. Your choice."

"Bleeding and weak" wasn't acceptable. But then, leaving to meet Dragovich wasn't exactly the answer as far as she was concerned either.

And where in the hell were Raeg and Falcon?

She was gone.

Falcon searched the crowd for her as he hurried across the distance to where her family sat—the last place he'd seen Summer before his view was blocked for precious seconds by half a dozen half-drunk guests asking him if he'd seen some blonde who had said she was going to dance with him or Raeg.

No blonde had approached them. It wouldn't have done her any good to do so either.

"Falcon." Cal and his sons came to their feet as he glared at them.

"Where is she?" he questioned her father. "She was here and then she disappeared."

"I thought she was with you," her father snapped as he and his sons hurried from the table.

"She wasn't with us." Fists clenched, he stared around the area again, fury beginning to build inside him.

Summer's brothers quickly began questioning guests, grabbing arms, stepping in front of laughing couples, demanding to know if they'd seen her.

"In the house," one of the hard-eyed Special Forces soldiers answered. "I saw her about five minutes ago. Everything okay?"

"Hell no," Caleb snapped as Falcon raced past them, Raeg close behind.

"Spread out!" Caleb yelled out to someone behind them. "Find her."

Pushing through the patio entrance, Falcon searched the crowd, ice beginning to fill his veins, the knowledge that she was in danger building by the second.

He was just turning to rush through the dining area when a gunshot exploded from deep within the house.

"No!" The denial burst from Falcon's lips as he began shoving guests out of his way, racing for the front of the house where the shot originated.

Dragovich had found a way to get to her. God, they were supposed to protect her. They were supposed to keep this from happening.

He was at a full run when he hit the foyer and came to a hard, agonizing stop.

Blood stained the marble. Too much blood.

Jerking the handgun from the small of his back, he moved quickly for the open doors and the shadowed entrance beyond.

The lights that had lit the area earlier were dark now, shattered glass on the landing attesting to the fact that they'd deliberately been blown.

Using hand signals, he directed Raeg to the blood trail leading from the house, then pointed to the rooms on each side of the entrance. Rushing into the room he chose for himself, he paused at the side of a window, crossed himself, then unlocked it and opened it just enough to ease through it, using the cover of the high shrubs to block his exit.

"Bastard . . ." He heard Summer curse from his right, somewhere from within the heavy growth of pine that grew along the edge of the house.

Checking for Raeg, he nodded toward the tree line.

"I hope you burn in hell . . ." Summer cried out.

Keeping to the cover of the trees, they moved quickly toward the sound. As they neared the side of the house he glimpsed Summer's brother Caleb and her father following, armed and obviously following the sound of her voice as well.

"They're heading for the swamp," Caleb snapped as he got close enough. "If they get her to an airboat, she's gone. We'll never find her."

It was night. The swamp was a primal, hungry creature at night, Summer's father had once told him.

He heard Summer cry out again and sprinted into the tree line, hoping his night sight adjusted quickly enough to allow him to avoid any of those damned alligators that seemed to lurk anywhere.

A light ahead of him pinpointed Summer's location. Spreading out, Caleb and his father moved in parallel to the glow of the flashlight.

"Caleb will kill you, Mike," Summer cried out, pain and fury filling her voice.

"You bitch. You deserve it." Mike Taggart's voice carried through the night air. "You fucking neutered me when you took that knife to me. Ruined my life!"

She cried out again as the sound of laughter met the crack of flesh against flesh.

He'd hit her.

He'd kill the bastard, Falcon told himself.

"You tried to rape me. I was thirteen," Summer yelled as Falcon caught sight of her struggling between Taggart and another, larger male.

"You deserved it, you stuck-up bitch," Mike snarled. "Always thinking you're better than everyone else. A little sedative to your daddy's drink, and he was out like a light. You shouldn't have fought me."

The fury building inside was a dangerous thing, Falcon thought distantly as he caught Raeg's eye and directed him behind the two men, Russians, one being supported by the other as they trailed Taggart and the silent captor as they dragged her through the trees, moving closer than ever to the water and no doubt an airboat waiting for them.

He was obviously wounded, Falcon thought with satisfaction. Trust Summer to shed blood. She was damned good at that.

"Mike." Caleb stepped out in front of Summer, Mike, and that bastard helping him drag Summer through the night. "Let her go."

Falcon glimpsed Mike's face as the other man laid the barrel of his gun against Summer's head.

"Well hell, and here I was hoping you wouldn't know it was me." Mike's laugh was bitter, filled with anger. "You should have given me that loan I asked for, Caleb. Then I wouldn't have had to do this."

Falcon slipped closer, edging in from tree to tree.

The two Russians behind Mike and the larger abductor weren't nearly as dangerous as the one holding his gun against Summer's temple.

As Falcon moved into position to attempt to draw the lead kidnapper's attention, he found Raeg to make certain his brother was in place to fire a killing shot to take the bastard out.

Raeg was lifting a rifle to his shoulder another guest, one of the Special Forces soldiers Falcon had seen earlier, had handed him.

There were others moving through the trees, silently, no more than shadows as they blocked any attempt to reach the boat waiting at the edge of the swamp beyond the glow of the flashlight Mike held.

"Just let her go," Caleb suggested reasonably. "All of you can walk away then."

Like hell, Falcon thought. Not a single bastard involved in dragging Summer from the house was getting out of there. At least, not alive.

"She's not worth it, Caleb," Mike snapped then, having obviously lost his senses. "She's trouble. She always been, and you know it."

"She's my sister," Caleb reminded him. "My baby sister. The one you tried to rape!" he snapped then. "Did you think I didn't hear that shit? You betrayed all of us. We were family and you didn't give a damn."

"I'm losing the farm . . ."

"There's no excuse," Caleb snarled. "Now let her go."

"She will die." The Russian pressed the gun tighter to Summer's head. "You will move, or I will kill her now."

"Yeah?" Caleb sneered. "She's the only thing keeping you alive, you dumb bastard. You really want to do that?"

The big Russian grinned as he moved the gun from Summer's temple. Before he could reposition, a shot rang out.

Falcon watched as brain matter exploded from his big head and splattered against Summer's face even as she tore herself from Mike's grip and threw herself to the ground.

That shot wasn't theirs. Neither were the three successive ones that took out the two Russians trailing Summer, and left Mike on the ground, groaning from a shot to his abdomen.

Falcon rushed for Summer, aware of Raeg at his side. Reaching her, they hauled her from the ground as half a dozen male guests followed, surrounding them as they quickly moved Summer from the line of fire while Caleb and his father dragged Mike behind the thick trunk of a nearby tree.

"Summer, baby?" Once within the cover of the trees, Falcon pushed Summer behind a stack of boulders resting against a pine, his hands running over her quickly as Raeg cushioned her against his own body, holding her close to his chest. "Are you okay?"

"Fine." She nodded, her voice shaky, her face bruised. "Who took that shot?"

"Don't know." He shook his head, the vibration of the satellite phone tucked in his jacket pocket drawing his attention.

Jerking it quickly from his pocket, he stared at the

display, shock resounding through him before he handed it to Raeg.

Dragovich at the Taggart hunting lodge.—Father

Raeg read the message and knew in an instant who had taken the shots.

"Caleb," he called out.

"Who's taking those fucking shots?" the other man answered.

"Your dad with you?" Raeg called back.

"Here," Cal answered the questioned.

"Cyclops is taking the shots," he called back, knowing Summer's father would connect the codename.

Silence filled the night for long seconds.

"Cy? You out there?" Cal called out then. "Come on now, answer me. Tell me you're not gunnin' for my little girl tonight."

The fact that Summer's father knew things he shouldn't would surprise him later, Raeg told himself as he searched the darkness, looking for the man who had once been a hero, only to turn into a monster.

"She's a tough girl." Laughter filled Roberto Falcon's voice, the hint of a Spanish accent fluid, not at all what a merciless killer should sound like. "Reminds you of a young Leasa, doesn't she?"

The familiarity in the disembodied voice was apparent. Summer's father knew far more than he'd ever let on to any of them.

"She does, Cy," Cal called back. "I need to get her out of here though. You gonna try to stop me?"

Silence filled the night again for long, tense moments.

Raeg could feel his heartbeat slowing, could feel the night filling with a heavy foreboding as he shifted to help

Falcon cover Summer further, to keep her from coming into their father's crosshairs.

"Go after Dragovich, Cal," a voice called out, the night distorting his location. "Your daughter's safe. For now."

For now.

Falcon hung his head, relief and desolation sweeping through him.

She was safe, *for now.*

"Move out," Cal ordered. "If you're going with us, we'll meet at my truck. Move it."

Shadows began shifting through the darkness. With a fluid, almost natural flow, they moved quickly back toward the house.

As much as he'd hated the damned parties that had been planned, he gave Summer's family credit for inviting the very type of man needed in the event Summer was actually threatened.

"I'm going," Summer snapped as he and Raeg helped her to her feet. "Don't even start . . ."

"I would never imagine you wouldn't go," Falcon agreed, and though Raeg agreed too, the thought of having her anywhere where Cyclops could get her in his crosshairs terrified him. "Let's go."

Chapter
EIGHTEEN

Roberto Falcone, "Cyclops," had obviously beaten them to the Taggart hunting lodge.

Dragovich lay in the middle of the wood floor, a broken bottle of vodka next to him, the back of his head mixed into the brain matter staining the floors and the blood seeping into the rough planks.

With him were three of his top lieutenants, the worst of his followers. Cowering in a closet was a young woman, bruised, her clothing torn, terrified and in shock.

On the table next to Dragovich's body was a note.

You're welcome, sons. I'll be in contact.—Father

He would be in contact?

The bastard.

Raeg grit his teeth, the muscles in his jaw bunching as Summer stepped around the dead to get to the table. She'd changed clothes in the back seat of her father's pickup as they raced for the hunting cabin. Rather than the dress and strappy sandals she'd had on at the party, she wore the black mission outfit she kept in the go bag she'd tossed into Falcon's SUV before they'd left the house.

Falcon had braided her hair, cursing the thin chains her hairdresser had woven through the curls as he plucked them free. Surprisingly, he hadn't damaged a single one of the little trinkets that he'd dropped into her palm.

The long, heavy mass of hair was neatly confined from the crown of her head to the middle of her back, showing off her high cheekbones, slightly tilted witchy eyes, and pouty lips that were thinner now with displeasure.

"What is this?" Lifting her gaze from the note to meet his, Summer stared back at him with a level, demanding look. "And why are we suddenly worried your father's going to kill me, Raeg?"

Her expression was cool, almost knowing, the persona she pulled around herself as Belle, revealing the highly capable agent she actually was. She had the ability to do that, to separate the agent from the woman, to become the cool, deadly powerhouse determined to survive and complete the mission at all costs.

And that was the woman he was facing, Raeg realized. This wasn't the woman he'd gotten used to over the past two weeks. The softer, sometimes emotional, always sensual lover who blew his mind in her acceptance of both him and Falcon.

She was the agent Raeg had refused to accept for so many years because the last agent he'd allowed into his heart had betrayed not just him, but his brother as well, in her attempt to learn the location of a man so dangerous that his own country had feared him. Even now, more than a decade later, his enemies in Spain were still searching for him.

"What is going on?" she demanded when no one spoke.

Her hands held the assault rifle with steady confidence, but as he stared back at her, Raeg could see the anger that flickered in the back of her gem-hard violet gaze.

"Might as well tell her. That secret was never as buried as you thought it was, Raeg," her father told him softly from where he stood on the other side of the room. "You tell her, or I will."

Because she was in danger now. Because Cyclops knew his sons would give their own lives for her, and that alone made her a weakness as far as their father was concerned.

"You knew him," Summer accused her father then. "You knew things about Raeg and Falcon you never shared with me." The promise of a later confrontation filled her face as she shot her father a hard look.

Raeg had a feeling Cal wanted to roll his eyes at his daughter.

"Girl, sometimes a man needs his secrets just to keep his own sanity," her father snorted, the hard purpose in his gaze assuring his daughter he didn't regret his decision. "But now, the time for this secret has come." His head turned, his stare slicing into Raeg once again, then into Falcon. "The time for it came when you made the decision to involve her in that part of your lives."

When they'd made the decision to become her lovers. The accusation, though unsaid, came through loud and clear.

"Cal's right," Falcon breathed out roughly as he stood behind Raeg. "But now isn't the time to explain it."

Not here where Summer was less secure, where the stench of blood and death permeated every corner of the room, Raeg thought in disgust.

Not here where the proof of Cyclops's icy competence was more apparent than ever before and where he had to stare at his father's efficiency in eliminating anyone or anything he deemed a threat.

God, how he'd fought not to become a part of the "shadow world," as he called it. Falcon had tried to stay out of it too, but the fiery, adventurous nature he possessed had responded to the pull of the secretive, dangerous life both of them abhorred.

That was the reason Falcon had opened the security agency, Raeg knew. A way to be a part of that life, but separate from it. To pick how deep he stepped into the shadows, and what secrets he'd come away with.

Raeg had denounced it completely, yet, he'd ended up working for two shadow agents who were even more adept at hiding in plain sight than his parents had been. Davis Allen and Margot Hampstead.

He worked for them, he reminded himself, he wasn't one of them. That thought remained with him as they began searching the room while one of the Special Forces agents contacted his commander to request cleanup and transport to a clinic for the young girl sitting still and silent on the other side of the room.

This wasn't something the world needed to know about. The assassination of a top Russian mobster related by blood to the Russian Ambassador to the United States could have serious political consequences if it wasn't handled just right.

Once Cal and Caleb Calhoun determined there was nothing in the hunting lodge that could possibly tie any of them to the Russian's death's, he left two soldiers to wait for cleanup and gave the order to load up and head out.

The fact that he didn't want Summer or his sons there

once cleanup arrived was more than apparent. The world might not know what happened, but someone within that shadow world would receive a report, and having his children's names in that report wasn't something Cal wanted, and Raeg couldn't blame him.

The shadows were filled with rogues and monsters in disguise. He and Falcon knew that one from experience, and evidently, Cal was well aware of it too.

They weren't going to explain a damned thing to her, Summer thought as she pulled on soft lounging pants and a matching camisole several hours later.

Unwrapping her hair from the towel she'd put around it, she tried to still her anger at the thought of everything they were hiding. All the time that they'd spent in her bed, that they'd bound her heart to them, and still they had no intentions of telling her why they couldn't stay.

No, why they *wouldn't* stay.

The story Steven had related to her was terrible, she admitted, and she understood their fears to a point. But just to a point.

The agent who had deceived Raeg in an attempt to learn his parents' whereabouts had deserved to die. She knew Raeg and Falcon had a sister no one ever saw. Margot had told her about the girl years ago. Summer knew herself how protective her own parents were of her and Aunjenue. They would kill anyone threatening their children to that extent, in a heartbeat.

By betraying any information she could have learned while sleeping with Raeg, that agent would have endangered his sister's life and placed her in a possibly fatal position. She could understand his father's decision to ensure that threat was eliminated.

Her daddy would decimate anyone determined to hurt her, no matter who they were. But, if his sons were involved with the person intent on such deceit, he'd go to them first. He'd try to make it right with his boys, because he loved them too, and he respected their intelligence and family loyalty.

He wouldn't just eliminate one of their lovers, then allow them to believe that any woman they cared for was in danger.

And it was possible, Summer thought, that she didn't have all the facts. Because she did know her brothers and because she did know the nature of strong, stubborn men, she knew Raeg and Falcon may well have set themselves up for someone just as determined and hotheaded to make such a threat.

From what Steven had told her, that was highly possible.

And they'd walk away from her rather than trying to fix it. They'd leave her there, her heart shattered, without a care, rather than let go of their pride enough to deal with the situation and with the man causing it.

Men would just cut their own noses off to spite their faces, she remembered her mother saying often. And this was a perfect example of their ability to do so.

Finishing her hair, she picked up the bracelet Steven had given her earlier and ran her fingers over the silver, gold, and crystal elements, frowning at the display of light and color in what were supposed to be fake diamonds.

Cubic zirconia perhaps? But they didn't appear to be that either. From appearance alone, she was beginning to get the feeling the bracelet was far more expensive than Steven had let on.

To be certain, she'd have to show it to Brody. Her brother could look at a piece of jewelry and instantly ascertain exactly what it was.

First, she had to figure out what to do with the lovers

driving her completely insane, she thought wearily. A woman really shouldn't have to treat two grown men like little children who needed to be taught the truth. They should be mature enough to see the truth when it was punching them in face.

At this rate, *she* would end up punching them in the face.

She was in the mood for it too. Their father was a greedy ass, she decided. He could have at least saved Dragovich for her, to allow her to get her own little thrill on since it was her life the bastard had tried to snuff out.

Struggling with the clasp of the bracelet as she attempted to secure it, she stepped from the bathroom into her bedroom, staring down at her wrist at the thought.

"He could have left us some blood to spill," Summer informed Raeg and Falcon as she glimpsed them waiting for her.

"Yeah, he's a fucking prick like that," Raeg told her, stepping to her and taking the bracelet from her. "Here, I'll—"

He seemed to freeze, staring at the jewelry in shock.

Raeg stared at the bracelet, his world narrowing to the links of the silver and gold heirloom piece, the sapphire, amethysts, diamonds, and rich gold accents as familiar to him as a past he rarely allowed himself to remember.

"Raeg?" Summer questioned him softly. "Did I break it?" She stared down at the piece of jewelry in his hand. "It's so pretty, but the clasp is kind of fragile."

She was aware of Falcon's breath catching as he moved to see what held Raeg's attention.

"Where did you get this?" Raeg asked her numbly, his thumb brushing over the interlocking gem-studded links and the priceless diamonds held between every third link.

Three links. The rumored liaison centuries before between two Falcone ancestors and the lover the cousins
had taken together was well known within the family.
The bracelet had been given to the lover, it was said. A
gold link surrounded by two silver ones and bridged by
priceless diamonds was said to represent that once-sordid
affair.

Their father, Roberto Falcone, had gone a different
route though. He'd taken two female lovers because, he'd
told sons, their love for each other was as deep as their
combined love for him.

"Summer, where did you get this bracelet?" Falcon
questioned her imperatively, the suspicion filling his
voice matching the suspicion only growing in Raeg's
mind.

"Steven," she answered them, confused. "He said it
was his mother's. He was supposed to give it to his son
but he said not every man was blessed with sons."

He hadn't told her he didn't have sons, just made a gen-
eralization, Raeg thought, aware of how Roberto Falcone
could weave lies.

Then he frowned. "Steven? Your damned hairdresser?"

The older man had been Margot Hampstead's hairdresser as well. Raeg had seen him often in the Hampstead mansion before Margot's death as well as after.

Roberto would have never been able to fool the highly
perceptive Margot. She'd known him far too well, had
worked with him for years. If Steven was the shadow
agent also known as the former CIA's Cyclops, then Margot would have known it.

The right height and build, but Steven and Roberto
looked nothing alike, he thought. Then again, Cyclops
had been known for his ability to hide in plain sight, that
was what Shadow Ops did. They could change looks as

easily as a chameleon, completely fooling those around them.

"What's wrong?" she asked, clearly confused as she looked between them. "Do you recognize it?"

"Recognize it?" he whispered, stunned, so completely confused by the sight of this once-treasured piece of jewelry that he could barely process it. "It was our grandmother's. It's been passed down to the Falcone heir for over five hundred years, Summer. Each diamond, each gem, is considered priceless, completely flawless."

She jerked her hand back, staring back at him in shock, then at the bracelet.

"A reproduction," she whispered, blinking back at him. "It has to be a reproduction." But he saw the suspicion in her eyes.

He turned it over, searching for the inscription on the back of one of the solid links, knowing it was no reproduction.

For our heart—Falcones

Rough, almost worn smooth, but there and still readable. He pointed to the words and watched her pale as she read them.

"How did Steven get it?" she whispered. "I know he knew your father and mothers . . ."

"He told you that?" Falcon questioned, his expression hard now, his gaze icy once again. "What did he tell you?"

Summer repeated their conversation. The events of the death of Raeg's lover all those years ago and some advice Steven had given her left Raeg reeling—and if the look on Falcon's face was any indication, his shock went just as deep.

"How did he fool us?" he questioned, turning to Falcon as he fought to process this information. "I've known Steven for years. He used to do Margot's hair."

Margot had been their mother's closest friend as well as Roberto's.

"Are you trying to say Steven is your father?" she questioned as Raeg felt a sense of unreality filling his senses.

"Steven has to be Roberto," he told her, staring at the bracelet, then back to Summer. "And he just gave it to you?"

Summer nodded, holding back the last piece of advice Steven had given her to tell them the difference between their relationship with her and Raeg's with the lover Roberto had killed so long ago.

Her own stubbornness in remaining silent on that conversation was in conflict with her desperate need for them and their presence in her life.

Pride could be a terrible thing, she thought wearily, watching as they exchanged looks. She knew those looks, knew the regret and longing in Falcon's expression, so at odds with the icy cast of his gaze. The torment that filled Raeg's gaze was just as apparent, yet neither man was smart enough to look to the past and see the differences between her and some stupid bitch who tried to use Raeg to further her own agenda as a double agent.

"Do you remember what I told you?" she asked both men, her chest tightening painfully. "If you leave me, there's no coming back." Gripping her fingers together she faced them, feeling the heaviness, the pain, like a familiar presence inside her chest now. "I love you," she whispered. "You'll let me face this with you, or I won't be a part of your lives when or if you return. Are we clear on that?"

Raeg's gaze went from the bracelet to Summer, his expression twisting painfully before he shook his head.

Stepping to her, he lifted her wrist silently and secured the bracelet around it. Once finished, he held onto her for several long moments, his thumb brushing over the links.

"Do you think we don't love you?" he asked her, lifting his gaze to hers, and the sorrow in his eyes went so deep that his declaration couldn't pierce the pain resonating inside her to allow her to feel even a moment's joy at the knowledge.

She jerked her arm back.

"No, you don't," she said, her lips thinning as she stared between the two men. "Love doesn't run away, Raeg. It binds lovers together. It creates a bond that danger can't break. I will not be left behind like some helpless little twit. Leave me behind and I promise you, you will regret it."

She didn't need protectors. She wasn't Cinderella and had no damned desire to be.

She would have shot the fucking stepmother and buried the bitch in the backyard if it had been her. And those stepsisters were just too stupid to live anyway, so helping them out a little wouldn't have been a problem.

"You don't understand what's going on here, Summer," Raeg protested, pushing his fingers through his hair before staring back at her broodingly. "You don't know Roberto as we do, or what he's capable of."

Her lip lifted in a bitter, sardonic smile. "I believe I was told what he was capable of, Raeg. But I'm not that woman, nor am I that damned easy to kill."

"Roberto won't care about facing you," Falcon continued the argument. "He'll catch you in his crosshairs just as he caught Dragovich, and then it will all be over with."

She could only shake her head at them sadly.

The same man who had given her a family heirloom

because she was his sons' lover, who had been a part of all their lives long enough to have realized both Raeg and Falcon's feelings for her, a man whose obvious fondness for her had been commented on by both of them.

He would put her in his crosshairs simply because she was sleeping with his sons rather than planning to kill them? She didn't think so. And they should know better.

"Then go," she told them without anger, without heat, as she waved toward the bedroom door. "Go now, while I can bear to watch you walk away."

He just stared at her, glared at her actually, the muscle at his jaw pulsing furiously. And for once, Falcon wasn't cursing in five languages nor was he angry. He was so incredibly somber, not at all the fiery, playful man she so loved.

"I'll make it easy for you," she told them then, steeling herself to make the only choice left to her. "I'll go. Then you don't have to see what the hell you're walking away from."

Turning, she walked away, certain they were going to stop her.

Any second . . . in the next heartbeat . . . before she reach the door . . .

Before she reach the stairs.

When she took that first step down, her breathing hitched and the first tear fell.

She didn't fight them, she couldn't fight them. But when she reached the landing she stopped, holding onto the banister as her shoulders shook with her silent sobs and the pain lanced at her senses.

She should just tell them what Steven said, she thought even as she shook her head desperately.

Oh God. She covered her mouth with her hand to hold back the ragged, gasping sounds that came with her tears.

She didn't do crying well, never had. If she lost control of the pain, she'd end up wailing like a five-year-old in the midst of a meltdown.

Finally, she regained control, wiped her hand over her face, drew in a hard breath, and opened her eyes to stare around the dimly lit foyer.

Just before she froze, the breath stilling in her throat.

Chapter
NINETEEN

She knew who they were, or at least she highly suspected. The problem, though, was that two of them shouldn't be there.

The slender, tall blonde held her finger to her lips in a demand for silence, then gestured to the living area and the other woman standing several feet away, with the weapon she held in her hand.

Dressed in dark jeans, a dark T-shirt, and a leather jacket, the older woman's coloring and regal features identified her as Raeg's mother. Selena Raegent was still a beauty, and obviously still in excellent fighting shape despite the fact that she had to be only a few years from sixty.

The woman leaning lazily against the entrance to the living area was as dark as the other was blonde. Mediterranean features, dark eyes, and shoulder-length black hair shot with threads of silver framed the strong, though still beautiful, features of her face.

She was dressed similar to the blonde, dark jeans and T-shirt, leather jacket and boots. She wasn't holding a handgun though. No, she'd gone all out and brought a compact assault rifle instead.

She grinned as Summer watched her warily, then nodded into the living area, indicating she should continue moving. Summer passed her, then she and the blonde followed along behind Summer until they reached the kitchen and the man sitting at her counter casually eating the leftover fried chicken her momma had sent the day before.

"Leasa always was a damned good cook." Steven, or rather Roberto, grinned as he waved a piece of chicken. "I would have joined all of you for dinner the other night, but each time she caught sight of me she did that frowning thing she used to do whenever she saw me in disguise. It was too soon to risk being identified."

Selena Raegent and Maria Mendoza moved to each side of him behind the center island, watching her curiously.

Roberto had never married either woman. It was rumored he'd named Falcon his heir to satisfy the family demanding he marry at the time—just for said heir. Though Margot had mentioned that Raeg was named as well, ensuring the two men would share equally in whatever they inherited.

"My hearts," Roberto said softly to the women at each side of him. "May I introduce the woman our sons are so enamored of? Summer Dawn Calhoun. Ms. Calhoun, Falcon's mother, Maria Mendoza, and Raeg's mother, Selena Raegent. Unfortunately, we could not bring their sister, Hailey Anne, this trip. Perhaps next."

Finishing the chicken, he laid the stripped bone on a paper towel lying on the counter before wiping his fingers on another.

"They're upstairs," Summer told them softly, feeling

the dried tears on her cheeks as Roberto's gaze flickered to them with a frown. "I was just leaving . . ."

Roberto's lips thinned. "You did not tell them what I advised you to say, did you?"

The disapproval in his pale blue eyes had her frowning back at him, wondering what it was about men that made them think they could control her. It had to be her short stature, there was no other explanation.

"They are highly intelligent men, I'm told," she informed him mutinously. "And they know it was you who gave me the bracelet when they recognized it. If they haven't figured out yet that you have no intentions of murdering me, then they're not going to figure it out."

"I warned you he was too stubborn for this," Selena muttered at Roberto's side as she shot him an irritated look. Roberto frowned in dark displeasure. "Raeg will not accept that you're not a threat to her."

"And here I have always claimed he was the smart one," Maria snorted, propping one hand on a curvy hip and glaring down at her male lover. "This is unacceptable, Roberto. We grow weary of our sons ignoring our requests to see them. And our daughter does not even know her brothers."

Those were two very unhappy women, Summer thought.

Roberto leaned back in the stool and regarded Summer silently, almost accusingly.

"It's not my fault your sons are far too stubborn for normal good sense," she pointed out, frowning back at him. "I suspect they came by it naturally too."

"I told you how to handle this." He leaned forward, his gaze narrowing on her. "I was quite clear on it, Summer. You are just as stubborn."

Her lips pursed at the accusation.

"Excuse me," she bit out, deeply offended now. "I am not the one who created this situation, Roberto, Steven, whatever your name is tonight. You created it. Let's not forget that."

He stared back at her for long moments before speaking.

"Did I not tell you she was a cheeky little creature?" he asked the women watching him as a grin quirked his lips. "Reminds me of the two of you at that age, she does."

Summer shook her head. Impossible. Now she knew where Raeg and Falcon had gotten the habit of driving her completely crazy.

"This is not solving the problem at hand, Roberto," Maria reminded him, her voice hardening. "I grow weary of this fight between you and our sons. Because you were too stubborn to listen to reason, they punish us. Now fix it."

He grimaced at the demand. "What do you think I am attempting to do, my love?" he questioned her, frustration evident in his tone. "They refuse to cooperate with my efforts. This is their fault, it is not mine."

Summer saw the two women staring at him with the same look of disbelief she knew was on her face.

"God, I know where they get it from now," she muttered, brushing the curls that escaped from the braid, back from her face. "It's obvious insanity runs on the paternal side."

Maria shot her an amused look. "Not insanity, my dear, they simply become spoiled far too easily. It makes them difficult to handle."

And Roberto looked far too satisfied at the accusation that he was indeed spoiled.

"Well, he's yours." She shrugged. "As are Falcon and Raeg. You can deal with them, my part in this is finished."

"Summer, do not be difficult," Roberto admonished her, the look on his face similar to the one her father used when he accused her of being too hard-headed. "We will explain things, and they will see they are being stubborn, nothing more. Everything will be good then. I promise you."

"Explain?" She propped her hands on her hips and glared at him. "You don't understand, Roberto. When they let me walk down those stairs tonight, they were letting me walk out of their lives. This is over. I will not beg and I so don't need two men who have to have things explained to them by their parents as though they're children. If they stay, and if we have children, I want our babies to have fathers strong enough to be adults."

"Babies?" Selena seemed to latch onto that word, her expression suddenly softening. "You want babies, Summer?"

"How many?" Maria's voice was somehow softer, almost dreamy.

Roberto was no better. His expression filled with such male hope it was pathetic.

"She has told me she wants five babies," he told his lovers then, his voice soft as each of them gripped his shoulder, their fingers clenching in the fabric of his shirt. "I did not tell them of your desire for babies, Summer, forgive me. They are mothers who long to hold their grandchildren to their hearts. Just as I do."

When had reality become this warped? A woman should get a warning before having her lovers' crazy parents explode into her world in this way.

"This is crazy." The two women looked like her own mother whenever anyone mentioned grandchildren.

"We would be excellent grandmothers," Selena stated almost regretfully. "Can you not try? Just once? Reason with them . . ."

"Explain the impossible, Summer." Raeg spoke behind her. "Go on, reason with us. Make murder seem just, and the threat of future bloodshed understandable. Go on, I'm waiting."

Uh-oh.

Summer lowered her arms as she looked toward Raeg and Falcon's mothers and father.

Selena and Maria watched their sons with hope and pain. Roberto was less easy to read, but Summer could sense his waiting silence as he tried to choose his words carefully.

She, however, wasn't waiting.

She turned on them, her hands going to her hips once again as she stared at him furiously. They actually seemed surprised that she was angry.

Go figure.

"Summer . . ." Raeg began warningly.

"Oh be quiet, Raeg," she snapped, watching as his eyes narrowed on her, his arms going over his chest, his feet shifting until his legs were braced solidly beneath him.

"Summer, if you would await us upstairs," Falcon suggested.

"Like hell. Here's what I'm gonna do," she told them, making her mind up in that second. "Since the two of you refuse to see sense, I'm goin' to Momma and Daddy's. I won't be coming back until you leave. And when the weekend comes, I'll be choosing a partner I can trust to put love and family before pride and a request for explanations. I will marry, have my babies, and regret every day of my life that the men I love don't have the balls to live in the present rather than the past. That's what I'm gonna do."

Raeg caught her as she tried to pass them.

Hooking his arm around her waist he pulled her to a stop before she could flounce past and cause him to murder some son of a bitch in a week.

He knew that tone of voice, and he knew Summer. She was not above getting pissed enough to do something just that stupid when her pride or her beliefs became ruffled.

"We were coming for you," he growled. "But just because our anger has cleared enough to realize that murdering bastard wouldn't hurt you, doesn't mean *we* have to deal with him. If you'll just go upstairs . . ."

Disappointment and uncertainty flickered across her face. "But Raeg, that's your momma," she whispered. "And your daddy. If there's any way to fix this, you fix it."

"There's no way." Surely she couldn't believe there was.

"Those would be my babies' grandparents," she reminded him softly. "Would you hurt our babies by denyin' them the chance to know grandparents who would love them and protect them, no matter what? They've proven they'll do whatever it takes to protect those they love, no matter the consequences. Would you take that from our babies? From us?"

Babies?

He swallowed tightly, his gaze jerking to Falcon only to see the soft bemused expression on his face that proved he was having just as hard a time processing what she was saying as he was.

Babies.

Summer growing round with their children, cuddling

them to her breast as she had cuddled her cousin's infant, humming lullabies, and filling their lives with things they'd never known they could have and were too wary to wish for.

"Raeg, would you do that to us?" she whispered, her voice gentle, dreamy. "I don't want our babies sad because we deny them their grandparents. Do you?"

He swallowed tightly.

Glancing at his mother, he saw the tears in her eyes as she tried to hide them, just as Maria was. Roberto looked completely devastated. Raeg had never seen him look anything but arrogant and snide after he'd killed the agent Raeg was sleeping with.

"Summer," he whispered.

"Whatever you want." Falcon interrupted him, the words taking a moment for Raeg to process.

"Dammit . . ." he tried to protest, his gaze jerking to his brother.

"Whatever she wants," Falcon bit out, his teeth clenched, his pale blue eyes filled with a demand so intense it took Raeg by surprise. "She will have what she wants in this. We will discuss boundaries." He looked down at Summer, his look softening. "Perhaps. If she wishes it."

If she wishes it.

She was perceptive, Raeg thought, intelligent. It was hard to fool Summer. And she would listen to them, just as she expected them to listen to her. She would never take Roberto's side against them, as long as they discussed it with her. As long as they trusted her.

"Whatever she wants, Raeg," Falcon repeated firmly.

Raeg nodded slowly, unable to help himself. The word "babies" was still whispering through his mind.

"Boundaries," he almost begged, his voice low. "He's like a child himself. Give him an inch and he's miles away."

The smile that lit her up, filled her eyes, and flushed her face seemed to reach inside him as well and fill him with warmth.

"I'm a damned good negotiator," she reminded him. "And I have a feelin' Momma and Daddy know those three better than we think. Trust me, he won't get by an inch, let alone miles."

"They can come back later . . ." He tried, he really did try to get rid of them, at least for the night.

"We have time." Lifting her hand she touched first his cheek, then Falcon's. "Your mommas have missed you and I need to go reassure my own that everything's fine before she and Daddy—"

The doorbell rang imperatively even as a heavy fist landed on the front door.

Dammit.

Falcon cursed, in Italian.

"Show up," she finished, grinning. "I love the two of you, until nothing or no one else matters. But now is probably as good a time as any to learn about family . . ."

Family.

She was their family, Falcon thought, staring into her beautiful eyes, feeling the love, the dreams he didn't dare have until Summer.

She was their future, they'd cleave to her and let her lead the way where family was concerned. They'd love her, and be loved, raise the babies they gave her, and protect her and their children against anything or anyone who would threaten them.

They were home, he realized, watching her move to

the door and open it to admit her family. Her parents, her brothers.

And their Summer.

"You did good," his father murmured as he passed them. "Both of you. You did very good."

EPILOGUE

The place was a madhouse.

Outside, a heavy fog surrounded the house, hiding the landscape and giving it an otherworldly appearance that became irresistible. It beckoned him out, teased him with the promise of hidden places and sheltered peace until Raeg found it impossible to resist.

Summer's entire family was gathered in the living area with his and Falcon's parents with Summer, her mother, and Aunjenue keeping sandwiches and coffee flowing as everyone talked. Roberto, Cal and his wife, as well as Davis Allen and Margot Hampstead, had gone through the CIA at the same time, and worked together often.

After Roberto, Maria, and Selena had begun their relationship, and their sons were in their late teens, Roberto's identity as Cyclops, the CIA assassin, and his lovers' identities as his partners, were betrayed by another agent to Roberto's enemies in Spain. That betrayal had nearly cost all of them their lives. Raeg and Falcon had been in California at the time, supposedly unaware of their parents' locations.

For two years Roberto had searched for the enemy threatening them while Maria and Selena stayed behind to protect Roberto and Maria's daughter, Hailey Anne. Not long afterward, Raeg had met Marilyn Dempsey, a college student, he'd believed. She'd played the shy, sweet little co-ed perfectly for months before he'd moved in with her, certain he was in love with her, ignoring the loss and longing he'd felt when he realized the woman he'd taken as a lover was adamant about not sleeping with him as well as Falcon.

A young man's adventurous nature, Marilyn had excused his need for it. Something he would grow out of. The truth was, she'd known she could never hide the fact that her motives for being with Raeg had very little to do with love. She was monitoring his phone calls, his emails, searching for any contact by his parents that would lead to their location.

When she and her handlers had realized they weren't going to learn a damned thing, they'd planned to kill Raeg after he returned from his meeting with his brother, then they'd go after Falcon.

Roberto had learned of the agents' plans nearly at the last minute, certainly not in enough time to warn Raeg. He'd arrived at Raeg's apartment, intending to incapacitate Marilyn and have her waiting for a confession when Raeg arrived. Her handler had arrived earlier than Roberto had been told he would and caught him unaware. In the ensuing fight, the handler escaped, and Marilyn had died just as Raeg walked in the door to see his father kneeling next to her, the knife he used in his hand, still dripping with Marilyn's blood.

"What have you done?" Raeg had stared in horror at the scene before him. "What have you done?"

Roberto rose slowly to his feet, his gaze completely devoid of expression.

"She would have killed you, you young fool," his father snarled. "I warned you about the agents they would send to find your family, but did you listen? You do not listen. You and your brother, so certain you know it all . . . She's your lesson." He stabbed his finger at Marilyn's dead body. "If you cannot choose wisely, then you won't choose at all. Each time you make this mistake I swear to you,. Raeg, I will make certain they die . . ."

It was simply too soon, those memories too stark, for Raeg to handle too much time in his father's presence.

Raeg slipped from the house with the whisky decanter and a glass to the relative silence of the back porch with its little enclosed seating area and collapsed onto the padded sofa placed in the darkest corner. Placing the glass on the table in front of him, he uncapped the decanter and poured himself a healthy amount of the dark amber liquor.

Recapping it and placing the decanter on the floor next to the sofa, he leaned back, swallowed a mouthful, and let it burn its way to his belly before closing his eyes and tipping his head back to rest against the cushions behind him.

The fog surrounded him, steamy and warm, faintly scented with the smell of the water it rose from and the earth it hugged so closely. The faint dampness was barely felt, though the concealing tendrils enfolding him were welcome.

How long had he fucking wasted? He and Falcon could have had Summer years ago, even before she'd joined the security agency. They could have already been raising those babies she dreamed of, living in this house, surrounding her at night. Because he'd been too damned stupid to understand what Roberto had been trying to tell him. Too stubborn to see that it wasn't just any lover his father would kill, or even any other lover who was an agent as well. It was any lover attempting to betray him or his family.

He barely knew his sister, hadn't seen her in years. He and Falcon had refused contact with their mothers, had isolated themselves from their families, because Raeg hadn't heard exactly what his father had been trying to say.

Not that Roberto or their mothers had tried to explain anything afterwards.

Stubbornness. They were all cursed with it. Except Falcon, he thought.

How many times had Falcon railed at him to go to Roberto, to find some middle ground, to come to terms with their father and give them a chance to have their own futures with Summer?

And he'd refused.

Like a fool. He'd refused.

"You take too much on your shoulders, son." Roberto's statement had a sigh slipping from Raeg.

He didn't want to deal with his father right now.

Maybe if he just kept his eyes closed and ignored him, then he'd go away.

Instead, Roberto settled into the chair next to the sofa and Raeg heard him uncap the decanter.

Surely to God he wouldn't drink out of it?

Opening his eyes, he watched as the other man poured the whisky into a glass he'd obviously brought out with him.

"Go away," he sighed, lifting his head to take another drink of his own whisky. "I came out here to escape, you know."

Roberto grinned back at him as though he expected nothing less.

"Wasn't your fault, you know," he said then, his blue eyes, so like Falcon's, staring back at him intently. "I was enraged. Terrified I wasn't going to make it to you and Falcon in time, furious I hadn't dug deep enough, fast enough, into her past to know what she was, and there you stood, those eyes of yours, so like your mother's, staring at me as though you didn't know me." He shook his graying head, his expression turning somber. "I guess, like a fool, I was punishing you because all I could think was, what if I wasn't fast enough the next time?" He tossed back his drink and poured another before lifting his eyes and staring back at Raeg once again. "And there was a next time. About a year or so later. She targeted Falcon. The two you were just too wary at that point to allow her into your lives."

"Jennifer?" Raeg pulled the name out of the past. "Brunette, big breasts, and brown eyes."

Roberto chuckled, nodding. "Yep, that was her."

Raeg shook his head. "Falcon wouldn't have been taken in because I despised her." His lips quirked in amusement. "He's even more set that we both agree on our lovers than I was."

Roberto sipped at the whisky, regret filling his gaze. "Falcon reminds me much of my grandfather," he sighed. "He and his brother desperately loved your grandmother, but were forced to marry different women. They each suffered the loss. My grandfather told me once that there was no pain so great as seeing my grandmother's loss when the other half of them was gone. She cried often, he said. Even when his brother could slip away to join them, it was always with the knowledge that he would return to his own home, his own wife."

"Yet you didn't seem to feel that need," Raeg pointed out. He'd always wondered about that.

"Not true." Sitting back in his seat, his father grinned back at him. "It was only different. When I met Maria and Selena, their relationship was already firmly grounded. They were, and still are, deeply in love. They love me as well though, just as deeply. From the moment we first met, that attraction between the three of us was instant, enduring. I would trade it for nothing else, Raeg. Those women, and our children, are my reason for existing. And should you and Falcon have children, then my grand-children will become part of that reason, and just as treasured to me."

"I should have tried to fix this . . ." Raeg began.

"No, I should have fixed it once I realized the impression you took from that night." His father leaned forward again, staring back at him somberly. "I am your father, you were a young man. But, we are both stubborn." He grinned ruefully. "I thought you should know I would never harm someone who loved you in return. You thought I meant to keep you from loving to ensure you were never betrayed again. I was the adult though, the father. It was my place to fix this."

Raeg finished his drink rather than speaking. The hell if he knew what to say at this point.

"You were always the one who had to think things to death before agreeing with anything," his father snorted, a little too amused to suit him. "I remember the first time I saw you with that young woman you've claimed. She was in your face giving you a what-for, shaking her finger at you, her face flushed with what appeared to be anger. But in both of you I saw the future of what you would have. You, that young woman, and your brother. Falcon was watching the two of you with that look he gets when I know the two of you are going to agree deeply on something. And it was young Summer you were subconsciously agreeing to."

Raeg remembered the fight. Damn, she'd pissed him off that day, he thought, almost grinning.

"Forgive me," Roberto asked softly then. "At least pretend to so your mother will finally forgive me," he sighed. "She cries for you often and when she does, if we had a doghouse, she and Maria would push me into it."

They would too, Raeg thought, remembering his mother's temper. She was small, looked like an ice queen most of the time, but she had a temper three times her size.

Like Summer, he thought. A woman strong enough to stand up to those she loved.

"Family," Raeg said then, nodding as he lifted his glass to his father. "To family."

"To family." As their glasses met, Raeg felt that last, dark fear that had resided within him ease away.

Family.

Somehow, Summer had shown him the way where the rules of family were concerned. Disagreements would come and go, as would hurt feelings and angry words. But family, they were like his love for the woman who stole his brother's heart, they were forever.

The door into the house opened and Summer stepped out, Falcon following close behind her.

"The guest room is made up for ya'll, Roberto," she told his father as Falcon closed the doors behind them before leaning against the side of the house, just watching as Summer walked to Raeg.

He pulled her to his lap, settled her against him, and kissed the top of her head gently.

"Breakfast is early now," she told his father. "And Momma and Daddy will expect ya'll there."

"Expect us, she couldn't keep us away," Roberto chuckled, rising to his feet. "No one does breakfast like Leasa does." His gaze settled on Summer for a moment before he nodded slowly and stared back at Raeg, then Falcon. "It's good to be here," he said then. "It's damned good."

He turned and walked to the door, his hand settling on Falcon's shoulder briefly before he went into the house, the door once again closing, leaving the three of them cocooned in the fog as dawn began to edge over the horizon.

Moving into the small enclosed alcove of the porch, Falcon settled into the sofa next to him, accepting part of Summer's weight as she leaned against him.

"We're home," Falcon said softly, a grin tugging at his lips. "We're finally home."

They were home.

Right there, held by the woman they loved, her smile bright for both of them, her heart embracing them equally. That was home.

"We're all finally home," Summer promised them, her voice soft and resonating with a future filled with dreams they'd never imagined could come true. "Wherever we are together, we're home."

extracts reading groups
competitions books new
discounts extracts extracts
competitions reading groups discounts
books new extracts events
new books events reading groups
events extracts discounts
new extracts reading groups
interviews events new
events extracts events books
discounts new books events
events new events
discounts extracts discounts books

www.panmacmillan.com

extracts events reading groups books
competitions books extracts new